PRAISE FOR AMERIC..

"In *American Still Life,* James Naremore skillfully examines the complexities of grief and loss. Through honest and sensitive storytelling, this novel delves into the ways we deal with—or are consumed by—life-changing adversity. With searing and lyrical prose, Naremore explores the aftermath of trauma and the ways we memorialize what we've lost. This is a thought-provoking and poignant read that is sure to leave a lasting impact on readers."

—Beth Castrodale, author of *The Inhabitants*

"With a mix of lyricism and grittiness, Jim Naremore tells the story of photojournalist Skade Felsdottir, whose past recklessness becomes the true focus of her documentary project to shoot roadside memorials. Recording what's left of other lives soon leads Skade to reframe her own—on an alcohol-fueled journey of self-discovery and accelerating prose that carries us through the countryside. Until art and crime and friendship and love collide to form the montage that is *American Still Life.*"

—Tara Deal, author of *Life/Insurance* and *That Night Alive*

"James Naremore understands how hurt, insecurity, grief and guilt work on human beings. But the most important insight he reveals in his penetrating novel, *American Still Life,* is also the one that goes unacknowledged in words: that art saves people. Without philosophizing or even seeming to think much about why, Naremore's troubled, slice-of-life characters naturally embrace creativity as a means of coping with their lives and expressing what they feel but can't say. That their work blooms from the darkest of soils makes Naremore's story both harshly real and profoundly redemptive."

—Carolyn Jack, author of *The Changing of Keys*

"*American Still Life* is a harrowing, gorgeously-written account of one woman's struggle with addiction, self-loathing, and a terrible secret that binds her to the home she tried to leave behind. Jim Naremore's prose is gritty, evocative, and unrelenting, taking readers from the seedy parking lots of old hotels, to the breathtaking beauty of a savant's puppetry, to the stark sadness of roadside descansos. The heart of rural, post-industrial America beats within this story, in all its contradictory joys and sorrows. Through it all, Skade Felsdottir grapples with her demons, strives to express an artistic genius strangled by guilt, and must ultimately decide whether she deserves--or even desires--redemption."

—Ellen Parent, author of *After the Fall*

"Returning home to face her demons, Skade is precisely the kind of hero I prefer to root for—as fragile as she is brave, as thoughtful as she is dazed, vividly rendered yet blurred around the edges—you won't even realize until after you've read *American Still Life* that she's burned a hole in your heart."

—David Yoo, author of *The Choke Artist*

"Naremore depicts his protagonist's tormented travels with a photographer's keen eye, a puppeteer's otherworldly magic, and a tattoo artist's deft hand. Following her into her tragic past, readers feel the thrash of her struggle between self-destruction and redemption. At the same time, the novel invites them into a poignant exploration of the power of art to connect the living and the dead. Vivid and haunting, *American Still Life* is, at its core, a story of forgiveness."

— Megan Schikora, author of *A Woman in Pink*

"In *American Still Life*, Naremore has created Skade, a beautifully inked wonder woman of immense talent, complex motives, and hardcore addictions who unwillingly returns to her hometown, the site of a brutal accident, the last and most deadly place she wants to be. There, she must complete a critically important life project, a photography book on roadside memorials, called descansos. Through Naremore's skilled telling, these memorials become the pivotal lens and mirror through which Skade is forced to face her dark history, one that involves tattoo artists, an alluring puppeteer, and a renegade boat builder. In this quietly brilliant novel of loss and duplicity, the descansos also become a powerful means for redemption."

—Anne-Marie Oomen, Michigan Author Award winner, author of *The Long Fields; As Long as I Know You: The Mom Book; Love, Sex and 4-H; American Map*

AMERICAN STILL LIFE

Jim Naremore

Regal House Publishing

Published by
Regal House Publishing, LLC
Raleigh, NC 27605
All rights reserved

ISBN -13 (paperback): 9781646035052
ISBN -13 (epub): 9781646035069
Library of Congress Control Number: 2023950613

Cover images and design by © C. B. Royal

Regal House Publishing, LLC
https://regalhousepublishing.com

Printed in the United States of America

For Amy, Alex, and Patrick

"You are only as happy as your memory lets you be"

— The electronic sign in front of the
New Hope Assembly of God

1

She was a needle pulling stitches across a gas station road atlas of America. An in-and-out pattern along the roads that connected barely breathing towns full of formerly grand old Victorian homes that now looked like assault and battery victims. Her sutures ran roughly along the line where the names began to change from things like Manatoc and Muskeegum and Oswego and Kankakee—to Fortville and Columbus and English and Whitestown.

Somewhere along that seam, on the side of a state highway, she spotted a rabbit.

The smiling rabbit held a bright bouquet of flowers in its paws. She framed the shot and snapped the picture. Moved slightly to her left.

This is starting to feel like grave robbery.

The rabbit had once probably been pink. Now it was grayish. She framed the shot and snapped the picture. Moved in closer.

A stranger's death is someone else's property... Am I allowed to collect grief? What do I hold it in? Should I weigh it? Sort it? Should it be displayed by those that don't own it?

It was the long ears that betrayed its inherent rabbit-ness. Other than the ears, months out in the rain and sun had rendered it unrecognizable. One of its eyes twitched in the breeze, hanging from a single thread. She framed the shot and snapped the picture. Moved back and to the right.

The flowers retained their bright colors. They were plastic, made to withstand the elements. The sun, of course, would eventually fade them to the color of a ghost. But not yet. She framed the shot and snapped the picture. Moved in very tight.

The flowers were held in the rabbit's paws with gardener's wire. More wire held the rabbit to the vertical slat. A tear had opened up in the rabbit's chest, near its heart, and stuffing was being pulled out by the wind or by nesting birds. She framed the shot and snapped the picture. Moved back and squared up to the subject. Sighed.

A dirty, misshapen pinkish-gray lump of stuffed animal with a set of plastic graveside flowers was attached to a white cross planted in the tall grass, about fifteen feet from state route 221; on the far side, a drainage ditch filled with hard black mud, roadkill, and beer cans.

A twenty-first-century crucifix.

Joey in plastic letters glued to the crossbar of the cross.

She framed the shot and snapped the picture. Moved up to read a note:

> *Joey, I never wanted to let you go. But now I have to. And so, I do. Take my love and give me peace. Stay close.*
> *Called home to the Lord on this place on 9/15/15.*
> *Stacey*

A tuft of the rabbit's stuffing had hooked on the edge of the note. She freed it and pushed it back inside the rabbit and smoothed over the rip in the rabbit's heart.

Did I ever have someone like you? I can't remember.

She and the rabbit smiled at each other like two strangers meeting on the street who didn't speak each other's language.

Mud had splashed onto the bottom of the cross; she pulled a cleaning wipe from her camera bag and scrubbed it off. She fixed the angle of the memorial, which had begun to list, and pulled some weeds and trash from the front of it. She sat quietly for a moment with her head bowed. She framed the shot and snapped the picture. Moved to her Jeep.

Her body rang with a dissipating hangover. She climbed into the driver's seat, leaving the door open. Carefully wiping the mist off her camera lens, she snapped on the lens cap and set the camera in her camera bag on the seat next to her. She reached down into the space between the seats and lifted an energy drink. Half full, maybe a little less. Reaching down in front of the passenger seat, she picked up a bottle of vodka from beneath a pile of press releases; the headline caught her eye: "…one of the young lions of documentary photography today. Intelligent, sympathetic, unflinching, blessed with a gentle, emotional, deeply human vision, and a brave eye and braver heart. Please congratulate this year's winner of the Klaustermann Prize…"

She poured the rest of the vodka into the energy drink can. It was now mostly vodka, with energy drink as the vermouth in her martini. She looked in the rearview mirror, avoiding her own eyes, and waited as a car blew passed and disappeared in the distance. Now only the wind and the quiet question of distant thunder. She closed her door and touched on her phone. A text was waiting. Eileen, her agent.

Quit ignoring my texts or I'll start calling

She looked out her window at the memorial. Her mind was full of static and noise. She took a long drag from her drink. Tension squeezed the back of her neck. The heat of ugly memories in her head as she glanced again at the cross in the grass. She looked back down at her phone screen and typed:

Not ignoring. Busy.

A reply came almost immediately.

We need to talk about next steps.
Manuscript is due soon!

She looked up at the empty two-lane. Even without the sun—an absentee today behind a high cloud deck—a royal heat had built again. She watched the compound leaves on a line of locust trees across the road toss like fur on the back of some giant deep-green animal in a hot listless breeze. The afterthought of far-distant thunder whispered again from nowhere. She gulped down something metallic and sharp with the last of her vodka, like a mouthful of tailor's pins. Fear. Or panic.

Yeah. Soon. Almost finished. Working on a few last shots

Did you get those totem pole shots? Those are important!
You had us thinking it should be a National Park.

Not sure we need. Manuscript is better without them.
That was just a bad example. What I've got is better.

Didn't seem like a bad example to me. Meeting Chancery later today.
Will get back.

Then a pause.

You doing okay?

Curses ran through her head.

Fine.

Good. Talk soon. Love.

She touched off her phone.

☙

She drove through another town; basically, the same. Salvation Army stores and meth clinics. This should be fertile ground, but not a single descanso appeared. It felt like they had started hiding from her out of spite, especially the good ones. Big fish retreating to the hidden depths of a river.

Sunset, and the sky was going through the colors of a bad bruise. She pulled off the road before it got dark, and climbed stiffly out of her Jeep, her camera around her neck.

The shapes of late swallows and early bats swooped and danced in the darkening sky. The heat was insistent, and the humidity made the deeper shadows feel like hot fresh black milk. The raging of thousands of insects and amphibians started up in earnest and the stars began slipping out from their hiding places over her head. Fireflies did a spar-kle-and-fade in the trees on either side of a pasture. The sweet summer smell of clover and alfalfa lay heavily around her.

Another day and nothing to add to the book.

Sure, the rabbit…but, really, that wasn't so much different than a dozen *descansos* she already had. She breathed in the scents of nighttime on the new wind stirred up by the oncoming stars. And she mixed her-self another drink with a warm diet Coke she'd brought from the Jeep.

Everyone was excited for the book. Except her. Eileen and the pub-lishers at Chancery were already beginning to talk about design and marketing strategies. But she felt like she was on a treadmill. Procrasti-nation, creative block, and lack of focus led to fear, which led to more procrastination and creative block and lack of focus, and on and on. It was making her nauseous. But everything was okay as long as everyone stayed happy. They stayed happy when she told them she was almost finished. It would be fine. She just needed an extension and a few good weeks of work. Maybe she really was pretty close. Everything was going to be fine.

But she wasn't fine.

She stared up at the sky and started naming stars out loud to herself in a worn-out contralto and tossing down her drink to fight off the shame and deep-purple self-loathing that sparked out of reach with the fireflies that now rose up around her knees. More stars came out and she rattled off the names and astronomical numbers of every one she saw. Eventually she stopped her celestial roll call; the alcohol had fogged her up enough. She turned and walked back to her car.

She'd pulled up into what looked like a service-vehicle turnaround, far enough off the side of the road to not be in any danger. She moved her Jeep deeper into the darkest shadows under a scrappy grove of ash and walnut trees and curled up again in the driver's seat and begged for a drop of sleep.

What came was unconsciousness without rest or redemption.

2

Her sympathetic nervous system went off like a roman candle.
Anger.
Danger.
Violence.
She felt like she'd been tossed into a frozen pond.
Loud angry banging.

Fast, sharp.

Light.

Too much light.
She blinked and jumped and tried desperately to orient herself. Her brain began to catch up.
Car.
She was in her car.
It was daylight.

She tried to focus.

The banging again.
She flinched and bared her teeth toward the noise and felt herself growl and curse.
A cop.
A cop was outside banging on her side window.
Her heart raced, and her head was foggy and throbbing. Her body felt made up of used, mismatched parts. She blinked again and rolled down the window. Cops used to terrify her, but that fear had worn off about the same time she'd started feeling better about using her real name.
"Are you all right, miss?" The cop sounded suspicious.
"Yeah," she muttered and grabbed the first lie that drifted past. "Yeah. I'm good...I was driving all night and got tired. Needed to pull over before I got into an accident..."
"Can I see your license and registration, please, miss?"
Grateful her vodka was out of sight, she dug her papers out and handed both to the cop.
"Where are you headed Miss...Felz....?"

"Felsdottir. Just like it looks. People always make it complicated. My first name rhymes with shade, Skade Felsdottir."

"Is that your real name?"

She knew from experience not to get shitty with the cops. "Yes."

"It's unusual."

"I know."

"Where are you headed Miss Felsdottir?"

"Home." The second lie. It was the first thing that entered her bruised mind.

"Where's home?"

"Owensville," she lied again. It was the next town on the map.

"Stay in the car, please." The cop walked back to his cruiser.

Skade watched him in her rearview. She could have just told the truth. The lies were reflex. But that probably would have required a lot more explanation beyond her strange name. She wasn't doing anything wrong. Fuck it. The cop didn't need to know what she was doing.

In a few minutes, the cop slow-walked her license and registration back to her.

"Sleeping in your car can be dangerous, Miss Felsdottir. It's not a great idea. Sorry to have startled you."

Skade knew the cop would wait for her to take off, so she got herself more or less in order, and said a silent prayer that her car would start on the first try this time. It did, thank God. She headed off in the direction of Owensville.

Owensville turned out to be yet another town dying of its habits. Skade pulled into a gas station. She brushed off the glances—leers—of the four men hanging around out front. So many flies. It wasn't just her. Her car drew looks too: a decades-old Jeep Wagoneer that probably looked like a bomb had gone off inside it. She'd been living in it for several weeks. It had been having issues lately.

But mostly it was her.

She stalked off toward the restrooms, dragging a train of eyes behind her. It was already hot enough that her skin felt like burlap. The smell of the gas and oil and a vague undercurrent of fried food didn't help her hangover.

She put her shoulder into the door of the women's room, sticky from the humidity, and went inside, locking it behind her. She leaned over the sink, opened the cold-water faucet, and gathered herself for a quick look in the mirror. This was never good.

And there it was. It took her a moment to recognize herself. She looked as bad as she felt. How long had it been since she'd slept in a real bed? Or taken a real shower? She took a bath in the sink and tried to feel better. She ventured another look in the mirror before she put her shirt back on and ran a gentle hand over the tattoos that covered her shoulder and ribs. Most of the ink made her happy. She brushed her teeth, gathered her long black hair up to keep it off her neck in the heat, dug out her sunglasses, popped open a brown pill bottle, and dropped a couple of Percocets into her palm, chasing them down with some water from the sink.

Skade slid into a booth at a coffee-and-eggs place in town and got a cup of coffee from a young waitress with acne scars who seemed completely enthralled with the ink on Skade's arms but was too shy or intimidated to ask about any of it (something for which Skade was grateful). She pulled open her email, feeling her throat tighten. Eileen had sent something last night. That was probably a bad sign. Texts were annoying. Phone calls were four-alarm fires. Emails were either very bad news or very good news. And this was probably not the latter.

Skade,

I met with the team at Chancery this afternoon. The work you've sent us is incredibly powerful. Even those few images have been enough to get Chancery to go all-in. They are clearing the decks for this book! You're getting their best team at every level. Congratulations! Because of all the effort Chancery is putting into this, we are on a pretty tight schedule. No more extensions. I need the manuscript in four weeks so we have time to cut and polish and get it to Chancery on their timeline.

We really wish you would reconsider the Fieldings Totem Poles. Your description of the Fieldings site hooked them. Nate Harlan— Chancery's lead visual editor—actually went to the site. He was in Chicago and drove all the way out to see them. Blew him away. He can't stop talking about it.

I think going back to where you used to live is a good idea. A good personal angle for the book. But at this point I think time is more important. Because of the big rollout, there isn't time to go get those shots.

Skade, you've been a joy to work with this entire project. Everything has been smooth. You really should be proud of your work. I know we will be when we see it, I'm sure. We are all so excited to see the rest of your manuscript given that you've kept us mostly in the dark for so long!

Love you,

Eileen

Skade felt the fear rising in her gut. She dug her phone out and called Eileen, something she almost never did. She tried to summon the right words to say to make this all okay.

"Eileen, it's me… I just got your email…"

"Yeah…look…"

"No, I know, Eileen…I know…but listen…I think I need a little more time."

"I know what you said!" Skade realized she was talking too loud when a guy at the counter turned to look at her. She attempted to lower her voice, despite her screaming anxiety.

"Because…I'm just not sure it's quite where I want it…"

"Eileen…listen…"

"I know Chancery has a schedule…"

"I know it's important…"

"I don't care…"

"Shit. Look, I was thinking about what you said about the totem poles and how much that guy from Chancery liked them. I was thinking about going to get those shots. You know, like you said? A personal angle? I just need a little bit more time…"

"Yes, I know…"

"A month?"

"I know…I know… Okay, a week. Give me another week. I'll get it to you in five weeks."

"Yes. A week."

"I will. Thanks, Eileen."

And she hung up.

She'd rather set herself on fire than photograph the Fieldings Totem Poles, but it was the only thing she could think of. If she didn't finish the manuscript, she might need to pay back a twenty-five-thousand-dollar advance, and she would fail in capital letters. But honestly, going back there might be worse. To Carleton.

She typed a reply to Eileen's email like dry grass in a lightning storm:

E.,

I'll get the shots. I'll get the manuscript. Thanks for the extra time. You won't regret it, I promise!

Love you too,

S.

She went to pay her bill. The guy that had turned around to look at her was staring at the waitress's tits while the girl pretended he wasn't.

"Sorry about that phone call," Skade said, leaving a five-dollar tip on a six-dollar check.

She got in her Jeep. The totem poles weren't really the problem, those things were fine. It was that town. Carleton. She was only four hours from there now, in a direction she never ever wanted to go in again. Why was she even this close?

She'd lived there twelve years ago, for most of high school. She knew the ins and outs of the area like any bored adventurous high school kid would. She knew how to get there. She knew how to get away too. She carefully refolded her map, making a hard, sharp crease just south of Carleton. The world ended on the southern edge of town. Her life ended there. She hadn't thought about the accident for a while. Now it was back in technicolor.

The shock. The sickening sounds. The blood. All of it.

3

Back to Carleton. Christ. She cursed the Klausterman Prize. She cursed the contract she'd won. She cursed herself; tears came to her eyes.

No choice now. She pulled out onto a state highway that was more or less going her direction and began the drive back into her future-tense past.

Maybe nobody knew? She'd been using her real name for almost twelve years and no one had come for her. She'd gotten paychecks and filed taxes. No cops had knocked on her door. But she knew.

By the time she hit Fulford, thirty-five miles north of Carleton, she was in painfully familiar territory. Some of the billboards hadn't changed in twelve years. The feel of the place was the same. The memories twisted her spine.

Skade pulled into the parking lot of an unchanged Sav-a-Lot grocery store and sat in a space as far from the doors as she could find. She felt disjointed. She caught sight of the inside of her left arm. The four-inch-long tattoo of three long-stem roses bound together with a ribbon in black and gray—the only remnant she had left from Carleton besides her wretched memories; this tattoo, the only item she hadn't been able to leave behind or burn. The only things that were permanent. What a nightmare. Just turn around and head in any direction other than the one she was taking. She gripped the steering wheel so tightly her hands went white, and she sucked in a breath. She got out of the car and slid into the liquor store next to the Sav-a-Lot.

❧

Forty minutes later, Skade Felsdottir passed a road sign welcoming her back to town. *Welcome to Carleton, A Friendly Place!*

A town full of haunted houses.

After the liquor store, she was just barely numb and insulated enough to pass over the psychic barrier of the city limits, and not crash into it and burst into flames.

Her one desire now was to get to the totem poles and not even stop for gas in Carleton. But it was too late in the day. *Why couldn't I have been fucking smart enough to time this better?* She grabbed a vodka bottle off the floor and drove into town.

The thick, heavy summer air surged with the buzzing pulse of cicadas. The seventeen-year-old Skade who had once lived here appeared and grabbed her by the hand, and she slowly meandered through town in her car, trailing along behind her memory as it made lefts and rights. Periodically she winced as little harpies intruded, reminding her of this or that embarrassment or bad behavior from her teenage years. Stains that never quite faded. Vodka always seemed like a terrific stain remover, at least for a while.

Her memory led her through town to Kensington Park. She sat in the parking lot overlooking what had once been the aquatic center, her home away from home. Swim-team practice, meets, lifeguard duty, parties, summer afternoons. But the old pool was gone. A construction fence surrounded the cracked empty pool deck. Just big pale-green concrete holes in the ground now. Dry and lonely.

A sleek new pool complex had sprung from the ground over the last twelve years just next to it. Familiar sounds came from it, half full of I-don't-want-to-go-home teenagers engaging in the chutes-and-ladders of summer coming-of-age. But Skade's eyes kept falling back on the old empty relic of her past.

She watched the movies in her head of her seventeen-year-old self playing seriously at being a lifeguard, giving swimming lessons to squirming four-year-olds, and tugging at parts of her swimsuit to get the attention of young men. This pool was the only decent memory she had of Carleton, and now it was gone. She sat in the car drinking until she couldn't see herself much anymore, watching the light drain from the sky, and the new pool drain of children, and her veins drain of anguish.

Lisa.

Lisa broke into her mind. Did Lisa Jorgensen still live in the big brick house three blocks away? Forever eleven in Skade's mind, Lisa would be, what? Twenty-three now? She'd be out of college. Eleven-year-old Lisa had been Skade's summer charge and employment during the day while Lisa's parents were working. Lisa had idolized the strong, athletic young woman Skade had been the way pre-teens idolize their made-up images of what's next. A big poster of Liam Sharp's classic Wonder Woman used to decorate Lisa's bedroom wall, and even Skade was a little taken aback by how much she'd looked like the poster. Lisa had even made Skade sign the poster.

The soft suede passing-into-evening of summer, and couples began showing up in the park, out for twilight walks. The air began to clean out a little. An evening clarity descending. Skade shifted in her car seat in the periwinkle light and remembered Lisa's twelfth birthday, when Lisa had eschewed all her eleven- and twelve-year-old friends to invite only Skade to a sleepover, ignoring the objections of her mom, who was sure a seventeen-year-old had better things to do. Skade remembered the *I told you so!* look on Lisa's face when her mom had opened the door to find Skade standing on their doorstep with a sleeping bag in one hand and a makeup case in the other. A night of doing hair and makeup and reading scary stories and telling truths and secrets. Of relaying information from the future to her twelve-year-old friend. The signposts along the road from twelve to seventeen—which ones to ignore and which ones not to.

The satin meat grinder that was the road from twelve to seventeen for a girl was bad enough. But that tea party between seventeen and twenty-nine, that was another game altogether. Ready or not, here it comes.

Skade wished she could hold Lisa's hand again.

The old Kensington Pool was where that thing with Michael Pullman had happened. Really it hadn't been Lisa's poster; the whole fucking Wonder Woman thing sprang from idiot parents letting their six-year-old loose in the pool unsupervised. What a grotesque joke that became. Another reason someone might recognize her now, given how big a deal they made of that in this nothing-ever-happens-here place. Karma lashed out hard on that one, didn't it? Those thoughts brought up all sorts of memories she couldn't look in the eye; she could only cast fleeting backward glances at the blood on the road, and the smells and the sounds.

After a half a bottle, things began to make a little more sense and she felt normal, and, for the first time that day, in control. The alcohol obscured the memories of the accident and all the hot grief of her childhood and her damn father. But little sparks and shimmers of humanity faded.

It pushed aside the small bright tendernesses and furtive happiness-memories, like laughing in the dark with a twelve-year-old girl when her Wonder Woman had come to her birthday sleepover. The vacuum of the absence of her feelings gave her some space to expand and move through the world.

She rubbed the three roses on her arm. It was going to be at least tomorrow before she could get out to the Fieldings site to take those fucking pictures. She needed a place to stay and hide—if a place to hide from yourself even existed. But she remembered a place.

Finally, she came to the forever-broken sign for the Skyline Motel. It was still here. The sign advertised rooms "by the night, the day, the week, the month, the year, or forever." The Skyline had always been a ready punch line to dirty jokes and a wonderful source of municipal embarrassment. She pulled in. Nobody would recognize her here. And if they did, they wouldn't give a shit.

Twenty minutes later she had a room. She wasn't sure she was pulling off sobriety at the desk, but the Skyline was not the kind of place that gave a damn. Behind the shock of actually being *here*—and the terror of her memories—she realized she was mortally exhausted. She stripped off her clothes, hit the bed, and began the inevitable game of hide-and-seek with sleep, with vodka being her ultimate cheat code.

The night was pushing down, drowning her. Skade sat on her bed with her knees drawn up to her chest, gasping. After sleep had left her, she'd gone through most of a bottle of vodka and wrestled with her pillow, watching the numbers change on the clock next to the bed, and felt the growing suffocation. Was it worse to be seen by someone who knew what had happened, or to be seen *through*, past her façade, to be seen for what she really was: a fraud and worthless? She tried to make herself calm down. But being in Carleton gave new strength and motivation to the arm holding the cat-o'-nine-tails that was her memory. The accident. The terrible sound like hitting a garbage can in the road played over and over again in her head. She couldn't look that memory in the eye. She could see it only obliquely, in her mind's peripheral vision, but it was monstrous and sounded and smelled of death.

And so she sat in the tossing darkness and endured her incessant vengeful lashing of herself and cried.

An excerpt from the introduction to
American Still Life

by Skade Felsdottir

A silent, cathartic, emotionally raw folk tradition has percolated up through layers of society and culture-making into every corner of America. Like all folk traditions, it comes without an instruction manual. Its naissance is ambiguous. It is sub-textual, sub-lingual, and sub-conscious. It feels like one of those "always-been's"—like ghost stories or urban legends—beliefs and practices without clear origin or explanation, revealing the darker, wetter, inner organs of what it is to be human.

Across the country our highways, country roads, busy streets, small town intersections, and urban street corners are decorated with a kind of memento mori—shrines, memorials, markers, and works of art commemorating the dead—and the event of death. *Descansos*

The word *descanso* comes from Mexico and the American Southwest, where centuries ago, pallbearers carried the dead from the church to the cemetery on foot. When the procession stopped to rest, a small white cross was planted where the coffin had touched the earth. The markers became known as descansos—literally, places of rest—and linked to the Via Dolorosa, the path Christ walked with the cross to Calvary. It's thought that the earliest crosses marking accidental deaths on roadsides appeared in the Southwest, where this ready-made name took hold. Now this term has spread to roadside crosses and altars all over the world.

Descansos are, in many ways, the opposite of what they most resemble. A gravestone is a cold, formal thing designed to reflect the permanent and eternal, to provide a systemic order to things. But a descanso is chaotic and emotional, sometimes humorous, sometimes achingly sad, always performative. Intensely personal and structurally ephemeral. Intimate, lively, direct, and temporal. And, most importantly, they are not the statements of finality like closed doors that most grave markers are in both essence and metaphor. They are ropes tossed into a void, a means of connection with people that are still present even beyond death.

Descansos act as libraries and catalogs. They tell us about our connection to time and place by galvanizing our senses against the flow of both. They tell us about our deep and vital—and often hidden, misused, misunderstood, ignored, denied, and railed against—connection to one another. They tell us about our sad and grasping materialism, and our connection to things—and the absurdity of those things, ultimately. They tell us about language and words, which fail us in the end. They tell us about mortality and death and grief and fear and the false identities we wrap ourselves in to hide. They tell us about a real spirituality through the profane inner workings of a mind alone and grieving, which merges with a hope of the spiritual and of the Higher Power. Not God, or at least not always, often it goes beyond the easy realm of the Sunday sermon and the dogma and the comfortable conservative organizing structure that gets left at the doors of the church. This is a current of spirituality that goes deeper into the common and collective psyche, steeped in magic and the irrational. In the end, they tell us who we were, who we are, and who we hope to be.

But more than libraries or catalogs, descansos are truly cabinets of wonders. They are made up of such a bewildering array of things—signs, metaphors, symbols, hieroglyphs, all bent toward communicating the ineffable. Ultimately indecipherable even to those who create them. And descansos, in their vast sui generis forms and emanations, are themselves tiny pieces of a larger human cabinet of wonders. They are mirrors that reflect us, and they are our own forlorn love letters to ourselves.

The small white crosses once only seen going from the church to the cemetery are now found on roadsides all over the planet in an uncounted number of guises and permutations, ironically pointing out the obvious—but avoided—statement: it seems all our roads still lead to the same place. But there is much more to these lonely markers that we all drive past at seventy miles an hour with usually nothing more than a passing glance. Much more.

-S. Felsdottir

4

She had no discernible sleep cycle.

Most days, the ragged specter that passed for her sleep got up and left before dawn, leaving her awake and skittish and ready to do anything to avoid lying in bed with herself.

She was up now.

She stood over the clamoring air conditioning unit in the picture window of her motel room, blearily scanning the parking lot through her headache and empty feeling. She watched a vigilant security detail of crows on patrol, poking at discarded beer cans and fast-food bags and acting like they owned the place. They probably did.

The Skyline was a single long, low building that sat under the highway bypass. Her room was on the back side of the building, away from the street. Beyond the parking lot was a wire fence, buttressed with random piles of trash blown up by the wind, that guarded the weed-filled slope running up to the bypass and the hiss and cackle of trucks.

Skade felt like she'd been in a fight. Before yesterday she hadn't said five words to anyone in three weeks, and probably hadn't touched another human being in six. But just being alone with herself was fight enough. She looked over her shoulder at the bed: a one-woman battlefield. She ached all over, still coated in a layer of her own sweat, a nightly ablution.

The sky matched her insides: dark and angry. The air outside was dense and close, like a hot, wet wool sweater. She cracked her door a little, and the wind, like a stray cat, invited itself inside.

Other than her Jeep, the only other cars in the lot were a rusty Monte Carlo and a green van with flat tires parked next to each other in the far corner. Their final resting place. Piles of leaves and trash eddied around them. She looked down the other way and saw the pool.

She immediately went for her swimsuit.

Unwearable. She'd put it in a plastic bag after swimming in a river in South Dakota and forgotten about it. It needed a washing—if not a flamethrower—now. She made a mental note to get a new one today.

She pulled off the sweat-dank roller derby T-shirt she'd slept in, worked back into last night's bra, threw a white motel towel over her shoulders, grabbed her phone and her keys, and walked out her front door in her underwear, heading for the pool. She didn't feel well enough to give a shit if anyone saw her. She was probably the only person in this cemetery-for-the-living anyway.

The gate to the pool was still locked: *10 a.m. to 8 p.m. May to September. No lifeguard on duty.* But the security fence was only about three feet high. Skade had no trouble getting over it, even barefoot and in her underwear. She tossed the towel onto a sagging, dirty chaise lounge, and took a quick skipping step and a strong hop up into a clean dive.

The water was cooler than she expected, given how hot it had been. The weightlessness helped the hangover. Gravity was a fucking bitch in the morning.

A warm dog's breath of a breeze blew a few brown leaves around on the surface of the pool like tiny boats. Dead june bugs collected belly-up near the drain. The pool was small, but Skade managed a hungover individual medley without counting laps until she felt less like a walking corpse.

She stood in the shallow end wringing the water out of her hair. Somewhere on the bypass a semi ground loudly to engine-brake, and a soft, distant roll of thunder went through her body. She dunked back under and mermaid-kicked to the deep end.

She surfaced and slid out onto the pool deck. She kept her feet in the water, slowly kicking back and forth, reclined onto her elbows, and dropped her head back, opening her throat to the angry gray sky.

A clanking sound behind her. She pried open an eye and craned her head back to see a heavyset chambermaid unlocking the gate to the pool.

"It's too early, but I might as well unlock it if you're here," said the woman wearily, seemingly unaffected by finding a worn-out bag of tattoos and bad attitudes, nursing an obvious hangover, in her now-translucent underwear, luxuriating on the trashy broken concrete deck of a closed swimming pool at six a.m. under a threatening sky.

"You might want to get a swimsuit," the chambermaid called as she meandered back toward the cleaning cart at the end of the row of rooms. "They got some rule about appropriate attire. At least when the truckers start coming in."

Skade retrieved the towel from the chaise, wrapped it around herself, and went back to her room. She took an extremely long, extremely hot shower, stripped the rank sheets from the bed, left them in a heap on the floor, hung the *Do not Disturb* sign on the doorknob, grabbed the unnatural-feeling synthetic blanket, and fell back onto the bare mattress.

Sometime after noon, she clawed her way back to leaden consciousness. She fished around in her duffle, trying to find anything that could lie itself clean. The smells of at least seven different places rose up out of it to greet her: wood smoke, beer and rain, diesel oil, Stargazer lilies, sheep runs, dawn rivers, chalk and rosin, sage and iron. Memories associated with those smells and places spilled into her head. The bones in her face began to hurt and she zipped the duffle closed. Her bag was full of voices and embers and winces.

She returned to her window, trying to give her brain something else to do other than go over the barren last eight months of her life, but her mind laughed and went back twelve years to spite her. Faces began appearing like the wind playing with a wind chime. The first one was most painful: Mike. Whatever associations Mike might have, pleasurable or otherwise, were obliterated by his face in the headlights on the road after the accident and his voice pleading to run. Those memories spilled like a waterfall into the physical memory of holding the broken body and all the blood and the smell of it and why wouldn't she wake up and what are we going to do and oh my god all the blood and breathe and count and compress the sternum and wake up please wake up and run.

It was too much. She forced those hideous memories away. She grabbed a bottle of vodka and took a long fast gulp from it. In the wake of the vodka, another face appeared. Lane. She looked at the tattoo of the roses on her arm and Lane became clearer. Poor, sad, intensely possessive asshole pain-in-the-ass Lane. She remembered sitting on the floor of a motel with Lane, stoned out of her mind, while he gave her this tattoo by candlelight. Lane was a terrific artist. Really terrible boyfriend, but a terrific artist. *Fuck, I can't think about this.*

She stood in the center of the room and nervously ran her fingers through her hair. Focus on the present. *Five weeks. Shit.*

She stared at her laptop, sitting closed and dark on her bed, and her head filled with the familiar noise and static. Just the thought of checking made her mind clench up. But she had to check. She had to see how much there was to do. She hadn't looked at her entire body of work for months. She sat down and tentatively went through her work files.

At least a quarter of her images were redundant. Her text was basically just notes. She was nowhere close to being done. She'd been lying to Eileen and Chancery for so long about progress on the book that it felt like the truth unless she looked directly at it. Now that she did, it was crushing. Just tell people what they wanted to hear, and everything was good. Until it suddenly wasn't. She'd known it the whole time.

Five weeks.

Those fucking totem poles better be God's Gift. An acceptable draft of the book was nearly impossible unless she suddenly found some really strong locations and a bag full of the right words lying by the side of the road somewhere to replace the twenty-thousand wrong ones she'd scrawled in her notes. Skade turned her attention to her road map, spread out like a shroud on top of the dresser. A stretch of highway circled in red ink. The Fieldings Totem Poles. Eventually she straightened up and stretched, trying to get all her pieces back into the right places, pulled on some jeans, checked her camera, and left.

Carleton—brick and depression, trying to put a brave face on emptiness. Skade followed the parade of broken promises that was Franklin Avenue out of town. On the way she popped open her Percosets. As she poured two into her palm, one escaped and disappeared onto the floor of the Jeep under the seats. *Shit, never mind.*

Ten miles down Route 416 she began to see orange *Road Work Ahead* signs, and *Fines Doubled in Work Zone* signs, and *Slow Down in the Zone and Save a Life!* signs. Another mile and she saw the detour and the barriers and the construction crews. Right where the Fieldings Totem Poles ought to begin.

She climbed out of her car with her camera and walked to where the first set of workers were standing. A crew member reluctantly came over when she flagged him down.

"Hey." She smiled. "I'm a photographer. I want to go down and take some pictures of the totem poles? Any chance I can drive around the barriers here just to get up closer to them?"

"Naw," said the workman, a short, heavy man with a dark tan and a scruffy gray beard. He turned to walk away.

Skade skipped around the barrier to catch up.

"Wait," she said, trailing quickly behind. "All I want to do is take a few pictures. I'll stay out of the way, and I won't bother anyone. I'll leave my car outside the barriers and walk in."

"Naw, lady. Can't do it," said the workman, trying hard to look too busy to talk. "It's against union rules, OSHA rules, SDoT rules, and management rules. You can't be on site."

Skade swung around in front of him. "Nobody has to know. Nobody even has to see me. I'll sign whatever I need to sign."

The workman put two fingers in his mouth and whistled loudly. A man dressed in a denim shirt with khaki slacks, a clipboard under his arm, came over. The workman jerked a thumb in Skade's direction and trundled off. "Can I help you, miss?"

"Yeah, I'm wanting to come in and take some pictures of the totem poles. I won't get in anyone's way, and I won't be any trouble. I'm a professional photographer," said Skade again, trying her best to not sound annoyed.

"I'm afraid we can't allow that," said the man. "My name is Brian Hardie. I'm site manager here." Brian handed Skade a card from his shirt pocket. "It's against several laws and regulations to allow non-contracted people on a worksite. I'm sure you can understand."

"Sure, I get it. Legalities," said Skade, feeling her temper slip a little. "I'll sign whatever waivers you guys have. I really need to get back and take those pictures."

"There are no waivers. Now I'm going to have to ask you to leave the site, please," said Brian, taking Skade by the arm and beginning to guide her back the way she had come.

"Don't fucking touch me," snapped Skade as she jerked her arm free. "What's the fucking big deal if someone wants to come in and take a few pictures? Shit!"

Brian gestured toward someone over Skade's shoulder. She turned to see a sheriff's deputy get out of a patrol car. "Listen, miss," said Brian. "We've had it up to here with you activists and reporters. We are following all regulations and laws. Please escort this young woman off the worksite and make sure she doesn't come back," he told the deputy. "Arrest her if she does."

Skade shook away from the deputy and stalked back to her car as they watched. She angrily forced her car around and headed back toward town.

A few miles down the road she stopped and grabbed her map. There was no way one asshole was going to prevent her from getting her pictures. Skade ran her hands over her steering wheel in agitation. The country around here was mostly farm fields; at least it had been twelve years ago, and there was nothing to suggest that much had changed. She found a farm-to-market road that ran parallel to CR 416 not far away.

Skade parked on a vacant stretch of road flanked on both sides by tall green corn, and stood for a moment in the heat and a silence so deep she could hear the crackle of the sunlight, looking at the unnatural order in the verdant plants. She did some quick navigation with a map and her phone. If she went straight, she'd come up on top of the hill overlooking the highway construction and the Fieldings Totem Poles.

She swung over the fence. The air was thick with lazy insects and the sensual scent of a cornfield in summer. The cornstalks towered over her. It had been hot and humid on the road, but inside the field it was like a sauna, and she started sweating as she slipped down the row.

Her map told her that three cornfields lay between her and the Totems, the last two divided by a power line cut. She came out of the first field after twenty minutes and took a long breath of fresher air. The powerful afternoon heat felt cool after being in the heart of the cornfield. She stood on the edge of an irrigation ditch and a dirt access path that ran along it. She navigated the greenish water and plunged into the second field, wishing she'd worn long sleeves even in the oppressive heat. The blades of the cornstalk leaves cut like knives, and the myriad little paper cuts on her arms stung in her sweat. When she finally hit the power line break, she felt the strange magnetic tingling in the air and heard a faint hum. The towers stood like the giant robots from *War of the Worlds*, marching off into the distance. The growth of weeds and wildflowers and first-growth opportunists in the break were harder to get through than the narrow rows of corn plants in the field. She reached the edge and pressed on into another sea of green corn. It felt like being swallowed by a living thing. The last field was strangely timeless and Skade's mind began to wander off into the shadows, but finally she came to the end.

There was a fence.

Not a wire fence like the ones she'd climbed over, but a tall reddish-brown wooden snow fence, clearly erected by the construction company to keep people out. A wide swath of grass ran between the edge of the corn and the wall that was the fence.

"Fuck," she muttered under her breath. She tried to look between the vertical slats. She'd come out about two hundred yards south of the totems, but she could just make out the first of the memorials—much bigger than she remembered. She didn't see anyone moving on the roadway, but she also didn't see any way through the fence. She didn't want to even try to climb it unless she had no other option.

Skade began walking up the grass alley, hoping she'd find some way through. As she walked, she kept looking through the fence slats. Her first impression had been right; the Totems site was far bigger now. Dozens of markers and altars lined the side of the embankment beneath her. The light was still good, but it wasn't going to last very long; the sun was beginning to set in a watery sea of lavender. She needed to get through.

Then she heard a voice behind her.

"Hey. What are you doing up here?"

5

Skade whipped around and saw a woman emerging from the cornfield. She didn't seem completely real. She wore dark-green work pants and a long-sleeve khaki shirt that camouflaged her. Coarse hair ranging in color from pale butter to dark straw fell out from under a yellow hard hat. She held a bright-orange safety vest in one hand. But most significantly, she was tall. The woman that appeared out of the cornfield was nearly as tall as the stalks themselves, as though she were part of them, and she towered over Skade.

"You probably shouldn't be out here," she said, in a halting voice.

Skade froze for a moment, unsure of what to say. Finally, she settled on the truth, mostly because anything else would sound completely preposterous.

"I just want to take a couple of pictures." She held out her camera.

"You with one of those papers that keep coming out here?" asked the tall woman.

"No! No, not at all. I'm a freelance photographer. I'm actually working on a book. I really just need to get some pictures of the memorials."

The woman regarded Skade suspiciously. "Why are you up here? Didn't you try just coming in from the road?"

"Yeah. Some guy named Brian ran me off with a sheriff's deputy. Guess he thought I was with a paper or something too. I swear I'm not. I won't cause anyone any trouble. I just want to take a few pictures while the light is good."

She snorted. "That's Brian. He's a jerk. Likes being the big shot. Don't tell me you walked all the way out here through those cornfields?"

"Yeah," said Skade, holding up one of her arms to show the red lace work of tiny cuts.

"You promise you're not with one of those papers?"

"I promise."

"Okay. Come on then. It would suck to make you go back the way you came without getting your pictures. There's an opening in the fence up this way. My name's Kit."

She moved off with an ungainly, uncoordinated stride. Skade followed quickly, hoping she wouldn't change her mind. They came to a place where two rolls of fence weren't bound together. Skade slipped through, and her new companion pulled the opening closed behind them.

"I go up there to pee," she said. "The guys play tricks on you when you go in the porta-john. Try and tip them over or take pictures of you and stuff. Plus, the porta-johns are gross anyway. So I go up there. It's more private."

"That sucks," said Skade, looking up at Kit. Now that they were on level ground Skade guessed she must be over six five. In work boots and a hard hat, she was nearly six ten.

"They're just being guys, I guess. Whatever," she said, more to herself than to Skade.

"So what's with the hatred of newspapers?" asked Skade.

"Seems like a lot of people are angry about us maybe tearing down some of the memorials. People are freaking out over it."

The wind whispered around through the construction area, and Skade looked at the hillside. It was truly stunning. Altars of innumerable sizes and shapes and colors. An uncountable number, and she wasn't even near the original poles yet. Skade started framing shots as fast as she could. She'd sort through them later. She started by taking long shots of the entire hillside, or at least as much of it as she could get in the viewfinder, then she took details.

"I hope you're not going to get in trouble for letting me in. Is anyone going to catch us?" asked Skade, framing and shooting as she talked.

"Naw, everyone else is back down at the trailer, or they've gone home. You should be okay for a little while. The deputy will cruise by here about dark."

"So you work for the construction company?" asked Skade as she moved up the hill.

Kit had walked a little way up the road, looking at all the markers. "Yeah. I'm labor. Mostly they tell me to hold the sign. Because I'm a girl. They think it keeps me out of the way or whatever. But that's probably the most dangerous job out here. Holding that *Stop/Slow* sign out where the traffic merges into the zone. That's usually where I am. With the sign. More workers get killed holding that sign than anyplace else when jackasses aren't paying attention, going too fast or whatever. But today I was down here helping to pour some gravel."

"Lucky for me," said Skade. "Thanks again for letting me in, Kit."

Dust from the road settled like fine volcanic ash. The ambient light was still strong, and the air had gone clear like pure water.

Skade remembered coming out to this site with her friends in high school, before it was this big, and just sitting on the hillside and talking quietly. She looked over and saw Kit poking around in the shrines. She had her hat off now, and the wind tossed her straw hair. She moved as if she were on stilts, as if her legs were not her own, halting and insecure chords behind her movements. She was thin, loose jointed, and pigeon-toed. Skade guessed she must be in her twenties, but as she watched her drift through the hillside shrines, she just saw a sad little girl.

The arrogant heat of the day was beginning to subside. The light was running away. Skade took a few more pictures: a small stone horse, a guitar tied to a fence post, a shrine with a plastic-covered photograph of a plump couple from the '50s, a tall ghostly cross draped in a gray sheet. Then she walked over to where Kit was wandering.

"I'm out of light now," said Skade, looking around. "Could you get me back in here? I got some pictures, but I had no idea how big this place was. I haven't even seen the original totems yet."

"I suppose so. We could try," Kit said, looking around at the memorials like she'd never paid any attention to them before.

"I'm Skade," said Skade, taking Kit's long hand in hers. "Skade Felsdottir. And before you ask, yeah, I know that's a weird name. It's Norwegian and Icelandic."

"Nice to meet you, Skade, and before *you* ask, I'm about five eighteen or so. It sounds a little better that way than a girl saying she's six feet six. And also before you ask, how am I supposed to know? People always ask, 'What's it like to be so tall?' It's like being me. Probably just like being you except taller." A smile composed itself in sections across her face.

"So Kit? Is that short for Katherine or something?" asked Skade.

"It's short for Kitten. My name is Kitten. My dad was an asshole."

Skade grimaced. "Sorry."

"It's okay. My sister got it worse."

Skade smiled and looked around at the hillside again. "Do you really think you can get me in?"

"Sure. I think I can do that," said Kit as they started walking back to the road. "It's going to start getting dark soon. Where are you parked? I can give you a lift back to your car. You don't want to be hiking back through that cornfield in the dark."

The two of them walked up the road to a red pickup truck. Skade pulled open the passenger's side door and was confronted by a doll sitting patiently in the seat secured by the seatbelt.

"Sorry," said Kit, climbing in behind the wheel. "You can move her."

Skade undid the seatbelt and picked up the toy as she climbed in. The doll, about twenty inches high, looked like one of those specialty creations you'd order off the internet, made to look as much like a "real girl" as fifty bucks—or whatever it cost—would get you. She had a blond pageboy, and her face was stunningly lifelike and beautiful. She wore a long white eyelet-lace dress and black Mary Janes. She sat up properly in the seat with her hands in her lap as if she were waiting for something. It was evident when Skade moved her that this was more than a doll; it was a puppet. The puppet felt warm. There was something magnetic about it.

"That's Janeyre Thinksquickly," said Kit, watching Skade looking at the puppet. "Her last name changes a lot. Last month she was Janeyre Travelsbynight. Here, let me have her."

Kit took Janeyre from Skade and gently nestled her into a cardboard box behind her seat that was stuffed with crumpled newspaper. "Don't mind all that other stuff," said Kit motioning toward another box on the floor, full of little heads and limbs and articles of clothing—eyes and hands and shoes and tiny umbrellas and suitcases; sticks and strings and paper fans; fishtails and feathers and claws and snouts; parts and pieces of dolls and toys of all kinds.

And off Kit drove.

❧

"Keep low for a minute," said Kit. "We're gonna go past the trailer."

Skade slipped down in the passenger seat as they shuddered over the bare roadbed. The window on her side was most of the way down, and as the truck slowed she heard the sound of several men's voices.

"Hey! It's Lurch! Hey, Lurch, when are you gonna give me some of that long tail?"

"G'night, Lurch!"

The laughing and the shouting died away as Kit sped up on the finished roadway.

"Well, that sure sucked," said Skade, sitting up and glaring behind them. "You shouldn't let those assholes talk to you like that, Kit."

"I guess. But what am I gonna do? If I get mad at them, they just laugh and get worse. It's better to just ignore them. I've been talked to like that pretty much forever anyway. It doesn't bug me too much anymore."

But Skade saw clearly that Kit looked hurt and embarrassed.

Kit wound her way toward where Skade had left her car.

The sun was now well down, but its light was still in afterglow, and it dressed in shades of indigo and grapefruit. A reflexive unbuttoning and untying came over everything with the ending day. Skade felt her body relax from a tension she hadn't been aware of except by its leaving. The dusk-light spun around with the dust kicked up by passing pickups and farm equipment—and the pollen and humidity rising out of the cornfields—to knit a veil like powdery dragonfly's wings that softened everything. Skade sat back and let wisps and fingers of memory wash over her with the air sucked in through the open truck window. Skade remembered singing with the radio at the top of her lungs with Theresa and Rachel on car rides like this. No place to go but where she was going. Everything was painless then.

She looked over at Kit. Her hair switched and snapped in the wind; she was constantly brushing strands of it out of her eyes and compulsively chewing her fingernails. The fierce red stripe from the rim of the hard hat she'd been wearing laughed across her forehead, and dust collected in the sharp angles of her face where the sweat had dried. Hawk-nose. Too much eyeliner. Her face rummaged through expressions like a child going through a box of dress-up clothes without her being aware of it. She was richly tanned from standing in the sun all day, and she had a sheen of freckles over her nose and cheeks. She was certainly neither conventionally beautiful nor graceful, but there was a naturalness about her appearance and demeanor that Skade found appealing and attractive.

"So you're taking pictures for a book?" asked Kit.

"Yeah. Of those roadside markers you see everywhere for people killed in accidents. They're called descansos. I'm nearly done." Skade's gut hitched and she felt the uncurling need for a drink to mix with the lie. "I wanted to come take some shots of the totem poles, since they're so famous. Maybe see if I can find a few more while I'm here. The problem is," Skade sighed, "I'm running up against a deadline. I'm not sure I can get it finished in time."

There was a hesitation in Kit's breath. "I know where a lot of them are."

"What?" asked Skade.

"Those markers. Working on a highway crew you get to see those things all the time. I get assigned to take them down sometimes. There's a crew that does it. I know some pretty special ones. If you'd like, I can show you?" Kit said.

There was more than a hint of hopefulness in the way Kit had said it. Weird puppets and a strange uncomfortable awkwardness aside, Kit seemed eager and kind.

"Seriously? That might save my ass, Kit," said Skade. And something else clicked in her mind. Her drinking was worse. And it was worst when she was alone.

"And I don't know many people here," Skade said after a pause. "I don't like being alone a lot. It'd be nice to spend some time with somebody else."

Kit smiled. "Yeah. I don't have a lot of people to talk to either. I know how that is. Where are you staying?"

"Skyline Motel."

"I go by there almost every day."

Kit pulled up to where Skade had parked.

"Thanks for the ride, Kit. And thanks again for letting me in. Here," Skade fished a card from her camera bag, "and give me your number." She wrote down the number Kit gave her.

"I'll give you a call," said Kit. "We can get back into the totems next time I can do it, then go see some of the other markers I know."

As Skade climbed out of the truck Kit called through the open door. "It was nice meeting you like that, Skade. This will be fun." Kit's uncertain smile suggested it was not a facial expression she made too often.

6

It was just past the blue-to-black moment—evening to night—when Skade pulled into the parking lot at the Skyline. The drive back from the totem poles had been a long crescendo of the desire for a drink. Her expectation that the totems were going to be a quick in-and-out kind of shoot were dashed not only by the difficulty she had getting in to photograph them, but by the size of the site. This was going to take a couple of days at least—if she could even get into the site with any regularity. The one consolation was Kit; she might know enough good locations of descansos. But Skade would have to deal with another person. She had been alone for so long, she was beginning feel the edge of feral. People drained her energy. And she might need to be in Carleton for a while, the idea of which was almost too much to bear. She needed a drink to deal with this. She badly needed to go to the liquor store.

Skade stood under the bright fluorescent lights with two bottles of vodka. She was third in line at the checkout behind two young men—one of whom kept looking back at her with that damn look they get before they become an enormous pain in the ass—and an old woman who was buying an impressive amount of boxed wine. Skade's annoyance was rising, and she couldn't stand still. Everything was starting to piss her off. Why did she come in on a Friday night? Why hadn't she planned this better? Why the fuck was it Friday night, anyway? What was taking the old lady so damn long? Was she trying to give exact change in pennies for six gallons of blush chardonnay? Good Christ, hurry the fuck up already!

The old lady finally wheeled her swimming pool of wine out the front door, and Skade was leaning into the "don't even try it" vibe to put off the inevitable chat-up attempt she knew was coming from the guy staring at her, when she felt a gentle hand on her shoulder from behind. "Skade?"

She turned around and her already-compromised mental gears ground to a crushing halt.

It was Lane Barstow.

Lane was behind her in the checkout line, a six-pack in one hand and his face awash in surprise and happiness. Neither of them spoke for a moment. Skade cast about for something, but all her thoughts and ideas had scurried away to hide, leaving her blank.

"You're in town?" he said. "When…?"

"Uh…yeah. Yeah, I just got here a day ago, actually." She paused and gleaned some of herself from somewhere. "I'm sorry. I'm sort of shocked. I wasn't expecting—"

"Neither was I. Wow." Something in the way he said that was off, but there was too much static in her head to figure out what it was. "Twelve years. Long time. You look great."

"Thanks. You look good too. Yeah, it has been a long time." And he did look good. Better than she remembered. He looked good in his clothes. His hair was pulled back in a tight bun, a few loose strands framing his face. He wore a dark beard that needed a trim, which he pulled on absentmindedly. His dark eyes still held the familiar gleam that had been so alluring as a teenager. A new inscrutable look had been added since she'd last seen him, and he now paused a beat before he spoke; Skade could see his mind working.

"Shit, this is a surprise," he said, trying to fish a smile from her with one of his own.

"Yeah." She reluctantly offered one up. "I'm just passing through. Working on something." She fumbled through the checkout process, suddenly overly conscious of what she was buying and feeling a little bad for judging the old lady a minute ago.

"Let's go outside and talk for a second?" he offered as he paid for his beer.

Lane pushed through the doors out into the dark parking lot and Skade followed, clutching the paper bag full of vodka to her chest. The heat and humidity enveloped them, and the sounds of Friday night traffic played in the background.

"This is me…" she said, motioning to her Jeep, conscious of the state of her car, which looked like a tornado's aftermath. Lane glanced in one of the windows.

"Passing through? Where'd…?" He let the beginning of that question hang for a moment. There were many directions that could have gone, so Skade picked the one she wanted and ran with it.

"Wyoming. I've been out west for the last few years. I'm working as a freelance photographer. Photojournalist." She grabbed her camera, and then framed a quick shot of him. He smiled thinly and fended off the camera's advances with his hands.

There was another pause and a hard silence while he stared at her through her lens. "You're a photographer now?"

"Yeah," she said from behind her camera. "It feels weird to be back like this…"

The fledgling conversation snapped under the strain of the awkwardness. He seemed more at ease with the awkward discomfort, and she turned away.

"Hey, listen," he said. "I'm late for something. You were the last person I ever expected to bump into again. How long are you here for?"

"Few days probably. Not sure."

"You're working on something?"

"A book, believe it or not. Yeah…"

"Okay, you need to come by the studio. Tomorrow? Here…" He fished a card out of his wallet and handed it to her. He owned a tattoo studio now, something he'd always wanted to do. Good for him. "Gimme your number…"

Skade found one of her cards in her camera bag and handed it to him.

Lane paused, looking at her card as if he were memorizing it. A block of hot air filled with grit and a riot of street smells ruffled their hair.

"So, seriously. Come by tomorrow night. We can go get a drink. Catch up. It's been too long."

Skade watched him walk over to a green '70s pickup and climb inside.

"Tomorrow!" he said, pointing at her as he pulled away. Standing by her Jeep, Skade felt like she were drowning. She robotically went back to the motel with her paper bag.

Lane had taken the wind out of her. The first thing to rebound was her urgent desire for a drink. She had the cap off the first bottle before she got to the door.

In the dark motel room, memories of Lane barged through her mind, mixing with the vivid images of the accident. She was time-traveling. Twelve years felt like two lifetimes. The girl that had lived here once and the woman she had become on the road. She had become a professional photographer through talent honed by survival instinct, and something had come of it. She'd won a book contract and was no longer the aimless child she'd once been.

Skade switched on the lights and looked at the pile of papers that was her workspace. She turned her left arm over and looked again at the three roses.

She went back outside. The night wind and the sounds of insects and life on the roadways made her feel grounded—but grounded in a strange place. Like she were on a moon of Jupiter. She remembered the last summer she'd spent here, leaving other people's houses at dawn smelling of wine and sunscreen and sex. Teenage nights. Parties. Dancing. Orbiting the floor like insects around a porch light.

The movie projector in her head kicked on and replayed Skade Felsdottir's greatest hits. The montage of her breakup with Lane. It would be hard to even call that a breakup, really. No discussion, no fight, no finality. She was there and then she wasn't. Then she was with Mike. It had not been her finest moment in a past that didn't have many fine moments, and she felt the dry edges of regret. But the memories of Lane led to the memories of Mike, which led to the memories of blood and broken bodies, and so it needed to be shut down.

She reached for the vodka again. Unsurprisingly, the Skyline didn't provide glasses, so she just drank straight from the bottle. Easier that way. The alcohol lubricated the machinery of her memory, and Skade spent a couple of hours running through her past. She managed to stay away from her breakup and that final April. Better times. Seeing Lane made her aware of her loneliness in spite of herself. She felt small. She tossed down two Percocets. Her supply was getting low.

In the parking lot she leaned against her Jeep, feeling the hot breeze on her throat. The low, resonant hum of the painkillers set in, dulling her fears. Maybe she didn't need to hide. Maybe she could go and see Lane and prove to herself that everything was under control. Sure. Her priorities were straight. Why not be a grown-up about it and quit acting like she was seventeen again?

7

At two in the morning, Skade awoke with a violent start and crab-crawled up the headboard, shaking off her soaking sheets as if they were on fire. It took her a few long moments to realize where she was. When reality got through her watery senses, she realized she felt like hell. Her head throbbed, and her body was wringing itself out. She didn't reach for the vodka bottles—of course they were empty. She shakily pulled on her jeans, stepped into her boots, and tumbled out the door into the hot and humid night, one body part at a time, toward her car.

It didn't take her too long to find a twenty-four-hour drugstore.

Inside, the bright inorganic interior of the store echoed painfully in her head. Strange colors shouted from the shelves. The air smelled like it came out of a plastic bottle of insults. She tried not to look down the aisles at the cheerful, cheap consumer nightmare.

She leaned on her elbows at the checkout counter to keep herself from sliding to the floor; she had to wait for the shifty kid working the cash register to stop trying to look down the front of her shirt and wrap up her vodka.

Back out into the sweat of the night, she flopped into the front seat of her car and went for a drive through the steaming streets with the open bottle between her thighs.

She passed an empty ice cream store with a sign wishing success to the local high school graduates; the same school she'd left twelve years before. She flinched involuntarily and muttered, "Fuck you!" at herself.

She drove around aimlessly until a little after four, when the bottle was empty and all the belligerent smells and sounds and lights that had been bludgeoning her lost their interest in the activity. It got quieter in her head, and she breathed the night deeply into her lungs from the open window and felt herself expand into the space again.

Then she went back to the butcher's floor that was her hotel room and crawled into bed for a few hours of what she told herself was sleep.

❧

Morning came. Skade came to consciousness. The night before was a jigsaw puzzle on the dirty carpet beside her bed. She poked at it with her foot, trying to make it come together. She remembered seeing Lane and accepting his offer to come to his studio. The drugstore. After that it was hazy. She hauled herself like a bunch of dead branches to the shower.

Two hours later, Skade's phone went off. She'd been working on the book. Kit was calling. Skade watched the phone ring, not having the strength to answer it. But it kept ringing, and Skade got increasingly anxious. Finally, something made her answer.

"Hey, Kit…"

"Uh. Yeah, let's do that. That would be fantastic. You want me to meet you someplace?"

"Yeah, okay. I'll see you here in an hour."

Skade was waiting outside her motel room with her camera bag over her shoulder and a ragged notebook in her hand. The sun pinned everything where it stood. Cloudless. Windless. Lifeless. Like living inside a still photograph, except with heat.

Kit's dusty pickup drove into the parking lot, and Skade pulled her still-beaten body into the front seat.

"Hey," said Kit happily when Skade closed the truck door. A trucker's hat from the local Humane Society covered her straw-dry blond hair. Threadbare jeans, dusty cowboy boots, and a faded green work shirt buttoned at her wrists. It must be hell for a girl this tall to find clothes that fit right. Skade noticed that the box of doll parts was gone, but Janeyre Thinksquickly was still strapped into the seat between her and Kit.

"Thanks for helping me out like this, Kit," said Skade weakly.

"It beats hanging out at home on my day off. It'll be fun."

Kit headed out of town, passing auto repair places and used car lots and vacant ruins of strip malls, all flinching in the battering sunlight and heat. Skade looked to see if anything had changed. It hadn't. They passed the occasional bar, sitting dark and toad-like in its parking lot, and Skade made an unconscious mental note.

"So tell me more about this book you're doing," said Kit. "That sounds pretty cool."

"The working title is *American Still Life*. It's about descansos. It's a Spanish word that literally means *resting place*. A religious concept morphed into the practice of putting up memorials for people where they died. Mostly car accidents. You see those markers all over the country now. In cities, you also get markers and street memorials for people who died from gunshots and that kind of thing. There are elements of folk art in it. I've got some images of some incredible markers. And it's an interesting way of looking at how people deal with death and grief in a real, personal, individual way. Kind of a folk spirituality."

Kit glanced over at Skade before returning her attention to the road.

"Yeah," laughed Skade, "that was a big mouthful of crap, I know. But descansos can be beautiful, and they all have stories, and those stories can be great. Mostly they're sad, but sometimes not."

"Well, I think it's a cool idea," said Kit. "And like I said, working for the highway, you get to see a lot of them."

"How long have you worked for the road crews?"

"Four years now. I was happy to get it. It was that or fast food or...I know girls that are dealing meth or selling hand jobs. I hate to think about being there."

By now they'd passed out of town into the farmland beyond. Corn and bean fields stretched out in either direction, green and hot.

"How'd you hear about this town? Was it the totem poles?" asked Kit.

"Here? No..." Skade felt the fear flow into her body. "No, I used to live here."

"Really? When?"

"Long time ago. I went to high school here."

"Were you born here?"

"No. I was born in Canada. Halifax. My mom died in a car crash when I was little, and my dad moved around a lot. We never stayed in one place very long growing up. I wound up here for high school."

"Sorry about your mom. Is that why you're doing the book? You still have family here?"

"Yeah. I think my mom is why." Skade seethed inside. "No. It was just my dad and me. I took off on my own after high school. He moved to California, I think. I haven't seen him in twelve years. We don't talk."

"Yeah," said Kit. "I don't see my dad either. Just didn't come home one night. Guess he couldn't deal with it anymore. It about killed my mom when he left. She got real sick. She's in a care facility now up in

Monroeville. I don't see her much anymore either. We went through some hard times."

"Sorry."

"Happens."

Kit pulled around the construction barriers. "I'm not sure we can get to the big totems yet. But we will probably be okay on the edges of it, if that works?"

"That's great. Anything. Thanks," said Skade. The two of them walked up into the altars, and Skade began working.

Skade shook herself out of her concentration, realizing she'd lost all sense of time. She looked around for Kit and saw her standing over by the fence that separated the hillside from the cornfield, surreptitiously watching Skade work and playing with something in her hands. She had a strange way of making her tall, conspicuous body seem small, as if she needed permission to inhabit her own skin. "I've got a couple dozen good pictures," Skade said, walking over.

Kit had taken a couple of dry corn husks she'd found stuck to the fence, and she'd torn and twisted and tied them into a human figure—a puppet.

Kit placed her puppet on a fence post and with subtle and mysterious motions of her hand, the little figure suddenly came to life in front of Skade's eyes. It slowly looked left and right; then, using a stick to guide the doll's hand, Kit made it shade its eyes from the sun and gaze out over the fields. It walked gracefully over to the edge of the post, and Kit again used the stick to bend the body at the waist; the figure looked down, toward the ground. It knelt, then got on all fours to get a better look, then stood back up again, looked at Skade, and shrugged its shoulders. A perfect pantomime.

"Wow." Skade laughed. "That was amazing. I'm serious, Kit. That was really impressive."

"Thanks. I like to play with puppets and stuff," Kit mumbled, but she smiled and lit up at Skade's attention.

"Well, I'd like to see more of it. That was like magic. But I would love to get a few more shots first. You think we're still okay here? Anyone going to drive by or anything?"

"No. I think we're good," said Kit, still playing with her cornhusk puppet.

When Skade looked up again, she saw Kit several yards in front of her looking at another memorial.

"This one could be me," said Kit. It wasn't clear to Skade if Kit was talking to her or to herself or to the memorial or to the universe. The memorial consisted of a piece of wood stuck into the ground like a headstone. A poem had been written on it in white marker.

All the young dead.
They pass us by like wind
In the grass, and we mourn
But who grieves for the one
Still alive.
Left alone.
To sweep the floors and tend the flowers
And live the scraps of a life
Left behind.

Skade took a picture of it and moved on, watching Kit walk away with her head down.

༄

Skade stood on the top of the slope of the hillside looking out across all the shrines. Kit quietly joined her.

"You know what I need?" said Skade, more to herself than to Kit. "I need some old archive photos. Something that gives a sense of how this place has grown over the years."

"Newspaper," said Kit.

"Yep. Just what I was thinking. Newspaper. I bet they've got some in their files. I ought to be able to get them online."

"Not likely," snorted Kit.

"What?"

"I dunno. Maybe you can. But I'd be surprised. This place is still pretty 1980 for the most part. But if you can't, you can just go down to the office."

"Yeah."

After a moment of silence, Kit asked, "So nobody really died here?"

"Well, the original accident happened here. The four members of the Fieldings family died in a car accident here in the seventies. But the rest of these? No, not as far as I know. A lot of these people died in hospitals or overseas or whatever."

"So, they aren't really descansos then?"

"Strictly? Other than the totem poles themselves, no. But it's kind of a shifty definition, you know?"

"I can bring you again?" Kit offered hopefully. "And then we can find some of the real ones?"

Skade glanced up at Kit's face—she needed something so badly, and Skade wondered momentarily what it might be.

"That'd be nice. I do need the original poles, like I said. I got what I need right now though. We should go back."

At the truck, Kit laid a road map out on the hood and began chewing her fingernails while Skade carefully cleaned and stowed her camera.

"These are the memorials I liked, or wanted to know more about, or something...the famous ones too," Kit explained, pointing at red circles on the map.

"These three for sure you need to see. I'm down a few days on the schedule for some reason. But that's good, 'cause we can go out and see these markers, if you want?"

"Great. Thanks, Kit. And you should stop biting your nails like that. It's not good for you. Your hands are so beautiful. I want to photograph them."

Kit smiled weakly and turned away. But she did take her fingers out of her mouth.

They got in the truck, and as Skade was fastening her seat belt, Kit reached over and thrust something at her. Being with people still made Skade feel unnerved and tense, and she jumped a little.

"Here," said Kit awkwardly. "You can have this." She held out the cornhusk puppet she'd created.

Skade took the little puppet gingerly. "Thanks. Sorry. You startled me." Skade tried to put her fingers into it and make it do things like Kit had done, but it was clearly not going to happen.

Kit started back to town. Skade rolled down the window and put her face out into the heat blowing past. Her hair whipped and fluttered around her face.

"Careful, you'll get a bug in your teeth," said Kit. Skade pulled her face back into the car and pulled the long ropes of black hair out of her eyes. "Or up your nose. I got that once. Ugh. That was horrible. There's a famous marker on the other side of town. You want to go see that one next?" Kit asked, with a strange shade of hopefulness in her voice. "We can do it day after tomorrow or the day after that, I think."

"Sure," Skade replied. She felt caught up in some current she couldn't swim out of. People were still hard for her, and Kit was really pressing. Kit pulled into the parking lot at the Skyline and Skade got out.

"Thank you, Kit. I appreciate it," said Skade, holding her cornhusk puppet.

Kit smiled from her heart and drove away.

Skade needed a drink very, very badly.

8

The dust and humidity turned the air into dirty glass, and the streetlights buzzed in their golden halos. Skade parked her Jeep by a slab of crumbling sidewalk.

She'd spent the day alternating between holing up in her motel room trying to find the flow of her work, which was so elusive she felt like a stranger on her own page, and swimming in the motel pool. Nothing worked. The words felt as if they'd been written by someone else, leaving her feeling like an interloper. The shock of seeing Lane unexpectedly had worn off and the desire to disengage from this whole dance with her past pulled at her. But as the sun set, she'd found a precarious balance with the vodka and painkillers and decided to go through with her decision to meet up with Lane. The drugs and alcohol had even talked her into putting some extra juice in her appearance.

Out of habit, Skade grabbed her camera and began checking door numbers. The adrenaline associated with the shuffled deck of emotions she was playing with was wearing off and taking the high she'd built with it. She began to feel the pangs of a hungry exhaustion.

Light streamed out from inside an immaculately clean, brightly lit space. The wooden signboard hung over the doorway read *Barstow's electric pen and ink drawings. A Tattooing Establishment.* A loud whirring sound. She tried to give herself permission to walk in, and when it didn't come, she went in anyway.

The front half of the space was a waiting area. Dark-green vinyl benches lined one wall, samples and flash hung along the other, and three large catalog portfolios sat open on the long wooden counter that separated the front from the work areas in back. Hospital-style curtains, now pulled back, cordoned-off tattooing chairs, rolling tables, and stools. The sound Skade had heard was a vacuum cleaner. She watched Lane's back from the doorway as he went over the polished concrete floor.

She thought hard about turning and running, but she was still standing there when he shut the vacuum off. The sudden silence felt like cement, but she punched through it.

"Hey, Lane."

He turned around and looked at her, slowly coiling the vacuum cleaner cord in his hands. She had snuck up on him and caught him with his armor down.

"You showed up—"

"I said I would. Don't be so surprised."

There was a charged and glassy pause, then he smiled. "Hell, it's so good to see you again. Come on in. Grab a seat," he said, motioning to one of the benches.

Skade felt the once familiar feeling of being completely in Lane's world.

"So," she said behind a deep breath and a paper smile, "dream come true?" She gestured with her camera around the space.

"Yeah, I've been open a couple of years now."

"It's a long way from whiskey and joints in a motel room."

"Long way. You still have that? Christ, you have some really good ink now." He leaned toward her to examine her tattoos. Skade pulled back reflexively, regretting the amount of exposed skin.

She held up the inside of her left arm to show him the three roses. It was lovely, detailed work, even though it had grown softer with age. "First one I ever got."

Lane took the opportunity to close some of thick space between them, and he got up to look. She felt her body tense, and she was grateful he didn't reach out to take her arm.

"It still looks okay for a freehand motel room session. I should touch that up for you, though. I can add color if you want?"

"Maybe," she managed. Silence fell between them again, and Skade suddenly regretted her revealing clothes and dramatic makeup.

Lane pulled a box of Old Milwaukee out from behind the counter. "Want a beer?" he said over his shoulder.

"Yes. Very." Skade opened the can he handed her.

"You're not having one?" she asked.

"No. I've got a client tonight. A regular."

"That's not how it used to be. You used to work drunk or high all the time."

"Yeah, that was stupid. I'll wait until later tonight."

Skade turned to examine Lane's flash work. She paused at a framed custom piece: Puss in Boots.

The drawing was intricate. The expression on the cat's face was charming. "Are these all you?" she asked, gesturing toward the hanging artwork. "They're amazing. So beautiful."

"Thanks," he said, passing her a second beer. "I'm getting decent reviews from some of the ink magazines. Here's one." He passed her a copy of *Under the Skin* magazine with a banner article: *Memento Mori: New art of remembrance by Lane Barstow.* "I'm working on getting into some of the big tattoo conventions. There's a show in Chicago I want to do, and then maybe one out in LA next summer. I really need to put together a portfolio."

Skade flipped through the photo catalogs of some of his regular clients and their custom work. The beer had kicked in and Skade began feeling settled.

"I could shoot that portfolio for you if you want," she offered, then instantly regretted the impulse.

"You said something about working? I wouldn't want to get in your way." He leaned back against the counter.

"Yeah." And she paused.

Skade drew in a quick breath full of needles. "I'm doing a book on roadside memorials. Descansos. That's what they're called. Those crosses you see along the roadside where people have died in traffic accidents and stuff."

"Really?"

"Yeah. I'm nearly done. I just wanted to come back here and get a few shots." Something inside her was screaming and breaking dishes.

"What are you wanting to take pictures of around here?"

"Maybe the totem poles."

"Sure, that makes sense. But that's going to be tough. That stretch of highway is under construction. They've detoured all the traffic off onto 347. And there has been some talk about tearing those totems down, or at least moving them. They want to widen that stretch of the road I guess."

"Already discovered that. But I did get back in there after some hassle. I'm going back soon, even if I have to fight my way in. The totems are the only real reason I came back to this fucking place." She was tightening inside.

"Yeah, I got the impression you left here on bad terms. Just sort of vanished in a puff of smoke. I figured your dad had finally driven you over the edge, and you took off early for Harvard or Yale or someplace. You ever hear from Mike?" An edge in his voice betrayed a forced casualness.

"No," she said, like striking a match. "I haven't heard from him since I left. Since before I left. He was gone before I was." This conversation felt like sandpaper scouring her insides.

He smiled at her, genuinely, and the sharpness retreated from his tone. "I don't want to talk about that either. It's good to see you. Sorry. Let's drop all that old shit and start fresh. Come by tomorrow around seven. I don't have anyone on the books. We can go get something to eat if you want."

The front door to the studio clattered open again, and a 55-gallon blue plastic barrel was pushed through, accompanied by a great deal of bumping and cursing. Once inside, the man pushing the barrel stood up with a groan.

"Christ, Jerome," said Lane. "How many of those damn things are you going to need?"

Jerome was small and wiry with a bushy shock of dirty-blond hair. A wild collection of tattoos ran up both his arms to the sleeves of his La Mano Peluda T-shirt. He wore paint-spattered work pants and a pair of old Converse high-tops.

"Three more! I just need three more! I'm damn near done!" he said, grinning broadly at Lane.

"Skade, this is Jerome," said Lane. "Jerome is the other artist here. A damn good one too. Jerome, this is Skade, an old friend of mine who just got into town."

"Skade?" Jerome said, stepping around his barrel with a knowing smile. "Gotta be Skade Felsdottir, right?"

Skade felt a flutter of panic—she hadn't counted on anyone remembering her.

"Must be," Jerome continued. "Probably not two people named Skade in America, I'm betting?"

"Uh, yeah…?" Jerome didn't look at all familiar, but hell, was she even capable of recognizing now everyone she'd known then?

"Thought so!" Jerome grabbed her hand and shook it vigorously. "You're the lifeguard that saved Michael Pullman!"

Not that. Please, not that.

"Michael's in high school now. Thanks to you!" said Jerome. "I'm a friend of his brother's. Man, that's all they talked about for years. You're a superhero in that house."

"Wonder Woman," Lane said, taking a box of latex gloves off a shelf. "Remember that newspaper headline? *Local Wonder Woman saves kid at pool* or something like that?" Skade shot him a frown.

"Yeah, like that!" said Jerome happily. "Hell, you even look like Wonder Woman a little."

"Thanks," said Skade flatly. "So what's with the barrel?" she asked, hoping to change the subject and quell the fear and memory riot in her head.

"My boat!" said Jerome.

"Jerome's building a boat. He's going to float it to New Orleans. But we're probably going to be fishing him out of the river about ten feet from the shore after he launches," said Lane.

"Oh fuck no!" replied Jerome as he began setting up his workstation. "This is going to be the greatest boat ever!"

"So you want to get dinner tomorrow?" Lane asked Skade. "With a friend?"

Skade felt like a plug had suddenly been pulled out of her. The tension and apprehension slowly drained away and left exhaustion and resignation behind. Lane was somebody to talk to, even with all the evil baggage. She smiled honestly and wearily. "Yeah. Thanks. I guess I could use a friend. I'll see you tomorrow."

"So we're friends then?" he asked.

"Yeah," she said. "Let's not make it complicated, okay?"

And she turned and left, feeling small and worn out and trying like hell not to show it.

9

Unable to sleep, Skade sat on the floor of her room with some proofs and her laptop. The fear of not being able to finish— not being good enough to finish—felt caustic. But maybe it wasn't a lost cause.

It was just that something wasn't there.

She was trying to find that resonant piece—the feeling and emotion. She dove in and managed to get some work done. But periodically she would resurface into the tangled junkyard of her memories of her life in Carleton. The accident. She needed that to all go away. The cornhusk puppet Kit had given her sat next to her computer, and Skade would pick it up and play with it to calm her mind. Eventually that stopped working.

She finished off a bottle of vodka.

Finally, she got too tired to look at the screen anymore, and she fought with the bed in a frustrated pas-de-deux.

Morning again. Or was it early afternoon? It really didn't matter. Skade got up achingly and hit the shower. When she emerged she found a paper cup half full of day-old—two-day-old?—coffee on the dresser. She drained it and looked down at her scattered prints and notes on the floor and sank back down into them like she was wading into an ice bath. Trying to get something done before meeting Lane.

Hours later, she pulled up near Lane's studio and made her way through late-afternoon air that felt like molten caramel. Blessed relief inside the quiet studio AC. She found Lane.

"You doing okay? You don't look so great," he asked when she came into the room.

"I'm not sleeping real well. Shitty motel bed. I think I'm still adjusting from all the travel. I'm fine. I went down to the totem poles again."

"Did they bust you and haul you in for trespass?"

"No. I got back in there and got a few more pictures. I'm going to go back again in another day or two and see if I can finish." Skade took her laptop out of her bag and made a space on Lane's counter.

"Come here. Take a look," she said.

Lane leaned into the computer screen, running his hand compulsively through his beard, and slowly went through Skade's most recent images. She showed him several of the older files stretching all the way back to northern California and Nevada.

Many of the images were in black and white, and the play of the light on the lonely forgotten makers was exceptional. The color images were haunting. Shot after shot of visualized mourning.

"Christ, Skade. These are incredible," said Lane, lost in the parade of photographs.

Skade opened another folder. This one contained all the shots she'd taken that had been used by magazines in the last three years.

He stopped on an image of two climbers working up an icy granite traverse on a mountainside. The blue-gray granite and the white-blue ice brought out the severity of the darkening weather beautifully.

"Shit. This was you? I saw this one. This is spectacular, Skade!"

"Yeah. That's the one that got me this book deal."

"Really?"

"Yeah, the Klausterman Prize. It came with a publishing contract. So here I am. That was a good shot. Hell of a climb to get it. I was part of a climbing party of five women in the North Cascades. Me and Sarah and Margot were on the last pitch on the last day when a storm came up and beat the shit out of us. It looks like we're going up, but we're actually trying to come down. Scary moments."

"Seriously, Skade. This is some awesome work." His face was unreadable. There was nothing in his eyes to decipher or decode, everything was neat and staged.

"I feel like what I'm doing now isn't working. This book...I feel like I'm missing something. It sucks."

"I'm not a photo critic," he said, giving her another untranslatable look, "but it doesn't suck to me."

"You like them?"

"Yeah. I think they're superb. But it isn't any wonder probably. What did the school call you? The most gifted genius they had ever produced?"

"Like they had anything to do with it. I still wish I could punch the entire administration for hanging that albatross around my neck. Fuck."

"Yeah, well, you might not like it, but it's probably true. You were several levels smarter than anyone I ever knew. You were just better at everything than anyone else. I'm not the least bit surprised you are one of the best photographers in the country."

The praise, which seemed honest, helped her slip out of the shackles of her hangover. And it reinforced her façade.

"Hey listen," said Lane. "While we're here and nothing's going on, let me look at that old piece on your arm? So I can get an idea of what needs to happen."

Skade sat down only half reluctantly. She always felt deeply relaxed in a tattoo chair.

Lane put on a pair of reading glasses that looked out of place on him and wheeled a stool over. He examined the ink running up Skade's right arm. "You've had a lot of work done since you left. This is pretty high quality."

He slowly went over her other arm. "Christ, this is great work. Let me see the rest of it?" He began to undo the buttons on her dark blue rayon shirt. She brushed his hand away.

He straightened up. "Sorry. Didn't mean anything. Some of this stuff is master's work, Skade. I'm seeing at least four hands in this, just on the front of your torso and arms, not counting that little one I did."

She angrily straightened her shirt. "I've got maybe seven—no, eight—different people's work on me now. That's just the big pieces. More on the smaller work, not counting you." She fixed him with a quartz stare.

"Well, you should be in a museum." If her not-so-subtle sword thrust had found a mark, he didn't betray it.

"Thanks," she replied evenly.

Lane stood up and crossed his arms and looked her in the eyes. "A lot different than I remember. The last time I saw you—before you took off—we were swimming out under that haunted bridge out by the country club, remember?"

"Yeah." She coiled up in the chair and watched him.

"Yeah. The image of you climbing back up onto the bridge, naked, wringing the water out of your hair, caught in the headlights, moving like a ballet dancer over the planks, with that dangerous smile of yours? It's inked into my brain. And then turning each other inside out in the back seat. Jesus, you were breathtaking, Skade. You still are."

Skade wrapped her arms around the naked memory of herself. "That was a long time ago, Lane. Those were two different people."

"No shit. A week after that and suddenly it's you and Mike, and then you're gone like smoke."

"I'm sorry. But it's done."

"Yeah."

The only thing she could find in his face was exactly what he wanted her to get and nothing more.

They heard the sound of the bolt being thrown on the back door behind the curtained-off storage area and a light came on. Jerome appeared from behind the curtains; he had a cheap captain's hat on his head that looked a size too small.

"Well, hey," exclaimed Jerome happily when he saw them. "Lane and Wonder Woman!" Jerome was carrying a large white duffle bag and he set it down near his workstation. "Hey, you guys are perfect to help me pick a name for my boat. Lane hates the *Hillbilly Titanic*. What do you think, Skade?"

Skade was grateful for the interruption. "I agree with Lane. The *Titanic* sank. That's probably bad luck, right?"

"Fine, fine," said Jerome with an annoyed wave. "What about other names?"

"The problem is," said Lane, "most boats get famous for sinking. So, it's gonna be tough to come up with a famous name. Think about it, *Lusitania*? Sank. *Edmond Fitzgerald*? Sank."

"*Marie Celeste* didn't sink," offered Skade.

"Yeah, but everyone disappeared off her. Ghost ship."

"What about the *Argo*?" said Skade. "That would be a good name for your boat, Jerome. The *Argo*."

"Argo? What's that?"

"Greek myths. The *Argo* was Jason's ship. Jason and the Argonauts. They went and found the golden fleece. Or you could call it the Odysseus? After the *Odyssey*?"

"Argo sounds like a seed company and the Odyssey sounds like a minivan," said Jerome dejectedly.

"*Pequod*?" said Skade.

"Sank," said Lane.

"Y'all are no help at all," said Jerome, heading back to the storage area. "I need an epic name. I'll get one yet."

"So, let me do a touch-up on your arm. I want to do my work proud, especially since you've got some very high-quality art now. I've got a couple of ideas. I can draw them up for you? And it looks like there's some space to work with."

"Sure, maybe. I'll take a look at your ideas."

Lane took her wrist gently and turned her arm over to look at the three roses again. "Okay, yeah. Dinner. Come back to my place and I'll make us some food. I've got some half-decent wine. We can just talk. Bring your car and you can leave anytime you want. You feel like you could use some company?"

She drew in a long breath and let it out slowly. "Yeah. Okay. That would be nice."

10

Skade followed Lane out to his apartment building, feeling annoyed, but also knowing he was right. Being alone. Her drinking. Bad memories. She could take care of it though.

Lane lived on the top floor of a hundred-year-old five-floor walk-up. The aggressive direct heat on the sidewalk was replaced by a cloistered, mausoleum-like hotness that tried to stuff itself down their throats as they entered the stairway.

"It's not so bad in my place," he said over his shoulder as they climbed the stairs.

A heavy oak door opened into a small foyer with a battered oriental carpet and an old oaken coat stand. Skade's first impression was one of sandalwood with an undercurrent of onions.

The living room was deep and airy; a zoo of shadows with the angular sunset light streaming in the west-facing windows. Lane switched on a couple of floor lamps and most of the wilder shadows chased away into the corners and deepened into wells of dark. Two worn leather club chairs and a large, deep wine-colored chesterfield sofa. Lane started a large industrial-looking air conditioner which seemed to have organically grown out of one of the windows. It growled to life, and Skade instantly felt a wake of cold air blow across her skin.

"I usually turn this down and pop some windows. Hang on." He set about cranking open the casement windows. The curtains caught some of the air that rushed in and danced limply. Skade settled with the same lack of enthusiasm onto the chesterfield and watched.

Lane went into the kitchen, returning a moment later with a couple of glasses of wine.

"Here," he said, handing one to Skade.

Skade took a sip. It was good.

"So you gotta be hungry, right?"

"Maybe. I don't always notice."

"What?"

"Nothing. I kinda lose track of eating sometimes. Sure, I could eat."

"Vegetarian?"

"Nope. I eat pretty much anything that doesn't escape."

"Okay, hang on a minute…" Lane disappeared again into the kitchen.

Skade slid off the sofa and began wandering around the living room looking at the art on the wall, including a signed print from Jenny Frison. She briefly danced with the curtains to get a look out one of the windows and ran a finger over the books on a bookshelf: mostly contemporary art. She saw an old high school yearbook—her senior year—on a bottom shelf. That stung.

"So your place is really nice," she managed, trying to put some space between herself and the yearbook.

"Thanks," came his reply, mixed with the sounds of muffled efficiency in the kitchen. "Like everything, it's a work in progress. I inherited most of the furniture."

"I got down to look at the old Kensington Aquatic center when I got into town…"

"Not surprised," he called back from the kitchen. "Knowing you, that would be the first place you'd go."

"Yeah. So what's the deal with the old pool? Are they tearing it out?"

"Not sure. I heard they might be turning it into a skate park, actually. That'd be a good thing to do with it."

Skade continued to drift slowly through Lane's space. She found a brass incense holder on a table and picked it up. Vague memories flitted around it—something she remembered from before.

"How come you never left?" she asked.

Lane appeared from the kitchen carrying a couple of plates. "Here, see if you like this."

Skade took a plate, something smoky and sweet smelling. She sat back down on the sofa and took a bite. It reminded her how hungry she really was. When was the last time she'd eaten?

"This is great. Thanks, Lane," she said halfway through another bite.

"No trouble. Nothing fancy. What did you ask?"

"Why didn't you ever leave here?" Skade asked again, covering her mouth.

Lane took a bite and smiled slightly as he looked at one of the curtains expanding into the early twilight draft coming in the window.

"I don't know, really," he said. "I guess I never achieved escape velocity. The gravity of this place was maybe stronger for me. Or maybe my engines weren't as strong as yours were." He took a long deep breath and fixed her with his gaze for a moment. "Or maybe I never had a good enough reason."

Skade felt a wave of something from him, but let it go.

"A lot of it was probably not knowing what I wanted to do," he continued. "I got an art school degree and stayed put. It was easier."

"You think about leaving?" she asked.

"Yeah. I met somebody a couple of years ago. She lives in Toronto. She's been after me to come there." The look on his face was an open question of sorts. Maybe the first crack in his façade.

"Toronto's really nice. I love it there," she said, letting his overloaded energy pass again.

Lane went back into the kitchen and came back with the wine bottle and refilled their glasses.

"So…" He raised his glass and they touched rims. "A photographer? I was surprised. I guess we all assumed you'd be a scientist or a doctor or a fucking astronaut by now, you know? Given how big a deal everybody made about you being that gifted genius thing—which you were. How was college?"

"Fine. It was good. I decided photography was what I really wanted." The lie felt as if she were swallowing tacks.

"How'd you get in to take pictures at the totems?"

"Someone let me in…a woman who works for the highway department. She let me in after I hiked back there through an endless, horrible, stifling-hot cornfield. I was worried, at first, that she was going to turn me in. She was really nice, though. Tall as all hell. She says she might be able to show me some other sites she knows about. I had no idea what that place had become. My memory of it is being so much smaller. It's crazy now."

"I drove out past them a few months before the construction began," Lane said. "It's really pretty spectacular. But you can understand why there's been a constant battle over it. State-owned land, no permits, no plan. And if you're not ready for it, it can be an enormous distraction on the road. It's like suddenly driving into Disneyland. And it draws all kinds of goofy people. It wouldn't surprise me at all if half the reason they decided to do the construction was a cover to tear the whole thing down."

"Maybe," said Skade, sitting back on the sofa. "The state hasn't gotten around to outlawing them yet. Not that many people pay attention to those laws in other states, but it does give the highway department a legal reason to take them down when they get around to it."

"So this is your last stop then?"

"I'm on a deadline now. So, yeah, I'm hoping this is all I'll need. There's some other sites in other states I'd like to go check out, but I don't think I'm going to have the time now. What about you? How's the studio business been?"

"Mostly great. I have some really good regulars, and I've got people making appointments now from out of town. I'm becoming a destination, I guess, so that's pretty cool. I'm able to charge more and control my own schedule. Things would be damn nice if I could just keep people from screwing me over."

"How do you mean?"

Lane's energy changed abruptly, as if something under the surface was getting closer. Volcanic. "Fucking people screwing me over. Taking advantage of me."

"How?"

"Shit. I had a couple of women I took on as apprentices. Girls, really. Both of them pretty young. Fresh out of wherever, you know? I explained the rules to them. They signed my contract. I don't screw around with this. If you sign on with me, it's not always going to be easy, but you're going to know what you're doing when you're done. You'll be good if you can cut it." Lane leaned back in his seat, his face darkening.

"I don't play that whole just-do-your-time-and-here's-your-license thing. People need to put in the work. It's not just fun and art and screwing around. Anyway, they gave it a go for a while, but it was pretty obvious from the start neither of them was cut out for it. They weren't going to make it through the two years. They started whining and complaining about this and that. Not wanting to take it seriously, you know? And then one day, they both just quit showing up. We had appointments on the books and I had to cover them. Then I find out that they've opened a shop together in Danville. Complete violation of the contract. And to make it worse, they've scalped a few of my newer customers. Screwed me twice."

"Damn, Lane. That sounds awful."

"Yeah, well, we'll see if they get away with it. I've got their licenses tied up in the court, you know. No way I let them screw with me. If I can help it, they'll never work in this state. And I'm putting the word out to people I know. This isn't going to end well for them. I'll get mine back and then some." He sat for a moment and glowered as Skade watched. Then the storm broke and passed and the normal Lane returned.

He got up and took the plates back to the kitchen. "You still hungry?"

"No. I'm fine, thanks." Skade tossed another glass of wine back and poured what was left of the bottle into her glass and finished it. She looked at Lane's half-full glass sitting on the table. She reached out mechanically and drained it, then sat it back down in its place. She was feeling done now. Keeping up her façade was taking too much energy.

"Hey, Lane," she called out to him, standing up. "I should get going. I need to get some rest and get back at it in the morning."

Lane came out of the kitchen. "Where are you staying?"

"The Skyline, believe it or not."

Lane gave a mirthless laugh. "I think I was at a party out there ten years ago and I needed to take a shower just from being in the parking lot. It can't be a good place for you."

There was a noticeable change in the energy.

"It's fine. It's quiet. I'm good there. I've been in worse, believe me."

"You could stay here, if you want," he said with a casual gravity.

"No." There was more than a polite refusal in the flatness of her reply, and both of them knew it.

"Well, if you wake up with fleas; or worse, if it gets creepy—"

"No, Lane."

They looked at each other for a moment and she turned to leave.

"Oh shit. Hang on a second, Skade. I almost forgot..." Lane hurried back down the hall. She waited by the door.

He returned holding something that Skade fought hard not to recognize: a worn-out blue-and-white shoebox. *SF* was written in dark purple marker on each of the sides.

"Your dad..." Lane paused, not knowing what else to say after that. "It's kind of a weird story, honestly," he began again. "He came by the restaurant where I was working and gave me this right before he left town. He said to give it to you if you ever turned up again." He held the box out to her.

Skade felt as if someone were handing her a dead cat. She didn't take it.

"What?" said Lane, seeing the reaction play across her face. "You don't want it? It is yours, isn't it?"

"Yeah." She finally managed to get past the screams in her head. "Yeah, it's mine. How long have you had this?" Skade stared at the box in Lane's outstretched hands.

"Shit. Your dad gave it to me nine or ten years ago, I guess. When he left, he had a bunch of stuff he was getting rid of—"

"Yeah, I bet," Skade spat out angrily.

"But if you're asking have I just had it lying around here? No. It's been in a storage locker with a bunch of other crap. I got it out yesterday after you showed up. That made me remember I had it."

"Have you looked through it?" Snakes and alarms in her head.

"I'm not going to lie, Skade—"

Skade inhaled sharply through her teeth. "Fucking give me that!" Lunging out, she fairly ripped it from his hands. The box felt like molten lead.

It was her private memory box from the age of twelve, to the week before she ran away.

"Hey. I didn't read any of the stuff. I just looked at a few of the pictures. I'm sorry. Obviously, that was a shitty thing for me to have done…"

Skade wanted to throw the box as far away as she could, but it was stuck to her hand now. Just the touch of it—the feel of it—sent a furious rush of memories up her arm against her will. She writhed inside but managed to calm down and get some control back. "No. Thanks, Lane. Thanks. I'm just…I don't know… It surprised me."

"Yeah, sorry. Hey, listen—"

"I gotta go now," she said, fighting off nausea as she backed away, turned, and strode out the door.

11

The fucking box sitting on the end of her bed was already playing tricks with her mind, and she hadn't even opened it yet. Skade thought about the clay jar given to Pandora. Unlike Pandora, however, she knew what was in this box. *She* was in the box. The undeniable evidence of her existence in the past. And she wasn't at all interested in letting herself, or any of the rest of it, out.

It had to just be in her head, right? She could smell the utterly unique collage of scents—the smells of the substrate of her youth: her father's cigarettes, crawfish and red wine, Noxzema, tea, chlorine, her old shampoo, and a hundred other tiny things that made up the olfactory fingerprint of her past. Together, it was a smell so familiar it had registered in its absence only when she ran off into a new backstory of smells, the new canvas upon which her new world was painted.

She thought about tossing the box in the motel dumpster or setting it on fire in the parking lot. But something—masochism or vanity or some misguided hope—pulled at her.

Skade tentatively poked at the lid, and it came off. She'd ripped the lid off her own coffin. Letters, postcards, old photo envelopes, a splash of unrelated little objects, linked only by their relationship to her. A collection of ephemera charged with memory—each item a tiny Aladdin's lamp with its own genie ready to escape, called upon or not.

Skade sat on her bed without taking her eyes off the box while she opened a bottle of vodka and took a drink. It made her eyes water. The second one was always easier. She reached into the box of snakes and spiders and pulled out the first thing her fingers encountered before anything had a chance to bite her. A photograph. Of herself. Maybe thirteen years old, all arms and legs like a fawn. Skade might not have been able to identify the girl in the picture except that she'd once been told that that girl was her. It might have been taken at a carnival, but Skade couldn't be sure. In the photograph—a badly lit old snapshot taken by someone she couldn't remember—she was clutching an enormous green-and-white stuffed dog, nearly as big as she was, and she was smiling honestly, which was something else she didn't recognize. The picture had been taken not long before her mother died. Everything that happened before the crash and the funeral felt fuzzy.

"Jesus Christ…" She took another drink and stared briefly up at the ceiling.

Next out of the box was an ivory-colored bone tied to an old skeleton key with red cotton string. Something her father had brought her from someplace strange, when he'd reappeared after an absence. Her mother had thought it an awkward gift for an eight-year-old girl, and had said as much, but she let Skade keep it. The bone became the centerpiece in a coven she and two friends had formed one long-ago girl-summer.

Next was a battered plastic bag containing a collection of mismatched chess pieces.

Her mother had taught her chess when she was six or seven. She had gotten fairly good at it, by six- or seven-year-old standards at least, but the game itself hadn't captured her the way it had some of the other kids at her Montessori. What had fascinated her, however, were the pieces. The sheer variety of chess sets intrigued her. Some sets were realistic in their depiction of medieval warriors or Napoleonic soldiers or Vikings. Other sets where wholly abstract forms. They all seemed to be works of art. And all of them had a power to engage her imagination.

When Skade was twelve, she'd found an ancient set in a flea market while tagging along with her mother. One side was composed of miniature British soldiers—the rook, a log tower with a Union Jack. The opponents were Indians, ignorant stereotypes of how white people had imagined Native Americans, complete with tomahawks and a chief with feathered headdress. The faces of the pawns were strangely expressive. She picked up each piece on the board, one at a time, and slowly turned them around in her hands. Gazing at a British rook and an Indian bishop, a feeling of desire had come over her. She needed these pieces. Not the entire set, just a few pieces. She looked around—no one in the busy market was paying any attention to the twelve-year-old girl at the card table. She slipped the rook and the bishop into the pocket of her jeans. No one noticed. Her heart raced. She took a pawn from each side and put them in her pocket as well. She felt as if she might explode. Turning slowly from the table, she walked away to join her mother, who had floated aimlessly over to the other side of the market. She'd never stolen anything before.

When Skade got home, she dashed upstairs to her room, bathing in the feelings that washed over her as she held her four stolen chess pieces. A heady mixture of vibrating guilt and frothy elation, her body resonated with it. She had always been scrupulous in her observance of the rules, and she hated being scolded for doing anything wrong. Adults had always praised her for being such a "good girl." No one would have ever believed Skade Felsdottir could have stolen anything. This feeling was new and enlivening, but at the same time, it had to be kept secret. In her closet she found a blue-and-white shoebox, dropped her four chess pieces inside it, and hid it behind the books on her shelf. Then she went downstairs for dinner. From that moment on, everything special, private, or meaningful eventually found its way into that blue-and-white shoebox.

Skade stole only chess pieces. She took them from coffee shops and libraries and thrift stores. If there was a chess set at someone's house where a party was being held, she'd slip out a piece. Once she took three pieces from three different very expensive boards in a high-end game store. As she got older, she began to discover a lilting sexual feeling associated with lifting a chess piece, something stimulating and erotic. Eventually she stopped holding on to the pieces unless there was something very special about them. It became more about the act than the item, but there were pieces she found so fascinating and special that she did keep them, and these were the pieces in her plastic bag.

She reached inside and took out a pawn from that very first chess set, the Indian with the tomahawk and the scowl, but the sensation was now different. She felt a sense of distance and detachment, of disconnection. What had been *her*—that part that had been present in her life—was now missing. The rabbit hole of the past into which Skade found herself falling was hateful. She felt a fine sheen of panic shimmer on her skin, but she was too deep into the box to stop, so she kept digging, against her better judgment.

Photographs. The thought of them made her ill. She knew those letters were in here too, and the awards. The box was full of what should have been, of the reminders of all she lost, reminders of herself and a past that was no longer hers. She'd abandoned her past in a dumpster twelve years ago and she couldn't have it back now. And because she couldn't have it, she hated it. The box mocked her and burned at her heart. Tears filling her eyes, she tossed the pictures onto the bed and ripped into her vodka bottle. She took a long, ragged breath, then grabbed her keys and went out to find a bar before the rest of what was in the box found her.

An excerpt from the notes for Chapter 4:
"The material and the meanings" of
American Still Life

By Skade Felsdottir

And what of all this stuff? These great many things which oftentimes make up a roadside or street corner memorial? In some places (mainly in wealthier, antiseptic suburban areas) *descansos* have been derided as nothing more than garish displays of "mourning sickness," places where someone has vomited up an ugly pile of emotion on the side of the road. And that might be accurate. *Descansos* are a visible effluent of grief. An outpouring of the uncontrolled and uncontrollable: feelings, something considered anathema to many Americans ~~(the wealthier, antiseptic and suburban at least, who have jettisoned their feelings for a form of insulation against their messy, uncomfortable humanity)~~. But again, why all the things?

We live our lives in metaphor. Everything we see and touch and think and speak and do is, at many levels, a representation. These things we collect and incorporate into our lives and ourselves are metaphors. They are in a sense a language of ideas and concepts made manifest: stuffed animals are innocence, they become that. Flowers are the transcendence of beauty, they become that. Wedding paraphernalia becomes devotion, food becomes peace offering, simple written notes to loved ones lost are elegies or confessions. ~~Who will hear my confession?~~ The act of setting up a memorial itself becomes an act of communion. And the syntax and semiotics of that communication is this non-verbal representation, this physical metaphor. These things. Is it because there is something so frenetically material about our grief? We are confronted with something beyond our understood and comfortable existence: death, the great permanence of it. Mortality, those things which are immaterial and beyond the common sense of easy representation. We confront the immaterial with the material. We heap up something understandable and comfortable to cover up that which is not understandable.

To give us a measure of security, we wrap the invisible man in bandages of plastic.

These objects are also place holders for us. They become like the breadcrumbs left by Hansel and Gretel as they traveled through the dark wood. Touchstones. Mnemonic devices. Things left in our world for the people who are gone.

And, all these *things* are like Aladdin's lamps for those that set them out. It can be so strange to come upon one of these markers alone, out of context. There it sits, on an embankment on the side of a highway, a cross strewn with plastic flowers, stuffed animals, notes, names, words, dates, numbers, and all manner of the daily stuff of life. It seems to be some sort of strange code in the grass. A jumble of the vaguely decipherable, something on the edge of our conception—mostly recognizable parts that won't come to any kind of comfortable whole beyond the largely superficial. And we look at these conglomerates of objects, and we wonder what it all means? It means someone died. And someone else cared. But to the people who created the memorial, it's altogether a different thing than what you or I see. Each object, placed in its position, has in it a captive genie of memory, its individual reference to something real in the past. They are each physical, corporal memories.

~~Why do I dream in broken things? I dream in torn clothing and blood and crows~~

All those objects are voices, and in their context and placement and meaning they sing loudest to those who understand. Deeply personal and profound. And alone and nonsensical.

The words left at memorials are also just things, shifting metaphoric and relational. One of the most common statements seen in these lonely places is *Never forget.* Upon first encounter, this statement, alone or in the presence of a name or a date, seems to be a defiant oath, full of anger and strength and blood. Demands and orders. Vows and promises in the face of impermanence, to maintain something permanent. A shout of control and mastery over ourselves and the universe. A final martial marching order to go boldly into the fog, come what may. But then, with the passage of time and life, those same words transform into something closer to a beggar's request. A plea. A hopeless desire to not lose that which was never ours to begin with. Our memory is archival, and it becomes a cry to maintain the library, to give us a sense of place in the ever-changing river of existence. We want to remember. There was good there. Wasn't there? Please, let me have this much. Then, finally, the words transform into a prayer. An offer up to something larger and unknown for meaning, for context, for understanding, and finally for some measure of acceptance. Or maybe for a desire to no longer need any of those things. Finally, just a prayer of acknowledgment.

~~You cannot cure what you cannot acknowledge. I cannot acknowledge. I cannot be cured. I have no hope.~~

An important part of the material—the "spiritual kindling"—at many descansos are the photographs. In many ways, these serve as the bight in the cords that bind the living to the dead. These smiling photos of people, not thinking about their own mortality, and representing a completely different context than the descanso itself, act as receipts to the heart. They identify that this person was really there, and they certify that the dead are not really gone. They are there still, captured in light-sensitive chemicals, and they call up ghosts to smile and wave at us from the roadside. Or shake their fists. Or weep. Or simply stare blankly back.

These material metaphors of transience mediate and negotiate between the living left behind and the dead. Just as the altars set up for the visiting ghosts of recently departed ancestors, released for the day from the afterworld on Dia de los Muertos in Mexico, are acts of offering and communication left by survivors, so too are these lonely markers on the roadside. And the very act of them—the fact that they exist in time, even relative to their supposed ephemerality—helps to bind the living and the dead together. A cord made of the literal memorabilia of grief. An authentic manifestation. All this stuff—these things—are the mundane transfigured into the mythic.

-S. Felsdottir

12

Skade sat in the parking lot of her twenty-four-hour drug store with a fresh quart in her lap. Her body felt like a bell that had been struck and was still angrily resonating.

She pulled the rearview over to look at herself. She could only assume what was looking back at her was her.

She found a bar.

❧

The night passed in flashes of things. Visions. Images. Sounds.

A bar, dark-brown mahogany and polished pine.

A bartender. With a bad case of bartender eyes.

An Allman Brothers song: "Whipping Post." The long version from the Fillmore.

The pool tables, and the endless green glow of the felt and the quiet ivory balls. Winning. Winning again.

The drinks lining up along the rail. Four? Four.

Being told "no." No.

Maybe about a drink? Being behind the bar? Showing the bartender how to make a fucking triple V&T.

"No. Don't call the fucking cops. Christ!"

Things never change here. This place is exactly the same as I left it.

"In Memory of Elizabeth Reed."

No.

The next morning felt like the scene of a crime. Skade came to a vague consciousness and sat up in a state of confused panic. Her sheets were covered in blood. So was she. For minutes Skade choked back screams, did a quick body audit, and found a nasty but superficial scrape on the side of her knee, and another long one near her elbow. They were still oozing. It wasn't someone else's blood. Not this time. She calmed down a notch. She couldn't find the night before anywhere in her head.

Her neck and shoulders throbbed with pain. She swallowed the last two percs, hit the shower, and got dressed—just don't look in the mirror.

She had moved from *emergency-trauma* to *beleaguered* before Kit's truck rumbled into the parking lot. Janeyre Thinksquickly was strapped in her familiar place.

"Hey… Good to see you," said Kit happily.

"Thanks," replied Skade, slumping in her seat. Keeping it all together in the onslaught of light and motion and Kit was almost more than she could bear. She broke out in a sweat.

They drove on for a few miles. Kit's silence was bouncy, Skade's glowering.

"You okay, Skade?" asked Kit, casting worried glances her way. "You look like you're getting sick."

Skade automatically sat up in her seat, rolled her shoulders back, and put some energy into her voice, which cost her inside. "I'm just tired. I'm having a hard time sleeping. Bad motel beds and being worried about the book." Kit looked at her blankly. They drove a few minutes in silence again, this time worried silences from both of them. "And I probably had too much to drink last night."

Kit smiled. "It looks it a little."

Skade sank back into her seat now that she didn't need to keep up appearances. "I guess I was trying to sleep better, so I tried having a couple of drinks to relax and it backfired. Can't hold my liquor."

"I've had that happen. I don't drink much, so it usually bites me hard when I have more than a couple," offered Kit sympathetically. She reached out a tentative hand and gave Skade's shoulder an awkward pat. Skade found herself almost in tears but held it off.

"So where are you taking me?" asked Skade.

"Out 232. Do you know about Donna Mosier?"

"I don't think so."

"It happened about seven or eight years ago, I guess. I thought maybe you'd have heard about her. It was a big deal. Still is, I guess, to some people."

"Why?"

"You'll see. It's real sad."

They drove over the Black River and onto State Road 232, a river-hugging stretch of highway. 232 was a lovely road running in and out of the hills in the river valley. Overhanging forest dappled the sunlight and made for an idyllic summer's day. A mix of summer smells blew into Skade's open window: hot asphalt, the clean, green smell of fresh leaves, the pungent scent of manured fields, and the muddy fish-scent of a slow river. The heat muffled the sounds in the eternal quiet of a midsummer afternoon. Skade's hangover began to subside as they came around a long blind curve.

"Damn," said Skade.

A slope on the far hillside was cleared of trees and brush, and in the open space stood a tight grouping of identical crosses. A lot of them.

"I need to go up a little farther to cut across. Did you count them?" said Kit as they drove past.

Skade turned to look out the back window. "Eight."

"Sometimes there's nine."

At Skade's request, Kit pulled onto the shoulder about a hundred yards from the crosses. Skade checked her camera and climbed out. She immediately lined up establishing shots, then walked up and down the hillside looking for good lines of sight. Kit stayed a few steps behind, watching.

Skade circled the memorial twice, slowly, taking shots at various angles. Then she sat for a moment in quiet respect before finally moving to take close-ups. Even the remnants of a monumental hangover couldn't compete with her focus at work.

"Hey, Kit?" she called. "What name did you say? Donna Mosier? Don't bite your nails."

Kit quickly dropped her hand from her mouth. She was sitting quietly in the shade of the tree line above the markers, intently watching Skade. "Yeah."

"I see four Mosiers here but no Donna?"

"Like I said," said Kit, unfolding her long body as she rose to her feet, "sometimes there's nine up here. Do you see the hole in the ground?"

"Yeah, right here."

"Donna is the reason this descanso is here," Kit said as she approached Skade. "I guess you could say she killed everyone up here. Herself included. Some church put up the markers after the…accident? I'm not sure what to call what happened here." Kit shoved her hands deep into the pockets of her work pants and took a long breath. "Anyway, after the church put up the markers, somebody from one of the families came and ripped out Donna's cross. The church put up a new one, and they ripped it out again. That went on for a while, then it spilled over into the newspapers. People were talking about it all over town. There was this feeling like Donna shouldn't have one, since she was the one who did this, but a few people were talking about Christian forgiveness and how Donna was probably sick, so she didn't know what she was doing. Now, every once in a while, the church, or somebody at least, comes out and puts up a cross for Donna. It'll stay up until somebody notices it, and then it gets taken down again.

"It's kinda famous now. Sometimes the Donna cross gets stolen by kids. There's ghost stories about it. Donna's cross is like a witch's symbol now, or something. I don't know, it's weird. And sad. I think about it sometimes and I feel bad for Donna. She's become a monster in a ghost story, but she used to be a real person with some sad problems."

Skade knelt again to look more closely. "What happened?" she asked, glancing up at Kit's face.

"The four Mosier markers are for Donna's kids. Those other two," Kit pointed at two more markers for Marsha and Connie Rechter, "are for Donna's sister's kids. All six of them under six years old, I think. One of Donna's kids was just a baby, not even two. One day Donna loaded her kids into her car, got her sister's kids and loaded them in too, then she came out here and drove into oncoming traffic on 232. Right here, coming around that curve, she ran into another car head-on. Those other two makers are for the two people in that car. Nine people dead, and I don't think anyone really knows why, but the police and everybody are sure it was deliberate."

The two of them moved back up to the tree line and sat down on the grass. "So Donna was, what, mentally ill?" asked Skade.

"Crazy? Sure. I mean, doesn't doing something like that require you to be crazy? Sane people don't do that."

"Was it out of the blue?"

"I dunno. I guess there were some issues in her past. Who really knows? Crazy kinda works like that. I've seen crazy."

They sat for a while, quietly, listening to the slow sounds of the summer and the whisper of cars on the highway below. It was pleasant in the shade, above the site of so much tragedy. A warm breeze ruffled Skade's dark hair. She still felt Kit's touch on her shoulder. It was the kindest thing anyone had done for her since...?

"How do you know crazy?" asked Skade.

Several strange facial expressions passed over Kit's face in waves. Finally, she settled on a weak smile beneath eyes full of sadness. "Family stuff, I guess." There was more ready to come out of Kit, so Skade waited.

"My dad was okay when he was around. He was a long-haul trucker, so he was gone a lot. He was my mom's third husband. He'd come home and act like a stranger or a houseguest. A nice stranger or houseguest, but not exactly like family, you know? I didn't really know him much. My mom...well, that was different." Kit pulled up a few blades of grass.

"My mom was part of this church. It wasn't like a regular church. I guess you'd call it sort of a cult or something. That's what the courts called it when they stepped in and shut it down." Kit sat looking at her knees. Skade was as quiet as a stone and kept waiting.

"She'd been in it since before I was born. I don't really remember much about anything before I was about eleven or twelve. It's all fuzzy and disconnected, you know? Some things I think I remember but some stuff might be like dreams or stuff people told me that I just sort of put into my own head like memories. I had these big blank spaces in my head, you know? And they needed to be filled up, so I just took stuff people told me and pasted the stories and things they said in there. And I'm not sure anymore what's real and what's not from back before." Kit looked into Skade's eyes with an embarrassed, pleading look. "But it was mostly okay. Until my brother and sister died." Kit closed her eyes. Skade reached out and put her hand on Kit's leg. That felt strange for Skade too. "They died when I was eleven, just a few weeks apart. That's when stuff got bad. My dad left. He went to do a job and never came back. Mom was already sick. She sank deep into that church and took me with her. That was pretty crazy.

"There were six kids from families that were in the church. We didn't go to school, and we couldn't talk to anybody outside. It was just bad. Sometimes we went without food. They wouldn't take us to the doctor when we were sick. When I got my period for the first time—" Kit took a long, sharp breath and looked away.

"God, I'm so sorry," said Skade.

"It's okay," said Kit, turning back and smiling. "I guess somebody went to the sheriff about it. The kids got put in foster care, and my mom was put in a mental hospital. She was having a hard time telling real from fake because of all the stuff God's Glory Preacher was putting on her. That's what the guy that ran the church was called, God's Glory Preacher.

"I got to go to school again, and stuff got more normal. When I turned eighteen, I got the house. Mom's still in a care facility. She's better, but she's probably not going to be able to really ever care for herself. I'd like to bring her home someday, maybe." Kit stopped and looked directly at Skade. "So, yeah, I know crazy." She smiled.

The two of them sat in the shade of the trees, Kit watching the cars slip by and Skade staring deeply into the group of crosses.

"Thanks, Kit," said Skade eventually. "Thanks for bringing me here. This is a great site. I can get some back story from the local paper, I'm sure. This will be great for the book." She smiled up at Kit as they stood up. "And thanks for telling me about all that stuff. I'm so sorry you had to go through all that."

"Thanks for listening. Sorry for dumping all that on you. Did you get enough pictures?"

"Yeah. Let's go."

And they walked back down the slope to the truck.

13

Kit suggested swinging by her house on the way back. Skade stared out the window, trying to piece together images and words for her book. She told herself she might be making progress, but that felt like a lie, and she contracted around it. She didn't know. She just knew she had to finish and in the same space she was sure she couldn't. Her head filled with noise again and she looked at the scenery to clear it.

This was country Skade was familiar with. When she'd lived in Carleton, she spent a great deal of time driving from house parties to bonfires out here. Faces came to her memory, faces she'd only ever seen in the dark. Those faces were etched clearly in her mind. More clearly, in fact, than many of the faces of recent friends and lovers. They appeared to her now with only the occasional partial name—Guzman, Fox, Sammy, Trish—attached. Why had she never seen any of those people outside of intoxicated late-night parties? For all she knew, some of these night-phantoms hadn't even been real, just products of the chemicals she had been pouring into her brain.

The faces were followed by the usual parade of embarrassments, regrets, and little horror-shows of things she'd done or said, or things that had been done or said to her. The truly awful things were locked away in little boxes in the back of her mind so that she could live with herself and get through the average day. But the little ones, the random little offenses, real and imagined, they always slipped through her filters like tiny shards of glass.

Kit pulled into a gravel driveway running through a scruffy yard up to a faded light-blue-and-white ranch house. Haphazardly maintained, it was clearly on the back half of its life. Skade felt the need for a drink as she climbed out of the truck.

"You want to come in for a second?" Kit asked tentatively.

The heat from the front yard and the canned coolness of the air conditioning did battle in the entryway when Kit pushed the door open.

And Skade walked into a fairy tale—very literally.

Dozens of huge, beautiful butterfly wings crowded the ceiling over her head. But on closer inspection, Skade saw that they weren't butter-flies, they were fairies. The gossamer wings had been sewn onto the backs of marionettes, and they dangled, limp and lifeless, from wooden racks attached to the ceiling.

The modest living room resembled a blend of Santa's workshop and Dr. Frankenstein's lab, crammed as it was with little wooden and plastic body parts—arms, legs, heads, feet, and fingers; glass jars of doll's eyes; fur, feathers, and fins; torsos of all manner of creatures, even some that were vegetable or mineral or some mad combination of both. It was a Jackson Pollock painter's bench. And an explosion of some of the most intricate and beautiful puppets and marionettes Skade had ever seen.

Kit slid behind a battered chair near the doorway to allow Skade the full impact of an unobstructed view. She watched with the wide eyes of a little girl looking for approval, biting her nails anxiously.

Skade had stepped out of reality like Dorothy after the tornado. The light was diffuse and dreamlike through layers of gauze curtains on the big picture window and Skade drifted into the room, looking up at the hanging puppets. Some were skillfully realistic—a fox in a bright-red military coat; a thin and faceless ballerina; a black bird with a three-cor-nered hat and a bugle; a cat wearing a drum over its yellow-jacketed shoulder; a peg-legged pirate brandishing a cutlass; a purple octopus. Other puppets were made of kitchen implements and bits of scrap, and everywhere, on the tables and chairs, were creations half-finished and rolls of wire and fishing line. Skade wrestled her attention from the magic all around her and turned to Kit with an astonished smile.

"What is all this?"

"Puppets," Kit said, straightening up a bit toward her full height and smiling through her fingers, which she'd reflexively put to her mouth again. "I do puppets." She'd gotten the reaction she'd hoped for.

"Did you make all these?"

"Yeah. I've done it since I was little."

Skade reached for the ballerina. The puppet was soft, jointed like a foot-tall artist's manikin, and featureless, other than the powder-blue tutu she wore.

"Her name is Henrietta. She's not that fragile."

"Do they all have names?" asked Skade, gently holding Henrietta in her hands and looking around at the multitude of figures hanging and sitting and lying around her.

"Yeah. They all have names. And stories. And personalities. They sort of come out as I'm making them. Here. Let me. She takes some practice." Kit rushed to the table, in all her desperate ungainliness, and awkwardly knelt on the floor, taking the puppet from Skade's hands. "Like this." Kit picked up a long piece of stiff wire with a crook at the end.

Skade gasped as Henrietta came to life.

She lay in a heap on the table, but as soon as Kit touched the rods connected to her hands and feet and head, the little dancer raised her head and looked around. She delicately pushed herself up to a kneeling position, her back erect and her hands on her knees. She seemed to take a deep breath, and then pushed herself up to standing. Henrietta slowly lifted each foot in turn, before turning her featureless face to Skade. She came to fifth position, her arms gracefully raised above her head. Plié, battement tendu, sauté, écarté, épaulé, croisé derrière, effacé, then a slow, graceful turn on one toe with a leg extended into space—all done with nuance and grace and an extraordinary emotional presence. Kit used the four rods and the wire crook, two or three in each hand, like a musician. For all her seeming discomfort in her own body, her hands seemed to invest an inanimate body with a soul.

Slowly, Henrietta folded down into a cross-legged seat on the table, her arms gracefully extended in front of her, and her head sank down as if she were going to sleep. Kit released the rods, and the life left the puppet as if a flame had been blown out, and it was, again, merely a handful of wood and cloth on the table.

"Kit..." Skade breathed in wonderment. Henrietta's ballet on the coffee table in the cluttered explosion of Kit's living room workshop was as close to magic as anything Skade had ever seen before.

Kit smiled and turned away, a blush washing over her cheeks. She got up from the floor and brushed the hanging fairies from her face as she headed for a doorway.

"Want something to drink?" she muttered.

"Christ, yes...I'd love something," said Skade as she tried again to take in the room.

Everywhere there were pieces and parts of things and glue guns and needles and thread and wire and string. Skade reached down and picked up Janeyre Thinksquickly. She held Janeyre and caught sight of herself in a mirror over the mantel. A little girl she hadn't seen in a very long time looked back at her for half a blink of an eye.

"Hey, Kit? Can I take a few pictures?"

Kit reappeared from the kitchen with a couple of glasses in her hands. "Um…sure, I guess," she said uneasily.

"Are you sure?"

"I guess. It's just kind of a mess…" Kit trailed off, looking around the space.

"It's amazing." Skade grinned.

"Here." Kit took Janeyre from Skade and handed her a glass. Skade took a deep pull and gagged slightly, coughing.

"You okay?" asked Kit.

Skade covered her mouth and laughed a little. "Yeah, the water just took me by surprise."

"What do you mean?"

"Nothing. Thanks."

Kit slipped her hand in one quick smooth motion into the puppet, much like an otter slipping into a lake. "This, as you know, is Janeyre Thinksquickly."

She held her left arm up across her chest and used it as a stage.

Janeyre seemed to have just awoken from some deep sleep. She rubbed her eyes as she looked around. When her sweeping gaze finally found Skade, a smile of amusement and wonder on her face, Janeyre gave a start and cowered like a baby animal against Kit's chest; then, she gathered herself and slowly leaned in toward Skade's face, as if to get a better look. Janeyre's movements were uncannily realistic, conveyed with the most subtle nuances of attitude and motions, almost none of which Skade could accurately describe, but all of which she registered as being real and of-a-life—of a human being.

Janeyre then drew herself up to her full height, raised her head slightly with an unmistakable air of mischievousness, and made a beckoning motion.

"Come on," said Kit. "We'll show you around."

"Does she talk?" asked Skade, still transfixed by the puppet riding on Kit's arm.

"She does, but only in whispers. She's pretty shy until she gets to know you. Some of the puppets don't talk; they sort of grow voices when they need them. It's hard to explain. Janeyre has a thing though— she likes to give people new names. Sometimes she gives the other puppets their names too."

Kit and Janeyre led Skade around the small living room.

"You made *all* of these?"

"Most of them. I have some that I didn't make, but I like making them mostly now."

Through the strange multitude of things to look at, Skade began noticing little gatherings of puppets—gangs, clusters, and family groups. Some seemed grouped by color or clothing, and others seemed random in their associations. There were vignettes, too, almost like little stage plays frozen in a moment. Stories, Skade realized, were going on all around Kit's house, being whispered everywhere in voices she couldn't quite hear and in a language she couldn't quite understand.

One group, on a shelf, consisted of an old woman in a gray shawl, a doe with long eyelashes, something that looked like a fierce Hindu demon, an elegant woman in a long burgundy taffeta dress, a wild-eyed goat, and a frog in a kimono—all huddled together under a torn Japanese parasol. The puppets seemed worn and faded, wounded by time, each with a sense of deep antiquity. A sadness leaked from them.

"Those are the mourners," Kit said quietly from behind.

"They seem so sad," Skade said, framing them in her camera.

"They are sad. A flood came and washed everything away. They're all that's left."

"Shouldn't they be happy to be alive?"

"The dead ones aren't sad. Sadness is part of life, so it spreads to the living but doesn't go past the edge of death. Sadness, I think, collects in the ones left alive, and the fewer left living, the more sadness they have to carry," said Kit, looking as if she might belong on the shelf too.

Four small wooden boxes sat on a lace-covered table, along with an assortment of other things—Native American fetishes, a bowl of what looked like bear claws, old envelopes, road maps, a scrimshawed whale's tooth, jade tiki figures, pipes, some dried roses, a glass box with what looked like shrunken heads inside, and a triangle-folded American flag. It all resembled an altar.

"That's my brother and sister and grandpa and our dog, Rufus," said Kit.

Skade looked for a photograph and realized that she hadn't seen a single one anywhere. "Where?" she asked, perplexed.

"On the table."

"You mean those?" asked Skade, pointing at the boxes.

"Yeah. Ashes. Most of that other stuff is my dad's. He was in the navy and collected stuff from everywhere. Some of it's my brother's. He joined the army right out of high school. He died in the first Gulf War. The flag is his."

Janeyre reached out and gently tapped Skade on the shoulder.

"What is it?" Kit asked the puppet. Janeyre pointed emphatically across the room. "Fearnigal? You want to show her Fearnigal?"

The puppet nodded energetically.

"Janeyre wants you to see Fearnigal. He's over here." Kit and Janeyre led Skade to a trunk.

Kit gently sat Janeyre in a chair and an invisible light left the puppet as Kit withdrew her hands. She opened the trunk and retrieved a complicated set of wooden bars and wires. She raised the apparatus into the air and, as she did so, a hairy paw appeared at the edge of the trunk, followed by a second hairy paw; then, suddenly, out of the trunk leapt a hairy brown creature about the size of a Scottish terrier. It shook itself from front to back and wagged a feathery brown tail.

"This is Fearnigal. We think he's a dog, even though he looks like a dust mop." Fearnigal hung his furry head in shame. "I'm sorry, sweetie. I know you're not a mop," said Kit lovingly. Fearnigal perked up and began cavorting around the room. Had Skade not been able to look up at the wires in Kit's hands, engaged in an odd and intricate dance, she would have thought Fearnigal was alive.

Fearnigal raced around the living room, with Kit in tow, poking into corners and jumping up on furniture. He jumped down and began running in circles around Kit's legs. Skade was torn between watching the astonishing antics of the puppet and admiring the dexterity of Kit's maneuvers as she passed the control wires from hand to hand behind her back without missing a beat.

Eventually, Fearnigal jumped on an old sofa, did three clockwise turns, and settled down with his nose on his paws. Kit carefully set the controlling bars and wires down on the back of the sofa. Even lying still, with wires slack, the puppet had a lively energy, so long as Kit's hands were on the controls, but once she'd relinquished them, the puppet once again became a thing of rags and scraps, inanimate and without living dimension.

Kit sat next to the puppet and looked at Skade hopefully. From some unseen place, Janeyre appeared quietly, pulling herself up to sit happily in the crook of one of Kit's crossed arms. Skade was speechless with astonishment. Kit's incomprehensible skill and artistry were breathtaking. "Kit...you're an artist. An amazing artist," Skade finally managed to say. Kit blushed and looked away. "I'm serious. I've never seen anything like that. My God..."

Skade took a tentative sip of water. Kit was hiding, she realized. She was hiding herself away in a house full of hidden things. Skade felt a painful recognition, as if she were looking in a mirror.

An excerpt from Chapter 7: "The people."
American Still Life

By Skade Felsdottir

Six days before Christmas, thirty-two-year-old Donna Mosier loaded her four children—Kenny, five; Lisa, four; Tim, eighteen months; and Billy, six weeks—into her battered minivan and drove to her sister Laura's house on the north side of Whitestown. She collected her sister's two kids: Marsha, five, and Connie, two. Since Donna had recently lost her job at the local Kroger's, she had been helping her sister by providing daycare for Marsha and Connie while Laura worked the day shift at the Griffin factory.

It had been a bad autumn for Donna. In September, she had been picked up outside a local bar for disorderly conduct and public intoxication, and this time, unlike the last four times, the county sheriff couldn't just drive her home with a warning. Donna had tossed a beer glass through the plate window of the bar and had struck two patrons, and then she hit the sheriff's deputy that responded to the call. The ruckus prompted Donna's mother to take the four children to her house for a week and begin a custody battle for guardianship.

A court-ordered medical exam determined that Donna was suffering from bipolar disorder, an affliction she had battled as a teenager. For the three years prior to her arrest at the bar, her behavior had become increasingly erratic and her brushes with the law more frequent.

Luckily, Donna was active military, serving in the National Guard, and the VA got her into treatment, which began to get her stabilized. But still, her parents had deep misgivings about leaving the children with Donna unsupervised.

By Thanksgiving, however, Donna's situation seemed to be improving. She made amends with her sister—whom she'd regarded as siding with her parents in the custody battle—and she'd considered returning to school to work on an associate degree as a nurse's aide. Donna's spirits had been better—she smiled more, she began attending church regularly, and she seemed more comfortable in her own skin.

"Donna was making progress," said an acquaintance. "She was going to be okay."

But on December 19, nothing was going to be okay.

After loading her sister's children into the van, Donna headed north toward state road 232. She drove over the Black River bridge on Main to the 232-junction light, then, when the light changed to green, she took a right...heading north in the southbound lanes.

State road 232 is a lovely drive. It winds along the Black River through some of the most picturesque hill country in the state. In October, it's one of the main arteries out of the larger cities up north down into the fall foliage on bright, cool weekend afternoons. But 232 is also something of a death trap. Because of the hills and the river, the road is full of blind turns and twists, and people will always drive too fast on it. It has one of the highest road-fatality rates in the state in any given year. Ice, fog, alcohol, deer, distracted or inattentive driving.

Donna Mosier didn't make it even a half a mile up 232 going the wrong way in the southbound lane. In the middle of the first big, sweeping blind curve, which would be the last curve before home for anyone coming south into Whitestown, she ran headlong into a Chrysler sedan driven by Tom Miller. His wife Judy was next to him in the passenger's seat. Police estimates say both cars were probably traveling at over forty miles per hour. The Miller car was the only one that attempted to break.

Of the nine people involved in the head-on collision, seven died before any help could arrive. The coroner's office says all seven probably died instantly. Judy Miller, aged fifty-seven, died in transit. Only four-year-old Lisa Mosier made it to Forest County General Hospital alive. She succumbed to catastrophic injuries nine days later. It might have been the first Christmas she would have remembered.

What possesses someone to load six children into a car, and then drive at over forty miles an hour into oncoming traffic seemingly on purpose? Because aside from the evidence of no braking or counter-steering by Donna's car, she would have had to drive around a seven-foot-high reflective barrier with a bright red *Do Not Enter, Wrong Way* sign, and five sets of warning strips on the road. And at least two people who saw her and managed to avoid her on 232 flashed their lights and honked their horns as Donna sped up. One of the witnesses reported that it appeared that Donna was smiling at them as she passed.

Postmortem examinations found no drugs or alcohol in Donna's system, so that, theoretically at least, absolves one demon from the discussion. But if not that, then what? Again, I ask, what possesses? Was it mental illness? Obviously, no sane person does what Donna seems to have done that December morning. Infanticide is one of the most difficult to comprehend societal taboos, so it will inevitably bring insanity along with it for the ride. But by the same logic, all murder is committed by the insane. And Donna was in right-enough mind to go through the careful rituals of millions of working mothers across the globe that morning. Did the malevolent entity that is insanity descend upon her in the car at some point? What possesses?

We are so much more comfortable as a society when we can label our monsters. Label them, and they are not *us*. They are an *other*. Label them and they can be understood and addressed and studied and kept neat, like a four-year-old who doesn't want the food on her plate to touch. Nine people, including six children, died at the hand of a thirty-two-year-old mother of four of those same children. This must have a label. Because if it doesn't have one, how will we sleep? What is the name of this monster? This demon? How will we know it when it meets us in the street, or in the grocery store, or in our own beds at night?

When a search was made of Donna's house following the incident, it was noted by a family member that things seemed neater than normal. Everything was put away and picked up—the dishes were done, the floors were vacuumed. Artwork by the children had been hung up all over the house. There was no suicide note, no diary or journal to be found, no phone calls made. The only things found on the kitchen table were two pieces of paper. A grocery list: *Peanut butter, Cheerios, toilet paper, cigarettes, diapers, celery, chicken noodle soup.*

And a little note: *If we confess our sins, He is faithful and will forgive us. If we cannot confess, or lie or slander in its giving, then our sins shall be as ink on pure wool, and night in the heavens.*

That was passed off as a Bible verse at first glance by those that saw it: 1 John 1:9. But it's not. Those words do not appear in the Bible.

So maybe that's the label. Or all the label we get. Maybe that's what possesses. A night in someone's heavens.

Now a grouping of nine white PVC crosses stand in a tight formation a safe distance from the roadway on 232 on the last blind curve heading into Whitestown from the north. Nine names are printed on the crosses, which were put up and are maintained by the Whitestown

Knights of Columbus. On a summer evening, as the sun descends behind the hill on which the crosses are placed and the light levels in the shadows, the crosses seem to glow. Many descansos seem to glow in the evening. Heading into that night.

-S. Felsdottir.

14

S kade had been editing and writing all day. She felt physically exhausted; she wasn't able to sleep even at a distance lately. Now she stood in the doorway of her room at the Skyline watching the sun lose its way behind the high bank of the highway, holding the cornhusk puppet. Selecting a cassette tape at random from a pile on the floor, she slipped it into her portable stereo and returned to the doorway, singing "Strange Magic" along with Jeff Lynne and ELO.

She caught the smell of a barbecue grill over the top of the usual smells of parking lot and highway. She looked down the row and saw three motorcycles parked at the far end, but no sign of any people or a grill. She leaned back against the doorjamb. The barbecue smell opened up something in her mind and a sluice of memories surprised her.

She remembered a kind of fine, thin freedom. Her father drinking beers over a BBQ with friends, while Skade and her friends went off like rockets into the eternal evenings. She was shedding her skin then. Her childhood past was dissolving behind her. In front of her was a vast dark hallway out of which emanated all sorts of sounds, some seductive and some terrifying, the origins of which she could not see or even completely comprehend. Back then the future was everything. The smallest discoveries were earth-shaking, so much more important than anything would ever be again, certainly more important than anything was now. There was clarity, and an expanse of possibility.

It might have been the only time she'd ever felt that being-in-the-moment. Life had felt like a giant never-ending game of hide-and-seek from nothing she could define and for nothing she could understand. She remembered parties in basements with the lights dimmed. She remembered running wildly after dark through the neighborhood, climbing fences and jumping hedges and navigating backyards at top speed after throwing water balloons at police cars. She remembered the final summer of the Starland Drive-In and all the attendant teenage Shakespearian drama that went with it. She remembered sitting and talking to Theresa Mitchell's mom at their kitchen table and the fog of cigarette smoke and the smell of burnt coffee and the wonderful insane horror stories Theresa's mom would tell about being a nurse on the ER night shift, and about her growing up in east Texas and what life was like—all this she tried to impart to the newly minted teenage privateers and princesses sitting around her table with her at two a.m., trying like hell to bridge that Formica distance. Skade remembered living at Theresa's house more that summer than she lived at home, to the point that Theresa's mom let the two of them set up a second bed in Theresa's room. She remembered one night Theresa telling her in whispers about losing her virginity and the taste of hamburgers at the First Down Grill and being spied upon by besotted twelve-year-old boys and the feeling of her body not being able to contain what was inside her, nor could the room, nor could the town. Skade remembered confusion and the fear and the weight of adolescence pulling at her from all sides; she remembered the feel of her sheets in her room at night and the smell of the awful nail polish pushed by the other girls at school. She remembered and she remembered and she remembered. And slipping in and around all those memories and intertwining with them carnally was her desire for a drink.

She darted back into her den and came back out with her car keys, a swimsuit, and the blue-and-white shoebox containing all that used to be her. At the liquor store down the street she bought one—no, better make it four—quarts of vodka and headed out again.

Memory was pulling harder at her, and she followed Memory to the neighborhood where she had once lived, very pointedly avoiding the house she used to live in.

A few blocks from her old house used to be an apartment complex. One of her favorite escapes had been to sneak into the complex pool after the gates had been locked. She pulled up across the street and felt a shot of relief go through her. It was still there.

It was getting dark, but the blacktop parking lot felt like the top of a short-order grill cooling off as she crossed it. The collection of cars in the lot looked much the same as it had twelve years ago. Probably would never change. What had changed was the fence around the pool. In Skade's day the fence hadn't been much of a barrier against an athletic teenager bent on the water, but now the fence was something different. Eight feet of new hurricane fencing circled the cement deck, and it was topped with a coil of barbed wire.

"Somebody got sued," Skade said quietly to her cornhusk puppet.

She hadn't remembered bringing it with her, but she was glad it was there.

Ominous red-and-white signs were strung on the fencing, warning against all manner of things, first and foremost swimming while the pool was closed. Thunder rumbled. Weather had come up. Skade looked through the fence. The decking was in good shape, and the pool itself looked like it was pretty well maintained, unlike the storm drain that passed for a pool at the Skyline. This pool was demanding to be swum in.

Skade examined the gate latch. It was padlocked, but it wasn't a formidable barrier. Leverage could lift the door over the hasp. She looked up at the apartments. Lights were on in a few of them, but curtains were tightly drawn against prying eyes, as much to keep things in as keep others out. She went back to her car and changed into her swimsuit in between pulls from one of her bottles. She'd had lots of practice at dressing and undressing in her car. She took the Maglite, a long-shafted screwdriver, the bottle of vodka she'd started on, and her shoebox, and wrapped them in her towel and walked back to the pool gate. She fitted the shaft of the screwdriver under the bolt of the hasp on the gate and laid into it. The hasp rose easily, and she shifted it over the catch and the door swung free.

She slipped onto the dark pool deck. Soft cold drops of rain began to fall. She set her towel and her shoebox by the edge of the water and pulled a small plastic table over to cover them from the rain, then she dove longingly into the dark water. It felt wonderful. She surfaced and tread water for a moment, watching the raindrops explode on the surface of the pool. She swam over to where she'd put her towel and shoebox and checked to make sure the rain wasn't getting to them. She propped her elbows on the smooth tiles lining the pool edge, took a long drink form her bottle, twisted on the Maglite and put it between her teeth, and began to sort through the contents of the box. She fished out a small netsuke of a fox and rabbit curled into each other, an item she had taken from her mother's jewelry box. A sticky trail of memories flowed from the netsuke like a plume of smoke. Images of her mother—happy, lively, walking with her father while a very young Skade dashed about in front of them, turning back now and then to make sure her parents still followed. There was no narrative associated with that memory, no cause and effect, no point. Only images.

Another set of memories, darker, were of herself at sixteen in a volcanic rage. Her father had one day, without discussion with her, decided to get rid of "this junk," everything that comprised her mother's possessions—her jewelry box, some books and letters and photographs, and other sentimental paraphernalia, which had always been stored on a shelf in the attic and seldom visited, except by Skade when she was slipping down a tunnel of sadness or feeling wistful. This box, even though it had never been on display, had often been forgotten about for weeks or even months at a stretch; it functioned as the beating heart of that poorly formed thing of stitched-together thoughts and breath and colors and shadows that she called "home." It served as that wet string of flesh and bone that still connected her to her mother.

That three-day moment—when her father stood like a rock against the typhoon of her, and his response that he damn well didn't need to consult her over anything, certainly not finally clearing out this dead woman's things from his house—burned in her ears to this very day. It filled her with a choking ball of feelings that transcended emotion and became physical. She remembered kneeling in the dark corner of the garage in front of a gas can and a box of matches, a silent prayer of hate and destruction racing through her mind, until she finally calmed down, and the poison bled out, and she deconstructed her little altar-of-apocalypse and raced back into the house to find the box.

She found it sitting out in the middle of the attic floor, torn open, under the naked bulb hanging from the rafters. Her father had been at it, obviously. She stared into it and the sudden realization that she really didn't know what she was looking at overwhelmed her. She had been in this box many times since her mother's death, and in so doing, she'd formed her own stories and associations with the objects inside it, all of which eventually simplified back down to "mother." This stuff in this box made up her mother now, but she didn't really know what any of it was. Each object's inherent reality was made by its association and relationship to her mother. What was this hairbrush to her mother? What memories and emotions came to her mother when she picked each thing up in this box? That was the value of it all, and that was what Skade wanted but could not have, and now she knew it. She didn't know what was most important.

She went through the box as fast as she could. She handled every object, closing her eyes to try and feel her mother's emotions and memories and resonance. She had taken so few things in the end. She now wished she'd figured out a way to take the entire box and hide it from her father. But she wound up with just a single pocketful of her mother. She took what she took, packed a bag, and ran from the house, as if she had actually set it on fire, to spend the next three days with Theresa and her mom.

Skade set the netsuke down and pulled a small brown kangaroo out of the box. She must have been four when her father gave it to her. She had memories, like scattered tintypes, of clutching it in first grade and sleeping with it when she was very little. Next she found a gold ring set with a large square-cut garnet. It had belonged to her mother. Skade tried to recall her mother wearing it, but all the memories of her mother were foggy and faded now, like a foxed mirror, and nothing came to her. She examined the ring closely and tried to put it on. It was small, but Skade could slip it on her little finger. She held the ring to the light of the flashlight between her teeth. Her hand seemed pale.

Next she pulled out a man's brown leather wallet—her father's—worn to a glossy black and smooth as silk. It still bore the *Morocco* mark and the faint smell of French cigarettes. She snapped it closed and tossed it back into the box.

She turned off her Maglite, tossed it into the box as well, replaced the lid, and kicked off into a backstroke to the center of the dark pool. The rain became a fine shower, colder than the water in the pool, and Skade shot sinuously back to the side for another long pull from her bottle, then a strong dolphin kick down to the bottom, where she sat and let the submersion and the alcohol smooth out the jagged feelings the box had stirred up. When her lungs began to burn, she popped up to the surface and slowly stroked back to the side, climbed out, and gathered her things in the rain, which felt like tiny electric shocks on her skin as it fell. She slipped back to her car, the remnants of old feelings like a miasma around her. She finished off the bottle she'd opened, then drove back toward the motel. keeping her head down to avoid the ghosts in the neighborhoods through which she drove.

She didn't get as far as the Skyline.

Skade found herself in the dark empty parking lot at the aquatic center in Kensington Park. She shut her car off and looked down at the new pool complex, lit by security lighting. The rain had eased up to a fine drizzle, and nothing moved. Her attention shifted to the old empty pool. The security lighting didn't penetrate beyond the hurricane fence that surrounded its memory.

She slipped silently out of her car, her Maglite in the back pocket of the cutoffs she wore over her still-damp swimsuit, her box in her hand. She melted into the darkness and approached the old pool, taking a wide circular path to make sure no one else was around.

She put a tentative hand on the fence. Clearly it had been erected for show; the posts were leaning and the wire sagged. Police warning signs were enough, no doubt, to keep most people away. Moving around the perimeter, Skade came to an open expanse of park: a gray ocean of rolling hills punctuated by small clumps of trees that shone silver in the city lights. A sign announced the soon-to-begin project that would turn the old Kensington Aquatic center—*her* old Kensington Aquatic Center—into a new skate park. Directly below the sign, the fence gaped open and Skade found her way inside.

She had entered directly behind the diving well of the old pool. The diving platforms had been removed, but one old three-meter board remained. Skade looked up into the misty drizzle at the dark outline of the diving board, an object with which she had once been intimately familiar. The lifeguard towers were gone, but Skade felt them even in their absence.

This was where Michael Pullman had nearly drowned. She had been sleepy and distracted that afternoon, twirling her lanyard whistle on her finger. The sun, she remembered, had glinted off the surface of the bright water, and the sounds of yelling and splashing and shouting and quiet music (Al Green on the pool speakers?) all blended together.

And then she'd spotted the six-year-old floating face down.

Diving in from her chair.

Hoisting the body out.

Mouth-to-mouth on a child.

For what felt like hours.

Being told to stop, it was too late, by the guard supervisor.

The wail of the ambulance in the distance.

Trying a military lifesaving technique she'd just read about.

Michael spitting up water and breathing just as the EMTs arrived.

The boy had been so weirdly light in her memory—hardly weighing anything at all.

Skade trotted away from the wretched horrible spot where she'd saved a six-year-old's life.

The security lights at the new pool cast a reflective glow into the worn old pale aqua paint on the bottom. She sat on the edge, looking into the dark shadowy well of the deep end fifty meters away. How much of the darkness that collected there was her? Had a piece of what had gone missing from her found its lonely way home, like an abandoned dog searching for the place it remembers? She set her memory box at the edge of the pool and opened the lid. Maybe something would come back. Or leave.

The only thing that came was a crippling sadness. When she could no longer stand the weight of the dark deep end of the pool, full of her regrets, or the yawning mouth of the box next to her right hip, she put the lid back on, got up, and left the way she'd come.

15

Thankfully, the AC worked at the Skyline. Skade sat on the floor with her laptop, looking at an image she'd taken in Iowa. A wooden cross draped with carnival beads and a pair of track shoes had been planted at the top of an embankment surrounded by high grass. She remembered lying on roadside to take the shot, the cross framed against a bright blue sky dotted with white cumulonimbus clouds. The clarity of the photograph gave the clouds movement and the grass a moment of dancing in the wind.

Skade played with different cropping and focus settings and the zoom. The more she zoomed into the cross—into the details and the objects given to it—the more she moved from the public experience into the personal; and the more deeply into the personal she traveled, the less clear the image became. As she cropped out the contextual information the image became an abstraction, an invitation to consider meaning.

These reframed abstracts that life became in grief, she supposed, were the gifts of loss: snatches of songs that never existed, words in an unformed sentence. Memories. Her memories were not always reliable. A distant view of her mother. And her father. She remembered shouts and curses there. Now she only had sighs and moans in her aloneness. Loss opens new doors of course, but they were doors that went only one way, and it was natural that the weight of loss increased as life sped by. The weight of her losses felt especially daunting. All she had to balance the scales was a pyrrhic freedom. And she probably didn't even deserve that.

Her phone buzzed. A text from Lane:

Hey, got some time tonight?

She looked at her phone, annoyed.
Working.

A few seconds later came a reply:

Take a break? I wanna ask U something

Maybe later

Be here all night. Come by

She shook her head and tossed her phone over her shoulder onto the bed. She jotted down some notes and kept pushing her book forward.

Just past dark. The air was thick. Nighttime had brought lower temperatures, but the humidity spiked, and the breeze stopped altogether, so now the atmosphere just hung there, waiting. Skade pulled her Jeep into a parking place a couple of blocks from Lane's studio. The rat's nest of thoughts in her head had slowly gotten worse, so getting away from her computer—and the endless stream of images she was going through and editing and cataloging—and taking Lane's offer turned into a better idea.

The streetlights were lit up in diaphanous globes. The humidity kept the light reined in and created eddies of blackness outside the hazy glow. A wave of smells teased her as she walked. She passed a Chinese place with picnic tables and naked bulbs strung on poles. Three young guys were drinking beer and eating something that smelled ravishing. A couple could barely be seen in the shadows outside the square of illumination, making out tenderly over egg rolls.

She saw yellow light from Lane's studio spilling out on to the bricks and broken concrete. She walked into the sound of Otis Redding: "I've Been Loving You Too Long," and Jerome running a monologue while working on the shoulder of a middle-aged guy:

"...a meat cleaver. I'm dead serious, man—a meat cleaver! Carried that sucker around with him while he was out digging in the trash for bottles and cans, you know? I asked him about it one time and he said he was going to cut anybody that bothered him up into little pieces! Now he serves soup at the Commandos of Jesus shelter. Remind me not to get soup at the Commandos, man! But you know, that soup ain't half bad..."

The guy he was working on wasn't listening.

Lane was in the back talking to a bald guy with several lip-rings. Tattoos of flames roared out from under his T-shirt onto his neck. They were looking at some skateboard decks and motorcycle helmets Lane had obviously mocked up. Lane waved to her and made his way over.

"Hey, thanks for coming by."

"No problem. I needed a break anyway."

"I got some ideas for adding to that old thing on your arm." Lane handed her a couple of sketches, then he turned to Jerome. "Hey, can you close up for me tonight? My appointments are done."

"These are really nice, Lane. I like them," she said, looking at the images.

Skade and Lane pushed out into the heat on the street outside. "I wanted to talk to you about something. Want to go grab a beer?" asked Lane.

"I got a better idea," said Skade. "Let's grab some beers and go for a swim."

"At nearly ten at night? Where are you thinking about swimming?"

"Out at Chrysler."

Lane looked at her for a moment. "Yeah, sure. I'll drive. Your car is a piece of shit."

"No, it is not. But drive if you want."

16

Lane drove into the dark with the windows down. Skade reached into the back seat to grab a beer as the wash of air tossed and buffeted her hair and the night soaked into her body. The once-all-too-familiar road south of town kept nudging her insides. Memories of parties and days spent swimming and living in the sun.

"So why'd you ask me to come over?"

"I told you about that big convention, remember?"

"Yeah?"

"You said something about maybe helping me shoot a portfolio for it?"

"Sure." Christ, she regretted that again.

"I don't want to get in the way of your book or anything, but if you've got a spare night, I'd really appreciate the help. I've been doing them myself, but I think you'd really make my work stand out."

"Yeah, sure, I'd be happy to help. What are you thinking about?"

"I got ten or twelve people with some of my better work. We could set up a photo stage in the studio."

"Yeah, I can do that. No problem. I'm pretty sure I've got everything we need."

Lane looked at her in the dark and smiled. "Thanks."

The darkness was deepening, but Skade could still see a little outside the spray of the headlights. They drove past the shadowy form of the Rockland water tower, which generated another set of old memories for Skade—climbing the tower with Theresa to watch the Perseid meteor shower; lugging her telescope, strapped to her back, up the perilous side of the tower; trying to teach Theresa about meteors; fighting with her father when she came back too late and too drunk.

Then a sign exploded into view as it caught Lane's high beams: *Live bait, Worms, Tom's crawlers*. It guarded the gravel parking lot of Fulford's Bait-n-Beer, now empty and ghostly at night with its dim fluorescent lights glowing inside the big glass windows. That meant they were getting close. Soon Lane slowed and found a gravel service road.

"Hang on a second. They've put up a gate and combination lock since you were here last. Trying to keep riffraff like us out so nobody dies and sues the shit out of the quarry. It doesn't work, of course, but they can say they tried." Lane got out and fiddled with the lock until it snapped open.

"You know the combination?" Skade asked as he hopped back in and slowly pulled through the gate and stopped again.

"Several hundred people do, yeah. Someone got it the week they put the thing up. Supposedly bought it from one of the security guards at the quarry. A hundred bucks, a big bag of weed, or a blowjob, depending on who you ask—there are several colorful stories. But the combination has been passed around, and they haven't yet changed the lock, amazingly enough. We may not be the only ones here, but we shall see."

Lane got out, closed the gate behind them, and re-locked it, then they proceeded very slowly down the long, dark service road.

The darkness fairly roared with the sounds of insects and frogs as the ragged undergrowth of Queen Anne's Lace, coneflowers, Jimsonweed, lamb's quarters, sumac, milkweed, ragweed, and dozens of other rat-plants closed in on both sides. The smell of dirt and all things green invaded the car. Eventually Lane stopped and reached into the back seat and produced towels and a couple of flashlights.

"Here," he said, handing one to Skade.

"Got my own," she said, holding up her Maglite as she popped out of the car and began down a dark path that was twelve years past familiar to her.

She followed the bright spill of her flashlight down the rutted path, which at first was enclosed by young trees and weeds. Then the trees parted. Enormous stacks of huge, roughly hewn blocks of limestone appeared, like a forgotten Mesoamerican city. Some of the stone edifices loomed over fifty feet high in the dark. They encroached on the path until it became an alley in a canyon of giant blocks, and the star-washed night sky was squeezed between them above Skade's head. It was like being a Lilliputian in a giant's playground. The path took a hard right turn and began to feel like a maze. But suddenly another left, and Skade stood on the edge of a precipice looking out into a void. Lane appeared next to her and set the twelve-pack down on the ground.

"Chrysler Quarry. Is it like you remember it?"

"Tough to tell in the dark. But it feels the same." Skade caught the distinct scent of water coming up from below. She shone her light over the edge; it reflected, twenty feet below, on the dark surface of the quarry. She caught a dim view of the wall on the far side, which rose up 135 feet over the water.

"Water level the same?" she asked, kicking a small piece of gravel off the ledge.

"Yeah...varies with the rain, like it used to. It's a little trashier than it used to be, but that all collects down at the south end." Lane pointed off to the left into the black. "Come on, let's go down to the beach."

Skade's eyes were beginning to adjust to the low ambient light cast by the nearly full moon and the stars, enough to be able to turn off her light and look at the quarry. It was an almost perfect rectangle, two hundred yards by seventy yards. Abandoned decades before, it had filled with water to about seventy feet at its deepest point. A shelf at the north end provided a flat entry point, so it was called *The Beach* by everyone that swam there. Lane carefully clambered down a fall of blocks to the level of the beach and walked out to the water's edge.

"I don't hear anyone else," he said. "We might be alone."

Lane began taking off his clothes as Skade watched. He was as she remembered him, and she grinned in the dark. New ink had been added—unsurprisingly, given his career. Near the center of his chest, Skade caught the brief sight of a lotus flower and a tiger, with text, and she caught her breath and looked away. Lane waded out until the water was up to his knees.

"Your turn now," he said, turning his flashlight on Skade up on the ledge.

She smiled and began taking off her clothes, revealing a dark-blue one-piece racing suit. "Didn't have skinny dipping in mind, Lane." She shrugged. "Sorry."

"Well, come on down anyway," he said, sounding disappointed.

Skade took two steps back and rushed at the edge. She did a strong, hopping kick and arched into the air in a lovely swan dive and knifed into the black water.

"Fucking Christ, Skade!" shouted Lane when she surfaced and began a lazy backstroke toward him. "You could have fucking been killed doing that! That was insane! Badly insane!"

"Maybe," she said calmly when she felt the shelf beneath her. "But you said the place hadn't changed. I could do that dive in my sleep. And, yes, I have done it in the dark before, you know. You've seen me. So calm down. Come swim with me," she said with a bright smile.

"Hell no. You scared the shit out of me with that stunt. And I never liked swimming here after dark. The water freaks me out at night."

"Suit yourself." Skade ducked under and kicked downward.

Even at the height of summer, the water at Chrysler was never warm, but this long, hot season had made the top layer of water fairly comfortable. Skade hit a thermocline about six feet down. It was like passing from one reality to another, and the water became icy cold. She continued to dive until her ears began to hurt. She stopped and floated for a moment, using her arms to keep from rising to the surface. She opened her eyes, but nothing registered; the black was impenetrable. It was like being in outer space with no stars. She floated, suspended in the utter blackness until her lungs began to burn and the strange sensation of not knowing which way was up overcame her. Fear wrapped itself around her spine, and she cuddled it for a second or two, and then kicked herself into a streamlined arrow heading for the surface. With only the dark night sky above her she had no idea when she was going to come up, which only increased her fear. Suddenly—unexpectedly— she burst out into the air and took a deep gulping breath and let out a shout from her abdomen that echoed off the steep sides of the giant stone box, a shout of several things all together and at once.

"That was loud," called Lane. He was sitting on the edge of the shelf in the water with his legs dangling off into the abyss.

"I always have this image of some giant quarry monster rising up out of the darkness to swallow me," he said when she swam back over to where he was sitting. "The dark and the water together just freak me the fuck out. I don't see how you can do that."

"It's scary as all hell, but totally liberating." She pulled herself up on the shelf next to him.

"Remember when we pushed the car off Mile High?" he said after a quiet moment, casting the beam of a flashlight toward the highest side of the quarry wall. "You goaded us into pulling that old junked truck out of the woods up there and pushing it off. It was a feat of engineering just getting that damn hulk to the edge. The wheels didn't even turn."

"I knew you guys would figure it out once you put your minds and muscles to it. I can't believe Geno had those hand winches and come-alongs in his van. It took forever to hit the water." She laughed.

"Yeah, we counted to eight, but it probably wasn't that long. We were high and counting too fast, I'm sure. It's not called *Mile High* anymore. Now it's called *Suicide*. Some guy killed himself jumping off it a couple of years ago. You were the only one brave enough to jump off from up there, at least of the people we knew. A hundred and thirty-five feet. You were queen of this place that summer." He turned and looked at her.

"Duchess, maybe. Baroness? Countess? Probably not queen, though."

"No," Lane continued; the seriousness in his voice made Skade a little nervous. "Queen for sure. Everything you touched turned to honey or flowers or gold."

A wave of misery passed though Skade like a fluttering ghost. "Fuck. You and I weren't watching the same movie, Lane. Maybe I was queen in the eyes of a pack of horny teenage boys, but everything I touched turned to ashes and dog shit in the end."

"No, it didn't."

"I don't want to talk about this," said Skade coldly, pushing off into the water. "Come on, let's swim. I'll hold your hand, you 'fraidycat." She tread water up to her shoulders in front of him and held out her hand.

"The shit you talk me into..." said Lane, and he uneasily slipped off the shelf into the water.

"Come on...you can do it..." Skade teased as she slipped backward out into the dimensionless blackness.

Lane ducked his head under and shot toward her and caught her arm before she could kick away. He came up in front of her and wrapped his arms around her shoulders. Skade could feel his naked body pressing up against hers in the warm top-water and she could feel him getting hard. He pulled her closer to him and pressed against her.

She easily pulled her hand out from his grasp and shoved her index finger up under his chin.

"No," she hissed. "I am not here for that shit, Lane. I'm not here for sex or rekindling anything, or anything else like that. It was nice when we were kids, but all that is now buried under a pile of crap twelve years high. I'm not digging through it. Let me the fuck go. Now."

Lane released her, pulling away, and Skade took four powerful strokes to get to the shelf at the beach. She pulled herself up and waded out of the water to where Lane had dropped the towels and the beer. She wrapped herself in a towel and opened a beer, taking an angry swallow. Her cornhusk puppet had fallen on the ground, and she picked it up and clutched it.

"Hey. Skade. I'm sorry," said Lane, wading toward her. "I just...I don't know...anyway, I'm sorry."

She glared at him as she finished her beer and popped open another one. "Fine," she said finally. "But no more of that shit, okay?"

"Okay," he said, wrapping himself in a towel, then sitting beside her.

"What's that?" he asked, motioning toward the cornhusk puppet in her hands.

"Nothing. Something somebody gave me."

After a few moments of silence, Skade finally spoke. "You know where I can get some Percocets? Or Vicodins? Oxycontins, anything like that?"

"Yeah, probably. Why?"

"It helps me calm down and feel better on shoots. I'd like some." A flock of birds took flight in her chest.

Lane looked at her for a moment. "Sure. Gimme a day or two. I can get you some."

"Thanks."

And they pulled their things together and headed back to Lane's car. Skade felt her façade crack open just a little more.

17

Kit made a left off the main road into the flat farmland. She'd arrived early to take Skade to another descanso on her map. Corn rushed up to them on either side of the road, and Skade could smell the thick, musky corn scent. The air hummed with heat and jangled with sharp light.

"That's where we're headed," said Kit, pointing toward the tall towers of wind turbines in the distance.

Soon they reached the spot. The towers were part of a huge wind farm that ran in straight lines, almost from horizon to horizon. They were gigantic up close, over two hundred feet in height, not counting the gently rotating blades. Kit pulled off near a red dirt access road.

"It's just at the base of that tower," said Kit. Almost immediately Skade saw it.

She laughed. "That's pretty good!"

The symmetry was perfect. Skade could not have laid out a better image. The access road ran in a straight line directly toward the turbine tower. About twenty feet before the turbine, the road ended in a *T*, with another dirt path running perpendicular. Dead center with the tower was a small white cross surrounded by dozens of little ferociously spinning pinwheels.

Skade stopped every ten feet along the approach to get shots and change lenses. The juxtaposition of the marker and the giant turbine and the little toy pinwheels fascinated her, and she took dozens of pictures from various angles. She got a couple of great shots by lying down in front of the marker and shooting up at the top of the turbine.

"You kinda remind me of me," said Kit as Skade lined up another shot.

"How's that?" replied Skade distractedly.

"You get sucked into taking pictures, just like I do with puppets. I can lose whole days if I'm not careful."

Skade was too focused to reply.

"So where'd you go, after you left here?" Kit asked, trailing along behind Skade as she lined up shots.

"Hmmm?" said Skade, making an adjustment on her camera. "Uh… places? I moved around a lot. You know…lots of places."

There was a long silence broken only by the click and whirr of Skade's camera.

"I'd love to see them—"

Skade rose up from her viewfinder. "See what?" she asked.

"Your pictures. I'd love to see them. From all the way back. Did you take many when you lived here?" Kit asked hopefully.

"What? Yeah. Yes, absolutely. Sure. I can bring some of my files by and show you some of the shots I've taken. This is a great site, Kit. Thanks. I haven't even looked at the marker and I've shot a dozen good pictures."

"Yeah, I liked this one. I thought you would too. I even like the sound." The turbine was loud, with a thrumming pulse that sounded like a beating heart.

Skade turned and looked back over her shoulder. "Do you know whose marker this is? Or the story?"

The marker consisted of a white plastic cross, about three feet high, with the name *Annie* painted across the horizontal bar. The cross was strung with a chain of dried marigolds, and a small laminated snapshot had been attached to the center of the cross, showing a smiling young woman, probably a high school graduation photo.

"Annie Mendoza," said Kit as Skade took a few close-up pictures of the cross.

"Car wreck out here?" asked Skade. "Seems like a weird place for a car wreck."

"Boyfriend shot her," said Kit.

"Christ," said Skade, turning around and looking up at Kit.

"Yeah. They say she was pregnant too. I don't know a lot about it. I always thought she was nice, though. She worked at the hobby store out by the processing plant. I saw her sometimes out there."

"There's probably a story about it in the newspaper archives, right?"

"Don't know. I guess."

"I can find out." Skade stood up and made a note in her notebook. "I'd like to come back out here when the light is a little better. Let's head back. I still have a shitload of work to do."

Four a.m. The motel room was illuminated by the glow of a laptop. The

catalog of photos illustrated image after image of grief and loss. Crosses and shrines and heaps of flowers and stuffed animals and signs. All
handmade. Each one carved out of someone's chest or crafted of living
bone and tied together with strings of muscle. Personal reliquaries and
memento mori. The florid eruption of pain. What is ejected when grief
turns a person inside out.

The bunny on the cross was there, at the end of the parade.

Skade had woken up as usual at the stroke of three, feeling like shit,
and decided to occupy her troublesome mind with work uploading the
most recent images into the catalog. These were images of wounds, of
emotional disfigurement. But the images were detached; they rendered
the deep pathos of the subjective into the cold objective. The camera
couldn't scoop up enough of the feeling—it was like bailing water with
a sieve.

kade pushed a half-empty vodka bottle down into her bag and instinctively grabbed her camera as she climbed out of the car. Lane had suggested meeting at an old haunt—the Dairy Boat— before the portfolio photo session later that night. She caught her dark reflection in the windows of a storefront as she walked toward the light and sound in front of her, and she ran a quick hand through her thick black hair.

She'd spent a while on her appearance—art-gallery-rock-and-roll-tattoo-LA-scene-sexy—trying to prop up her psyche. She was treating the portfolio session like a gallery party, so she dressed accordingly.

The Dairy Boat was a relic, but very much a live one. In the center of a wide concrete lot on Franklin sat a miniature-golf-course version of a pirate ship. Inside the ship, high school kids dressed like pirates took orders for ice cream. Groups of teenagers hung together at picnic tables, eating ice cream cones and drinking milkshakes, and families stood in line at the window. Little kids chased each other in and out of the blaring lights. Rock music played out of speakers. The smell of baking waffle cones and hot fudge rifled through the air around the building.

Skade saw Lane sitting at one of the picnic tables and strode over to join him through a gauntlet of teenage-male eyes. "Hey," she said. "I can't believe this place is still around!"

"The Dairy Boat will always be here. It'll survive the apocalypse. Shit, you look fantastic, Skade."

"In honor of the photo-party." They got in line behind a young couple with three rambunctious little kids who seemed destined to climb the sides of the building.

"It's too crazy here. Let's go for a walk?" offered Lane after getting their orders.

They moved out of the loud island of light and down the street. Night wasn't much of a break from the day, though the hostility of the sun was gone and that was a relief. Heat radiated off the brick walls of the buildings as Skade and Lane walked by.

"Thanks again for doing this. I appreciate it. I'm sorry if it takes time away from your book," said Lane into the silence that had wrapped itself around them on the shadowy hot sidewalk. "How's the project coming, anyway?"

"Clock keeps ticking. But Kit—that woman I told you about—she's been a huge help. She's an amazing artist."

"Artist?"

"She's a puppeteer. And a puppet-maker—"

"Seriously?" Lane laughed.

"I'm dead serious. And I mean she's fucking amazing. I'm not some puppet expert or anything, but she does things with puppets I cannot believe. She's really gifted. She's kinda strange sometimes, though—"

"How?"

"She lives out on 443, north of town. Her house is like a fairyland—full of puppets hanging from the ceiling and on shelves and stuff. Beyond that, she's got most of her family, in ashes, in boxes in some sort of a shrine in her living room. It's kinda creepy. But I guess she's mostly alone now. Seems like she's had it hard growing up."

Lane paused a moment. "You said her name is Kit? She's helping you?"

"Yeah. She knows where a lot of descansos are around here."

"You actually getting much work done?" asked Lane. "You seem kinda ragged. I mean not right now you don't, but the few times we've talked you've seemed kinda the worse for wear."

"I'm probably not sleeping like I should," Skade acknowledged. "I'm worried about the project, I guess."

"And drinking too much? And the pills?"

Skade stopped walking and fixed him with a stare. "What are you? My mom now?"

"Nope. Just a friend. Don't want to see you burn out."

She studied him, fighting against the angry defensiveness that flared up. Finally, she marshaled herself and let out a sharp breath. "I'm fine. Sure, maybe I'm having one too many sometimes. But shit, Lane, we all do. We all did. You're one to talk. If you're even close to the same person you were when I last saw you."

"Maybe that's true." He smiled and looked away. "I guess I don't find myself in the same state I've seen you in too much anymore."

"Probably just travel and stress and lack of sleep causing me to make bad decisions. But I'm fine." Skade scowled and started walking again.

"Coming back here probably doesn't help," Skade continued, after a long, uncomfortable silence. "This place doesn't have a lot of fond memories for me start to finish. That fucking box you hit me with? Christ, that thing is like Joseph Cornell vomited my life into a shoebox. Maybe it is making me hit the booze a little hard. I'll keep it under control."

"Keep it healthy," Lane replied. "So you have no good memories of this place?" She caught an edge of broken glass in his voice.

"I have good memories, Lane. And, yeah, some are about us. But that was us being kids. We weren't capable of much beyond having some laughs and trying to get each other's clothes off as much as possible."

"I have good memories of it." His expression was unreadable.

"Like I said, but all that was over before I left."

"Yeah. What was that, anyway?"

Skade stopped under the golden glow of a thrift store sign. She put the straw from her milkshake into her mouth and bore into Lane with her eyes.

"Is it really that important?" she asked, releasing both her straw and her glare. "Can't it just be kids being stupid and emotionally clumsy and doing damage they didn't intend? Because that's really what it was. The arrogance of being eighteen. Isn't that enough of an answer?"

They walked on for a while in silence, but Skade could feel a storm brewing next to her on the sidewalk.

"Having you drop back into reality all of a sudden stirs it up," Lane said finally. "I guess I'm still confused."

Skade sighed in frustration, but something caught her attention across the street. "That's a descanso," she said, crossing the street between cars that drifted past like parade floats.

The pole was wrapped with stuffed animals, plastic flowers, and heart-shaped candy boxes, all tied to the pole with white plastic twine. The arrangement had a dusty, disheveled appearance, and dirt and road trash had begun to accumulate at the base. A laminated poster showing a smiling young African American kid was labeled *RIP Devon. God's Baby Angel.*

Skade took out her camera and began setting up some shots. "You know anything about this?" she asked Lane.

"Nope."

The window of a nearby Chinese restaurant cast red and green light onto the stack of toys. Skade dropped down on one knee to get a better view of a collection of candy wrappers, carefully pressed and formed into a garland that was strung through the arrangement.

"There probably isn't a real answer, Lane, as to why things happened as they did between us. I was just a messed-up kid." She framed a close-up of one of the teddy bears.

"Does that just dismiss it?" Lane asked, watching her work.

"Yeah. Probably. I didn't come back here to lick your old wounds, Lane," she said irritably. "I had spent my entire life moving from one town to another. New school, new town, new people. I never had a chance to learn how to be friends with anyone, at least the way that means to most people. The way I viewed relationships was different than yours. It probably still is. I'm sorry I was a fucked-up little girl, okay? I burned through a lot of people. You were better off rid of me." Skade took several more shots of the descansos, then replaced her camera in her bag.

"And besides," she said, fixing Lane with a fierce stare, "worse things happened at that time that made our little Disney melodrama seem really unimportant by contrast."

"What do you mean by that?"

"Nothing."

The thick smell of the Chinese restaurant floated around them as the moon above fought a losing battle with light pollution. Lane reached out and brushed her hair out of her face.

"Yeah, Skade. You seem lonely as hell and wound too tight."

"I am, Lane." The steam had left her voice, and she wrestled her camera out of her bag again and started playing with it.

"So, I say again, come back to my place with me." He touched her arm. "The Skyline is a waiting room for the mental hospital. Crash at my place. You could use that, I think. Another person for a while."

She looked up into his face. "No," she said.

Her emphatic tone clearly surprised him. "Why?"

"I told you. I don't need that, and I don't want that. I'm doing fine. I need things clean. I'm not interested. I'll meet you back at the studio. Thanks for caring, though."

She strode off into the shadows toward her car, feeling like a bag of rusty razorblades. Lane, standing in front of a pile of toys and candy boxes and flowers, watched her go.

19

The photo shoot at the studio had gone well the night before. Lane had been effusive in his praise for her photographs, and she'd set the whole thing up for him on a thumb drive. Her icy persona of professionalism was intended to make it clear that she was there only to work.

The next afternoon she found herself in the customer service office of the *Carleton Herald-Times*, a cramped waiting room with three teller windows, only one of which showed signs of ever being used. Skade leaned on the counter waiting for the woman stationed at the customer service desk—whose job seemed to be to say "no" to any customer requests—to return from asking her supervisor a question. Eventually, the woman returned from some nether realm, frowning, which Skade took as a good sign. Skade had hoped to skip this step. She'd spent several hours trying in vain to find background information on the Fieldings site and especially photographs from the early days of the installation, but nothing she found on the internet was even close to usable.

"We don't usually let people back inside," the woman repeated for the fourth time. Skade smiled and cheerfully waved her National Writers Union press card.

"What did you say you were looking for?" she finally asked, betraying the fact that she hadn't been listening the first three times.

"I need some historic photographs of the Fieldings Totem Poles. And any background stories or features you've got."

"Well, come on back then. I can take you back to the morgue," said the woman unhappily, and she unlocked a door to the side of the teller windows and ushered Skade through.

"We keep the photo morgue in here," said the woman, pushing open a set of swinging doors into a large file room. "Jerry can help you find what you're after."

A small balding man in a short-sleeved dress shirt and a tie smiled kindly and introduced himself as Jerry. "So, you want stuff on the totems? Sure, we got a fair amount on that. Have a seat and I'll get our files out for you."

Skade sat at a large worktable and Jerry returned with a stack of file folders. "These are stories about the Fieldings site specifically, and these are the files that reference the Fieldings site. The earliest photographs are of the poles going up, so you're in luck there. We had a photographer go out there when someone called the paper asking what was going on out by that stretch of highway. He got pics of Tom Fielding putting the poles into the ground. The earliest story is from about six months after they went in. Let me go back and find the related print files for you. That might take a few minutes," said Jerry.

"Thanks," offered Skade to his back as he slipped back into the file stacks. She began digging into the files.

After about twenty minutes Jerry returned, pushing a library trolley with a file box. "Seventeen separate stories either on the Fieldings site or referencing it. Thought there'd be more for some reason. I'll go back and give it a second look. If you need to make photocopies, just let me know. Normally they charge you ten cents apiece, but if you don't want too many, I can do it for you free."

"I've got about seven photographs I might want. Would that work?" asked Skade, holding out a small stack of prints. "I marked their locations in the file."

"Sure, I can do those for you, no problem. Be right back," Jerry said.

Skade opened her notebook and pulled a stack of files out of the box Jerry had wheeled out. In two hours she was down to the last two files in the box. Jerry had made her several copies, all for free, and Skade was happy with her finds.

The last two files were not on the totems specifically, but Skade decided to take a quick look. She opened the first file and froze. The story was short, a filler to hold the place of a breaking story as more information was gathered. It was twelve years old.

> The body was found near Fairfax Road. Cause of death is being listed as hit-and-run. The body was found partially hidden in a field a distance from the road, suggesting it was moved after the accident.

The note was paper-clipped to a stack of photographs:
Fairfax Road about halfway to the Lake. Long shot to the south.
Fairfax Road. Same spot. Long shot to the north.
Brush line on the side of Fairfax Road. East side. Four State Troopers.
East side of Fairfax. Past the brush line.

A sweeping soybean field. Two troopers and thee EMTs.

Close up of a knot of EMTs in short-sleeved uniform shirts, looking drawn and serious.

The bean field. Two EMTs and a trooper kneeling over something hidden under some branches and cover.

West, toward Fairfax. Two EMTs bringing out a gurney.

Two troopers looking at the ground. Searching.

A body. A girl. A shallow ditch in the field.

A closeup of the body. Twisted. Dirty. Early stages of decomposition. Her blue eyes staring up at something in the sky.

Skade's breathing was erratic and she felt numb. Moving the file aside, she looked at the one under it, dated to nine years prior.

> Michael "Mike" Curtis, 21, originally from Carleton, confessed yesterday morning to the hit-and-run death of 16-year-old Chastity Wilkes, who was killed as she walked along Fairfax Road three years ago last April. Mr. Curtis, who was alone at the time of the accident, fled to Virginia immediately afterward. His arraignment is Thursday. Thomas Verlaine, Mr. Curtis's court-appointed lawyer, pointed out that Mr. Curtis returned to Carleton of his own volition and confessed to local law enforcement.

And then, a second article, a week later.

> Michael "Mike" Curtis, who confessed to the hit-and-run death of 16-year-old Chastity Wilkes, was found dead of an apparent suicide at his parents' home Tuesday morning. He was to be sentenced later this month on charges of vehicular manslaughter and leaving the scene of an accident that resulted in a fatality. Wilkes was walking along the side of Fairfax Road in the late evening when Curtis struck her. Curtis, who was returning from a party at Windward Marina, tried to hide Wilkes' body and then fled the state.

Skade took her photocopies and her bag and quickly got up from the table. She made her way out of the newspaper building without saying a word to anyone, doing her best impression of calm. Her best impression of a human being.

Mike was dead.

Mike had confessed to the accident.

Mike had lied. He hadn't been alone.

The accident was wrapped up. Explained. Over.

Unused notes for a chapter to
American Still Life

From the files of
Skade Felsdottir

Judging by the rites and rituals of various world religions, nothing—not even birth—has more connection to the sacred and the holy (or perhaps instills more fear and trepidation?) than death. There is such a profound focus on the act of dying and on "being" dead (an oxymoron?) that at times the Church runs the risk of resembling a death cult, but there is a profound reason for this.

Birth is looked at as a creation of people: "We made a baby!" But death is seen as the province of the mysterious. It is the unknown. And it is the great transcendence. We are all standing nervously on the platform waiting for a train, and we begin speculating on what the train will be like and where it will be going. *Descansos* recognize the holy and the spiritual aspects of death. Originally, the Church saw these markers as a kind of populist insurrection into their Holy Territory, and they roused local governments to tamp down and regulate their creation. But the left-behind persisted and the practice only increased with the growth of American Car Culture. More cars, more deaths, more *descansos*. But roadside markers still face regulation. Many states have banned them from roadways, and many others have created rules and regulations around their make-up and placement. Some states have ready-made markers that they put out at the locations of fatal traffic accidents, lending a clean, modern, sanitized sameness to the memorials. Yet homemade markers appear, in all their individualized simple garish imperfect perfection, a powerful and haunting shout of human individual expression ~~in the face of modern mechanized lock-step,~~ and attesting to the presence of, and connection to, the dead.

Along with death, grief has also been given over. Grief is uncomfortable for society. It serves to remind the uninvolved viewer of the reality, the inevitability, and the impact of death, and our inability to control or stop it. So much so that cultures everywhere have created rules for grief: who may grieve, for how long, in what way, even what costumes to wear. At different times and in different places, industries of grief have appeared: from greeting cards and plastic flowers to professional mourners (it has even seeped into the folk tradition of the *descansos*. You can buy white PVC crosses for exactly that purpose at big-box stores across America now). Even convenience stores, especially those near cemeteries, deal in the stock and trade of death and grief and re-membrance: plastic flowers, cards, toys, etc. And so, the simple folkloric *descansos*, or roadside altars and shrines, seem to be the response of the individual in the face of this corporate shrink-wrapping. It is a way of re-personalizing the impersonal response to death. A way of bringing, if not the body itself, then at least the cemetery to the observer. A way of saying, "Remember this, damn it! Please!"

~~How do I forget? How can I remember?~~

Grief and mourning go hand in hand. Grief is the affect. It is the reaction. It is the thing itself. It is the sadness and anger and melancholy and inexpressible sense of loss and violation that happen in reaction to something like death. Mourning is a set of rituals and practices and performances that we all use to cope with that feeling. But there are differences too. Grief is usually thought of as a profoundly private ex-perience. Something unique to the individual experiencing it and calling for some kind of imperfect empathy or removed sympathy from those close by, but still wrapped in something impenetrable. Mourning, on the other hand, is considered very nearly a dramatic performance. Some-thing to be judged and criticized and compared, something needing to measure up to an objective set of criteria and not to be surpassed. Something controlled and ruled and laid out and quantified as well as qualified by others. *Descansos* bring these two things together. They ex-pose and reveal and lay bare the purity of grief in a public way, and they embody and sometimes twist and supplant what are considered standard practices and dogma of mourning at the same time. And in so doing they also forge a link between the living and the dead. It was long thought in some cultures that ghosts were the result of the dead improperly or insufficiently mourned.

~~There are ghosts all around me. Where is my performance? What have I done? What have I done? What I have done. There is no proper way.~~

-S. Felsdottir.

20

Skade's mind was seething like a disrupted termite nest. Seeing the photographs—the story about Mike—was more than she could deal with. She managed to get back to the Skyline, but ten minutes in the motel room was enough. She couldn't be by herself with all this in her head. The walls of the Skyline were sneaking up on her and it felt hard to breathe.

She followed an overgrown but well-scented animal track in her memory. She remembered a bar—The Slippery Slope—she had gotten into with a fake ID a few times. The bar used to have a quiet-place-to-hide-and-think vibe in the daytime, or so she remembered. Skade sat on the stool closest to the window, ordered a double vodka tonic, stared out at the street, and lost a game of dodgeball with her memories.

Mike had confessed. He told everyone he was alone in the car. He'd lied. Then he'd...? Killed himself?

For all those wretched years, she'd scrupulously avoided looking at anything relating to Carleton at all, let alone the accident. Not one time, even in her worst, darkest, most self-hating moments, had she searched for any stories or information.

Twenty minutes and the bottom of another double V&T later, Jerome and a friend of his she remembered from the photo shoot, a guy that reminded Skade of John Doe from the punk band X, pulled up a couple of seats.

"Well hey, Skade."

"Hey, Jerome," offered Skade, unsure she wanted company.

Jerome happily launched into the mostly one-sided monologue that seemed to be his normal style of communication. This was fine with Skade, since she was beginning to get a little foggy. The discussion quickly settled on Jerome's upcoming adventure. The boat, it seemed, was nearing completion. It still needed some decking and a cabin and a name, but Jerome was joyful and undeterred.

"Are you going to just quit the studio then?" Skade asked.

"Oh yeah. You know I should have left a while ago, and maybe I will once the boat is done," he said.

"Why should you have left before?" asked Skade thickly.

Jerome smiled into his beer. "Lane's a good guy. I like him. He's good to work with. But man... He can be a little crazy sometimes, you know?"

"How do you mean?"

"I dunno. Like, did he tell you about Chelsea and Amanda? Those two girls that apprenticed with him a little while ago? Yeah? Well, maybe the reality is a little different than I usually hear him tell it."

"Like how?"

"Well, this *contract* he has all his apprentices sign? That's bullshit, for one. It's not a real contract, it's just an agreement that they are basically going to be slave labor for two years. It's like he thinks he's being old-school or military or something. He wants to break them down or some such shit, you know? Well, of course they don't stand for all the bullshit and not getting even half of the money they bring in and all the criticism and shit, right? So, they're like *fuck this* and they take off and start a studio of their own. Oh my God, Lane hits the fucking roof! I have never in my life seen a more vengeful fuck than he got to be over that. I mean, they actually had to call the cops on him for harassment once when he..."

Skade had no memory of getting home.

Consciousness. She was on her bed at the Skyline. The room was spinning. She was still fully dressed. She even had her boots on. A piece of paper was safety-pinned to the leg of her jeans. She tore the paper off her leg and tried to read it, but her eyes wouldn't focus. In her confusion, she missed the feeling, but then it hit. Crushing horror-show sickness and pain.

Skade was desperate and needed something badly. She dug into all her bags, tossing her clothes and belongings around, going through pockets. She twice turned over everything in her bathroom, avoiding the mirrors at any cost. Finally, in between sobs and a blinding flash of head pain, she had a new thought.

She opened the front door. The sunlight smacked her hard across the face and the heat felt like she was stepping into a roaring fireplace. The assault of the morning was so overwhelming that Skade doubled over at the edge of the parking lot and vomited the contents of her stomach onto the blacktop. Her car wasn't there. She stared uncomprehendingly at the empty parking lot and then went back inside and grabbed the note again.

Hey, Skade. Hope you're doing okay. You had a little too much last night. At least you didn't break anything! We got you home okay. Your keys and bag are in the chair. Your car is still probably where you left it unless the cops didn't have anything better to do and towed it. Get some orange juice. See you soon. Had a good time!

Jerome

She cursed mournfully and called a Lyft.

The ride was pure hell. The more fully conscious she became, the worse she felt. She was used to bad hangovers, but this felt like she'd done some real damage to her mind and body.

The Lyft driver tried to talk, but she ignored him. Eventually he shut up. The smell inside his car was designed by some evil scientist to hurt her. But he eventually pulled up behind her Jeep, right where she'd left it.

She opened the door and shoved her hand rudely into the crack between the seat and the backrest and fished around. She bent down to examine the floor mat under the steering column and felt around under the seats, hoping to find it.

And she found it.

The runaway Percoset she remembered dropping. She swallowed her treasure dry and drove back slowly and carefully to the cool darkness of her room.

Her cells were still vibrating from turning her body into a toxic waste dump. After she'd gotten out of the shower, Skade saw the empty vodka bottles lying around. Just the sight of them made her body retch. She stood outside in the parking lot with her arms wrapped tightly around her body, gulping big swallows of air while her eyes watered, and her body shook with little involuntary tremors. Finally she worked up enough control to rush in and gather up all the empties in the room and her car in a pillowcase and take the sack full of vacant dependency out to the dumpster.

Now, she took a few halting steps toward her car.

Stopped.

Turned back toward her room and went inside.

She looked around while a small feverish voice shrieked in her head that maybe she'd forgotten a bottle someplace. She breathed deeply and tried to check in with the part that felt poisoned and battered. The part that didn't want anything to drink. She grabbed a bottle of water, took a long drink, and opened her window. But something still groaned in the deep dark corners of her mind.

Skade sat on the edge of her bed as tears came. She felt absolutely horrible. She found the corn puppet on the nightstand. She picked it up and held it delicately in her fingers and studied it.

"I gotta quit," she whispered to the corn puppet. "I can't keep doing this."

21

The day had been another punishment, and the wind, what there was of it, had mostly been a tired, seedy sigh. But now a different sort of breeze bullied its way through Skade's you're-not-supposed-to-do-that open window. Fresh and cooler, carrying a cinderblock vigorousness. The intruder rushed up to Skade and ran through her hair, so she went out into the parking lot to look at the sky, taking the cornhusk puppet with her. She hadn't let it go all day; somehow, it had helped her keep everything together. The wind was stronger out here, and far in the distance Skade saw a flickering in the billowing clouds. No thunder. Not yet. Just the wind and the sound of the trucks on the overpass. Skade went back inside out of the wind's playground.

"It's going to rain," said Skade to the cornhusk puppet.

She decided to drag a chair out into the dark current of freshness and await the coming storm. Sitting back in the shadows, away from her work, she felt the air ionize, and watched the sky become more intense, a steady beat of flashes lighting up the dark sky. Skade felt her body relax, and her mind began to follow. As soon as she became aware of the release, however, the fluttering of a hundred black butterfly wings between her shoulder blades and in her solar plexus pushed her peace away. A craving for a drink spilled over her. The desire came on with so much muscular power that it took her breath and folded her in half. She managed to grab some control again just as the first distant sound of rumbling thunder and the bottle-green scent of rain on the wind reached her.

And it began to rain. At least the rain gave the storm drains something to do.

Skade sat in her doorway, at the edge of the storm, and she grew dimmer inside. The wind brought her a meditative petrichor which soothed her a little. Memories began to jostle their way out into her consciousness. Mean, embarrassing memories. Things she had said and done over the years that she wished she hadn't. She felt the pressure for a drink began to rise up again like dangerous surf. Her body rattled with it. The liquor store. She grabbed her keys and the cornhusk puppet.

Alone she wasn't strong enough to keep herself at bay. She needed a person. She called Kit. No answer. She sat in her car and cried some more from the pain. She called again.

"Hey, Kit. It's me. I was…um…I don't know. I'm not feeling real good right now. If you're around, just call me. Please?"

She started the car and pulled hesitantly out of the parking lot and headed toward Lane's studio.

❧

The rain had begun to slacken. Light shot out of the front doors of the studio like steam from a geyser. Something else as well, Skade heard it as she locked her car. Lane was laying down some classics. *2112 Overture and the Temples of Syrinx* by Rush was blasting out into the rainy night air.

Skade pushed her way through the music feeling empty. She didn't see Lane. Instead, she saw Jerome. Jerome grinned at her and reached down under the counter and turned the music down. "Hey, Skade."

"Hey, Jerome, thanks for making sure I got home okay the other night… Sorry about that. Not sure what—"

"No worries!" said Jerome happily. "Happens. Hope you're okay?"

"Yeah, thanks. Lane around?"

"Naw, I'm not sure where he is. He's usually not here on Monday nights."

Skade could feel herself tightening up and a ghostly sense of urgency rose inside her again. "Okay. Well. I'll stop back by."

She got to her car just as the music cranked back up to full volume and the Scorpions began "Hurricane." Her phone went off. It was Kit.

"Kit. Hey…"

"Yeah, I'm okay, I was just feeling a bit off, you know?"

"No, seriously. Not an emergency. I promise…"

"Yeah…" Skade started to tear up again. The wave of sickness and desire was too strong this time. She hoped Kit couldn't hear her fragility. She was having a hard time fighting a crack in her voice. "Hey. Are you at home? Could I come by? I'm kind of needing some company right now. I guess I hit a rough patch or something. I'm feeling…I don't know… Are you sure? 'Cause I don't want to come over and be a huge burden or a hot pile of crap all over you?"

"Thanks… I'll be out in a few." Skade smiled through her tears.

She started the car and looked at the cornhusk puppet sitting on her dashboard. She drove past three liquor stores on her way to Kit's house.

22

Kit answered her door with a smile. "Hey, Skade…"

"Sorry for dropping by like this." Skade had built her walls back up on the drive. They weren't very sturdy, but they looked good so long as the wind didn't blow.

"No, no, don't worry."

Skade shrugged out of her jacket and left it on the landing to drip.

The cavalcade of puppets in various stages of completion again overwhelmed Skade's senses. Ones she didn't recognize from her last visit peeked out from behind pillows and corners. And the groupings had changed.

"What's going on?" asked Kit. "You sounded pretty stressed?"

"I just felt like I needed some company. You know how it can get sometimes? I was going a little crazy. I needed to get away from the work. What are you up to?"

Kit motioned to a table at the far end of the room. A work light shone brightly down onto a jumble of objects strewn across the surface. "Just building some puppets. Do you mind if I finish this?"

"Of course," Skade said, finding a perch on the sofa and beginning to unpack her camera. She fit a lens onto the camera body and made her way through the disorder to where Kit was sitting.

Skade framed images of the objects on the table. Kit's work surface was an indecipherable map of a territory of dreams: doll parts, feathers and bits of fur, old skeleton keys and wooden spools, tufts of moss and little bundles of twigs, wire and ribbon of every size and color, satin and damask and muslin and burlap and toile, fishing lures and Christmas baubles, wooden balls and sheets of aluminum foil, and dozens of other bits and pieces of things that were invisible in their normal context, but which glowed as Kit delicately pulled them together into representations of living beings.

Skade couldn't help but notice Kit's hands; they were long and thin like she was. They grew out of her tightly buttoned shirtsleeves like strange flowers, the backs freckled and laced with scars and cuts, the result, no doubt, of hard outdoor labor—all of which was in keeping with the rest of the animal to which they were attached. But there was also an elegance and grace in the smallest movement of her fingers that was incongruous with the rest of Kit.

Skade focused her camera on Kit's hands. They moved like dancers, with a dexterity and finesse that gave them a lightness that could be mistaken for delicacy. But Kit's hands were architectural things, like great suspension bridges shrunk to a personal scale. The tendons running from her wrists to her fingers stood out like steel cables as she worked, and the long spidery digits pulled and flexed with unexpected force. They moved with a sense of conveying, of signaling, of casting silent spells like the flight of birds and the dance of bees. She lowered the camera and wandered out into Kit's space. The idea of a drink was spinning like a top someplace inside.

What had been a confusion of flotsam and jetsam began to pull together into meaning. The puppets, which at first had seemed haphazard, tossed about by a child to lie wherever they fell, now seemed to have stories to tell. Skade stopped in front of a shelf full of odd beings. The puppets here seemed to be mutants. Cobbled together out of mismatched parts and sewn together in strange dream-like combinations.

"These look like those nightmare toys from Syd's room in *Toy Story*," Skade said with a laugh. "Are they the monsters?"

"Oh no." Kit seemed shocked by the question, and she hurried over to where Skade stood. "I don't have any monsters. Puppets are always a little ugly or creepy to people," she continued, somewhat sadly, Skade thought. "Even the most beautiful marionettes, because of the way they move or whatever. Some of mine are made from broken parts. Scraps. My puppets are like salvage come to life. Maybe that's what scares people." Kit picked up one of the ugly misshapen puppets. "It's stuff they've thrown away that has come back to talk to them. I mean, what would something you broke say to you if it came back?"

Skade's mind offered her a vision of a broken lifeless body lying in the weeds beside a road framed in the headlights of a car. Reflexively, she put her camera to her eye and tried to curl up inside the safety of the lens and hide. She snapped a picture.

"But that's why I love them. They need to have people pay attention to them," continued Kit. "I can't stand to throw stuff away, so I take spare parts and put them together in different ways." Kit reached out and caressed an odd-shaped wooden marionette. Skade felt something prowling inside her, chasing her down; a part of her wanted to lie down and give herself up.

"Where did you live?" asked Kit. She had folded into a chair. Skade sat hunched on the sofa across from her, a glass of water cradled in her hands. "I mean, when you used to live here?"

"In a haunted house out on Rosefield, back behind St. Agatha's and the brick kilns," said Skade, looking out the window at the rain.

"Really?" Kit asked, wide-eyed.

"I thought so. Probably nobody else did," Skade said with a wry smile. "The house felt funny to me. There were rooms I didn't like to go into…funny sounds…stuff moved. But it was probably just my over-active teenage imagination and a strong desire to be special. I got off on being the girl that lived in the haunted house. But given the way things were at home, I was probably the only ghost."

"Why?" asked Kit.

"My attitude. I didn't feel real special inside, so I guess I liked it when people thought I was. By the time we got here, my dad and I had lived in six or seven different places. All that displacement and upheaval had pretty well wrung the child out of me. I suppose kids need time and space to spread out and make friends and create themselves. Their own little kid mythologies and stories and stuff. I spent all my kid-time packing and unpacking and trying not to say hello to anybody after I learned what goodbye was all about. And riding around in the back seat of used cars and moving vans. When I turned fourteen and we moved here, I was more my dad's roommate than anything else. I felt like I was just biding time until I could get out on my own. Then I did. Anybody who lives like that probably thinks stuff is haunted. But the ghost is just your own shadow. That house was creepy though," said Skade.

A strange smile crossed Kit's face.

"What?" asked Skade.

"I was going to say I would be so afraid to just take off at seventeen or eighteen. But I was alone by then too. Except I just stayed. Everybody else took off."

"That must have been hard. I'm sorry."

"I don't know if it was or not. It's not like I have anything to compare it to. It just was what happened. But it's funny that you felt like you were in a haunted house. I guess I do too, but mine is inside out. This house is full of dead people and I'm the one haunting them, it feels like. I think my brother getting killed was what really just set it all off."

"What happened?"

"Afghanistan. He was the shining light of the family, you know? He was the only boy, which was enough for my mom and dad. He was the one that mattered. But he was good and kind. People were always saying he had *promise*, whatever that means. He was nice to me and my sister. Anyway, he signed up for the army right out of high school. He was going to save up for college and get into computers. They said his platoon came under fire. Supposedly Eddie saved two guys. Went back and got them. But he got hit. Some kind of rocket or grenade.

"He got medals. A couple of them. They're over there on the table with his flag. And a commendation. They made a big deal of it. Some general or commander came to the house, I remember. They had a ceremony down at the courthouse. His name is on some marker down there now. 'Heroes of Foreign Wars' or something. Hero that came home in a box. I know my mom would rather have had a coward that came home in one piece. After he died, that's when things got bad. It was like him dying killed the roots of the family tree. And then my sister died real soon after that and my dad left. That blew the tree down." Kit picked up a marionette, a clown in a bright red baggy suit and a jester's hat. The clown started looking for something under tables and chairs and under Kit's feet.

"We're opposite like that, right? I mean you wanted to go out on your own, and I just wanted to have everybody with me. I miss them." The clown seemed to have found something, and it got down on its hands and knees and began fishing behind Kit's chair. Kit didn't look at the clown.

"What did you do when you took off?" asked Kit, seemingly oblivious to the marionette in her hands.

"I worked my way through a lot of stuff. Jobs, guys, adventure and romance," said Skade, with a facetious wave of her hand. Kit laughed.

"What's the line from that movie? 'There's no such thing as adventure and romance. There's only trouble and desire. And when you desire something, you immediately get into trouble. And when you get into trouble, you don't desire anything at all.' That's the truth. That was the basic story of it. Trouble and desire and one leading to the other and back again."

The clown found a ball and began tossing it back and forth between its hands in a curious representation of juggling. The act was so surprising that it momentarily pulled Skade from the hunter-gatherer game with a drink and the smoke-signal-memories.

"That's amazing."

"Yeah, isn't that cool?" said Kit, smiling. "That took a while to figure out. There's a trick to it. But it's pretty neat."

The clown began to do a dance while it juggled its ball. "It's got to get lonely, right?" asked Kit.

"What?"

"Just going off like that. You must have felt real lonely."

"Not that I can remember." Skade picked up her camera and began to clean the lens. "I mean, I made friends when I needed to. And most of the time people tire me out anyway. Being around people always feels like a drain on my energy. No, I wasn't lonely. Bored sometimes. Horny. Angry sometimes."

"Angry?"

"Maybe more impatient. Frustrated when things wouldn't go the way I wanted or as fast as I wanted. It pissed me off when things wouldn't work right."

Kit watched the clown dance. "I'd be lonely."

Skade looked at her. "Kit, do you perform live? Do you do theater?"

"God no. No way."

"That's crazy! You don't do that for audiences?" Kit laughed and looked at Skade. "I'm serious, Kit."

"No way. I'm scared of people. I could never get up in front of people and do a show."

"But when you do puppets, aren't you usually behind a screen or under a stage or something? People wouldn't have to see you. They're watching the puppets."

"That doesn't matter."

"You just did stuff for me?"

"Yeah…but that was just playing around a little. That wasn't a show or anything."

"So nobody has seen you perform? Nobody knows you do puppet theater?"

"I don't do theater, Skade. I just play around for myself. Some people have seen the puppets."

"Who? How many?" Kit just looked at Skade and laughed. "I'm serious Kit. Who has seen you?"

"I did a show for some little kids at a daycare a while ago. I about barfed afterward."

"Did they like it?"

"Well, yeah. But they were four years old."

"So you've got some stories you can perform? Fairy tales and stuff?"

"Yeah."

"What about stuff you've made up?"

A wave of what might have been panic and pain crossed Kit's face. She looked down at the floor between her feet. Skade looked around the cluttered space.

"What's that?" Skade said, pointing toward a large puppet theater made of cloth and scrap wood that leaned against the dining room table.

"That's my theater," said Kit quietly, looking back at the floor.

"You do have things you've made up, don't you?" Kit didn't answer. "Kit. You should be a professional puppeteer."

Kit laughed uncomfortably and looked up. Tears filled her eyes. "No way."

"You could be. I've seen puppet theater. Saw some in Paris and London. You're the best puppeteer I have ever seen. It's not even close."

Kit wiped her eyes and her nose on the back of her sleeve and looked at the floor again. "I don't want to."

"Why?"

Kit looked like a terrified little animal in a cage. "I just want to have this stuff for me. It's not for other people."

"But you do have some stories you can do? You have some shows?"

Kit looked around like she was trapped by a predator. "Yeah. I have some," she admitted.

"Okay," said Skade, holding up her camera. "I can take a professional-quality video with this. And I have a light kit in my car. Will you do a show for me? And let me film it?"

Kit shrank into herself. "I don't know—"

"Please? Think about it?"

"Okay. Maybe." Kit ventured a shy smile.

"All right then," said Skade happily, then she felt a wave go through her and she arched her back. She felt the urge directly between her shoulder blades. She got up with a burst like she'd been kicked out of her seat.

"You okay?" asked Kit.

"Yeah." Skade stretched and felt the walls closing in a little. "I might need to run out and get something here in a second, but I'll be right back."

"Okay…" said Kit, her hand going to her mouth.

Skade swallowed hard and felt her throat tighten. She sat back down. "No. I'm okay. Quit biting your nails."

Kit smiled, releasing the strings of the clown. Her hands scarcely moved but some intention or energy drew back up the strings, into her hands, and back into her. The clown became a lifeless puppet again, and she lightly let it slip to the floor. She got up and went into her kitchen and came back with another glass of water and handed it to Skade.

"So you were saying you wanted to talk to people that were putting up descansos?" said Kit, sitting back down. She picked up a sheet of construction paper and began folding it and twisting it in her hands.

Skade took a big gulp of her water and looked up. "Yeah?"

"I know a woman that put up one. You can talk to her, probably."

"Seriously? That would be great, Kit."

"Yeah. Let me call her and make sure it's okay, but I'm pretty sure she'd be okay talking to you about it. We could go in a couple of days. Tomorrow nobody's working out at the totems site. We could go back there if you want?"

"That would be great. Hey, Kit?"

"Yeah?"

"Can I ask you a favor?"

"Sure?"

"I feel bad because I feel like I'm always asking you to do things for me…"

"Don't worry about it…"

Skade sat and looked at Kit, blinking. She felt like crying.

"What?"

"Can I maybe crash on your couch tonight? We can get a pizza or something? I'll pay—"

Kit looked surprised. "Sure. That would be great. I'd like that."

Skade's deep breath came out in big pieces. But she smiled.

Kit held out her folded puppet—a human form about six inches high. She tucked her fingers into the folds behind the figure's arms and it came to life, moving its arms with a tiny sweeping grace as it bowed and danced.

Kit set the little figure on a nearby dish and produced a box of matches. She lit a match and held it to the paper puppet, which quickly went up in flames. Kit dropped the remnants onto the dish and they watched it burn.

"Why did you do that? That was such a beautiful little puppet."

"I do that every day," said Kit quietly. "I make one of those every day, then I set it free."

23

The night was hit and miss. Skade slept initially, but she'd fallen awake around three. The world worked differently at Kit's place. In Skade's mental swamp, all the puppets had somehow shifted to look directly at her, their eyes glinting in the fairy light brought in by the moon. She tossed and turned on the sofa for a while, then got up and stalked the house quietly, part of her hoping to find a bottle of something or some pills in a cabinet, and another part happy in the knowledge that she wouldn't. The late-night-and-alone headspace was disconnected. She started gently touching puppets, lightly brushing them with her fingers, not sure if she was relieved or disappointed that each was cold and without a pulse.

The house was full of currents and eddies of smells that had probably been there all along but were hidden behind the bewildering fantasy of Kit's house in the light. Now, in the darkness, the smells took the stage: the smell of glue; of the medicinal scent of hand cream; of rose, lilac, and lavender. There was a soft fluffy smell of clean laundry and the water smell of the air-conditioned air. All these smells blended together in Skade's nose to form what she would forever remember as puppet-breath.

Slowly the haze of agitation lifted, and she grew quiet in the cool blue darkness of Kit's house. She wandered down the hall and lightly pushed open Kit's bedroom door.

The room was a vast shadow, and Skade pulled hard into her hearing. The soft whisper of Kit's even breathing came over the white noise of the air conditioner. The cool aqua gleam of a security light in the backyard shone through the leaves of ragged sumacs outside the window. She made out the silver-gray topography of Kit sleeping, sprawled under a sheet. Watching, she wished sleep were contagious.

❧

"There isn't much going on near the totems until the paving crew gets there," said Kit as they approached the construction barricades. Skade was feeling hollow and used up, but a spark in her felt a little healthier. Her cravings—those animals in her chest—were quiet now.

Kit parked not far from where she and Skade had first met. Skade began by taking a few long shots, then she and Kit walked up toward the center of the memorials.

It was like being on the edge of a strange forest. Dozens of memorials, some extraordinarily beautiful and complex, washed over the hillside. Skade stopped every few yards and took pictures of installations or the juxtaposition of several memorials together.

They came to the Fieldings Totem Poles themselves, the epicenter of the entire carnival. The four poles stood together in a tight cluster. Someone had come in the last twelve years and reinforced them with concrete. The original paint had faded, and each pole was scarred with the visitors' initials. The tallest pole, for Patricia Fielding, stood fourteen feet high. The other three, for each of the children, stood between ten and twelve feet high. Each pole was carved in the traditional Northwest Coast Native American style, but closer inspection saw that, while the style was correct, the motifs themselves consisted of stylized soccer balls, horses, schoolbooks, and a German Shepherd.

"Why totem poles?" Kit asked. "I mean that seems strange. There are no totem poles around here and no Indians either. Fielding doesn't sound like an Indian name. Were they Indians or something?"

Skade took a few more pictures and backed down the hill to where Kit was standing.

"Don't bite your nails," said Skade, without even looking at Kit. "Nope, typical American family. Well, maybe not typical. He was a nationally known artist. So was she. They had money and lived in a nice place out by Lake St. Vincent. The way I heard the story was that they'd all come back from a big family vacation out west about two weeks before the accident happened. They'd seen the real totem poles out in BC."

"BC?"

"British Columbia. Canada. That's what gave Tom Fielding the idea. Yes, it's cultural appropriation but this was the '70s, and that's what the white world was like then, if it's changed much at all."

"What's this?" said Kit. She'd moved a few yards past the totems and was standing in front of a brass birdbath. "Smells good."

Skade moved over to join Kit. Inside the birdbath were three bundles of pale green leaves tightly wrapped and tied with a string so that they formed dense little logs. Ashes sat in the bottom of the brass dish.

Skade inhaled deeply—the scent was clean and familiar, sweet and musky.

"This is a sage smudge," she said. "They're used in cleansing rituals. Drive away bad spirits. Or bad luck. I love this smell," Skade continued, smiling up at Kit. "I was out west a couple of years ago, in the California desert. Everything smelled like this, especially in the evening. I was doing a magazine shoot on a dinosaur dig. One day the light got really strange and hazy…then this smell came up. My God, what an amazing smell. I guess there had been a brush fire near us overnight. My stuff smelled like sage for weeks, but I didn't care. Being out in it felt so cleansing."

An expression of confused anxiety crossed Kit's face. "I mean, how? I don't… You've been everywhere…all over the world doing all this stuff. I don't think I've been more than a hundred miles from this spot ever."

"So, go," said Skade.

"What?"

"Go. Seriously. And, no, I have not been all over the world. I'd love to be able to say that someday, though." Skade touched Kit's shoulder. "Pick a place. Someplace not too far, maybe that you can drive to. Someplace you've always wanted to see. It doesn't take a lot of money if you don't mind sleeping in your truck or camping out and eating cheap. Where do you want to go?"

"I don't know…"

"How about the Grand Canyon?"

"I don't even know where that is…"

"It's in northern Arizona, not too far from the Utah border. You could be there in three days; two, if you're insane. Everyone should see the Grand Canyon. North rim, not the south rim."

"I've seen pictures—"

"Not near good enough, believe me. You need to be there to experience it. It's like looking at…I don't know…one of God's faces, or something."

"I don't know…I can't just go—"

"Why not?"

Kit paused and looked at Skade with a bemused smile. "I can't. I have work."

"Take time off. Or quit. You can always get another job. And besides, Kit, you're an artist. Take your art. Use it. Work up a few puppet shows, load your theater into the back of your truck, take your puppets. Or some of them, all of them probably wouldn't fit in two trucks. You could make a decent living doing traveling puppet shows."

"No. No way—"

"That's what I did. I didn't start out wanting to be a photographer."

"What do you mean?"

"I was kind of in a freefall for a while. Photography was with me when I finally landed. It was what I had left." The sudden need for a drink took her, but Skade managed to find enough of herself to recover. "That's the beauty of your art, Kit," Skade continued. "You will always have it. You could do that."

Kit snatched a lock of her hair up into her mouth and chewed it with an anxious smile as she wandered off.

"Grand Canyon, Kit! You need to do it. Don't make me drag you," Skade teased, then she snapped a couple of pictures of Kit, who tried to turn her back and duck out of the shot.

"Why'd *you* go?" called Kit happily, trying to dodge the camera lens.

"What?" asked Skade, taking the camera from her eye.

"What made you go? How'd you just do that?" Kit was still laughing, but Skade wasn't playing anymore.

"I just went," she said quietly. "I hated it here. I hated my father. I just left…"

Kit looked at her and stopped asking questions.

Skade was taking photographs of a wooden chair covered with small stones and coins when she heard a soft cracking sound quickly followed by Kit's voice: "Oh shit…"

Kit was standing in front of an old department store mannequin dressed as an angel with large cardboard wings. The angel's arms had been raised in a prayer, but now one of its arms had broken off in Kit's hands. "I didn't mean to…" Kit began, mortified, holding the arm out toward Skade. "It just popped off when I touched it." Skade snapped a quick shot. "Don't take my picture," Kit pleaded.

"Need it for evidence," said Skade seriously. "The cops are going to want to know who did this." Kit's face went pale, and she looked as if she was about to start crying. Skade started to laugh. "Kit, don't worry about it. I was just teasing. No one is going to call the cops."

"I just wanted to see if it moved," Kit said, on the verge of tears.

"It's okay. Don't worry. Seriously, these things are not designed to last forever. They aren't like gravestones. Water and the sun get to them, and they start to fall apart. The most elaborate ones are usually the first to go. Haven't you noticed how many of these things are broken? Some people probably come out here once or twice a month to rebuild them, but if they don't, they start to fall apart within days."

"But this one was so pretty," said Kit mournfully.

"Yeah, it was a nice one, but look, the robes are dirty and stained by rain and the paint is coming off. It was coming apart. Don't freak out over it. I've had them fall apart in my hands a few times. Besides, I figured you, if anyone, ought to be able to fix an arm on a mannequin."

Kit brightened a bit and looked closely at the end of the broken arm, then at the shoulder where it had been attached. "Yeah, I can fix this. It just needs a new peg. I think I've got one in the truck. Here, hold this." She handed the arm to Skade and dashed back toward her truck.

Kit returned with a red metal toolbox and diligently set to work. Skade took a few pictures of her working, then moved on before the light dimmed.

"If the people who made that angel come back, they are going to have a heart attack," Skade said with a laugh when she returned.

Kit had not only fixed the angel's arm, she had transformed the entire tableau. Before, the angel had been standing erect, arms over her head; now she was kneeling down on one knee with her hands held before her in a gesture of giving and supplication. The figure had been transformed from a lifeless object to a living emotional being with a quiet and profound energy.

"I hope they won't be mad. I think it looks better like this," said Kit apologetically, chewing on the ragged end of a thumbnail.

"Nails. It looks amazing. That's probably what they were going for but didn't know how to do it."

With a smile, Kit looked around the hillside— other mannequins had clearly caught her eye.

"Hey, don't get any ideas, woman," said Skade. "Let people do their own work. The Fieldings Totems probably don't need a magic mannequin fairy animating the figures out here. Come on, I think I'm done. Let's get out of here before we get caught or you go crazy turning this place into Camille Claudel's sculpture garden."

And they headed back toward the truck together.

24

oly crap, you've got a tape deck," Skade said, glancing down at the dashboard of the old truck. "Why didn't you tell me you had a tape deck?" She rummaged around inside her bag.

"I'm not sure I ever noticed. I never used it. It might not work," Kit said.

"Nobody notices them anymore. Relic of the past." Triumphantly, Skade pulled three plastic cassette tapes out of her bag.

"You have tapes?"

"I do. Let's see if your deck works." Skade slipped a cassette into the slot. Kit's speakers came to life and "Learn to Say No" by Lydia Loveless began. Skade turned up the volume.

"It works." Skade smiled.

"How do you have cassette tapes?" asked Kit.

"It's a long story." Skade slid down in her seat and put her sunglasses back on. "When I left here, I was a mess. I didn't have any idea where I was going, so I went west because it seemed like the thing to do. I was thinking LA or San Francisco, but I wound up in Astoria, Oregon, because my aim has always been fucked up. I always wind up someplace other than where I'm going. So, I'm kicking around Astoria, out of money, sleeping in my car, which is nearly out of gas. Stealing food from supermarkets. It was pretty bleak."

Kit turned to look at Skade slumped down in her seat. "I can't picture you like that," she said quietly.

"Yeah," said Skade. "Long time ago and a galaxy far, far away. Anyway, everyone out there was listening to this wild free-form pirate radio station. All kinds of crazy theories about who was running it—everything from a pack of old Haight-Ashbury hippies, who made a fortune selling acid and bought a tanker to ship weed and put a transmitter on it, to a Mexican communist plot, to ghosts and aliens. They said you could sometimes get it as far up as Seattle or all the way down to Crescent City. Old tapes of radio shows, poetry readings, music, and spoken word. It was called Radio Artemis.

"One afternoon this guy comes up and drops a fifty-dollar bill on me. Older guy, short and fat and all scruffy. He looked down at me and asked if I wanted a job. My first thought was: *Great. Another dirty old man.* I'd had a few of those. Guys rolling up to me and offering me twenty or fifty or a hundred or a couple of hundred to do this or that on them or to them or with them. Some real freaks. I won't go into it. That's a whole 'nother story. I'm about to take this guy's fifty and run off with it, when he says he means a real job. He must have known what I was thinking by the look on my face.

"The guy says his name is Walter Arthur," continued Skade, turning the cassette box over in her hands. "And he wants to know if I know anything about music. I was at a point where if you'd told me I could have gotten a job as a brain surgeon doing a trapeze act, I'd have said I knew all about both, so I said, 'Sure, I know all about music.' He says I should get something to eat and meet him that night, and he hands me a business card with just his name and an address. He says not to worry, it's nothing creepy or perverted.

"I went out about four in the afternoon to the address to make sure it wasn't some Dungeon of Desire or phone sex setup or something."

Kit laughed.

"It was a warehouse down by the port. I didn't have anything better to do, so I waited, trying to keep out of sight, to see what was going on. Eventually I see Walter Arthur show up with a box of records. Nothing else happens, and after dark it starts to rain, so I figure what the fuck and I go and knock on the door.

"This is the only place I've ever been that comes close to your house for the 'wow' factor. Turns out Walter Arthur lives in this warehouse. He called it *The Archive*, a combination library and record store and cabinet of wonder."

"Cabinet of wonder?"

"Precursors of museums. Wealthy people created these curated collections: oddities and natural specimens and things, stuff they stole from native people. Walter's place was full of the craziest stuff. Anyway, Walter starts talking. First, he wants to talk about music (and he finds out I don't know shit beyond the obvious stuff), then he wants to talk about poetry, then politics, then science, and on and on. Eventually I get tired of the weird quiz-bowl conversation and ask him about this job thing, thinking that now it's going to come out there is no job, and he just wants to pay me to wear my underwear on his head for the evening or something like that, you know? But he asks if I ever heard about Radio Artemis.

"Turns out, Walter is the guy behind it. He told me he needed people to help him do the radio thing. Somehow, he had heard I was supposedly smart or something. Like, I'm some sort of genius living in a dead car and stealing bread from a Safeway, right? Anyway, I stayed about a year. I saved up some money. And he found out I liked photography. He pulls out a box with a bunch of old cameras in it and tells me I can have any of them that work. I took the whole box and cobbled together a decent set-up. Sold some of it to buy things I needed. But let me get to the tapes."

Skade waved the empty cassette box at Kit. "I couldn't stay in Astoria forever. When I got ready to leave, Walter gave me a box of tapes he'd made. He was always making these mix tapes. It was an obsession with him. He said whenever I could, to email him a mailing address and he'd send me new ones. So now, every time I get someplace where I can get mail, I drop him a line, and in a few days, I get a new shipment of Walter Arthur's Radio Artemis mix tapes. And, since you've got a tape deck in your truck, I can tell Walter to start sending some tapes your way, as my ward and apprentice."

"Yeah. That would be great." Kit beamed.

"Walter Arthur really did save my life, I think," said Skade. "He appeared out of the blue when I was in a dark place. I can name a couple of other people like that. Sometimes a friend who helped me out or kept me sane when I was starting to come off the rails."

"Guardian angels," said Kit. Skade made a face and laughed. "No, seriously. My mom used to say there were guardian angels all over the place, looking out for you. Sometimes you don't see them, and sometimes they take the form of people. Sometimes they step inside us and use us to help other people."

"I can buy that."

They lapsed again into a comfortable cohabitated silence, Skade looking out the window, letting her thoughts run with the wind and the heat.

"Weather's coming up," said Skade after a long pause. It had been hazy and heavy all day and storm clouds were building. The air felt charged.

"Can I switch on the radio for a second?" asked Kit. Almost immediately a weather bulletin came on—a tornado watch would last through the evening with severe thunderstorms expected.

"Normal this time of year," said Skade.

"Yeah," said Kit. But her energy had changed.

A long angry rumble of thunder heralded their arrival back at Kit's. Kit hurried through the house switching on lights. Skade's attention was drawn by a battered wooden dresser. Seven puppets sat quietly in a row, their backs to the mirror.

Most were former stuffed animals fashioned into puppets. All Kit's puppets seemed to possess a limitless patience, of things lost and left behind, cobbled together sums of miscounted integers that somehow created life when Kit slipped her hand inside. But where most of Kit's puppets seemed partly wired together with melancholy and sweet nostalgia and surprising little arabesques of remembering, the puppets on the dresser appeared to be trading on their grief—formed as they were of broken scraps of left-over regrets and sorrows.

"What are these?" asked Skade.

Kit picked up one of the puppets and slipped her hand into it. And it began to dance.

A former doll with blond hair, blue-glass eyes, and pouting lips, it wore a stained white chemise. One arm dangled and swung disobediently as the puppet moved. The dance suggested a frightened hope for understanding and connection, its movement subtle and fluid and lovely as its one good arm led in a singular waltz.

"These are hard to explain," said Kit, watching the puppet move as though she were uninvolved with its actions. "Promise not to be mad at me?"

Skade looked up at her and saw she was frightened and serious. "I promise?" said Skade.

"I told you that I sometimes got put on that crew that went out and cleaned up descansos? We had to before we did mowing or roadside work, like culverts or guard rails. We needed to clear the areas. So somebody had to go take down descansos if they were in the way."

"Yeah, you told me—"

"Well, like I said, I hate throwing stuff away. And these things were going to the dump. So I guess I took them. You know how sad these things are. The stuff that we had to clean up?"

"Kit, are you saying these puppets are items you rescued from descansos?"

"Yeah. Don't be mad at me, please," Kit said quietly.

Skade stood and stared at the puppets sitting in their sad, quiet file. "That's the most amazing thing I've ever seen, Kit. I mean it. I'm not mad. I'm blown away that you would do that. I want to put this in the book, if it's okay with you?"

"Really? You don't think people would be mad? If they saw their stuff made into puppets? Like I stole it or something?"

"No, not if the county was taking things down. I doubt anyone would care. And I won't use a ton of pictures. Just a couple. Is that okay?"

"Yeah, sure. I'd like that," Kit said, glowing.

Skade ran off a few shots of the descanso puppets on the dresser, then stopped.

"Quit biting your nails. Can we move them to another spot? I keep getting my reflection in the mirror." Skade finished her shoot.

A flash. Lightning exploded silently, then a shuddering crash of thunder shook the room. The air tightened and there was a strange clatter in the wind outside. A fat raindrop burst on the window.

"Crap," said Skade, looking outside. "I should get out of here before this gets bad. Let you have your place back." She took a step toward the door.

"Wait," said Kit quietly.

Skade looked at her. She was fighting something. Another blast of thunder.

"Don't go. Don't. Please?" Kit hugged herself and looked fearfully out the window. "Can you stay? Just for a little while? Maybe just until the storm goes away? I...I don't like storms." Kit was clearly terrified.

"Sure," Skade said. "Yeah, I can stay. Let's go into the kitchen, away from the windows."

Kit had left a kitchen window open, and she ran to close it, but not before the scent of rain and heat and high grass came rushing in on a bellows of cool air. Kit slammed the window shut. And the rain came down like running horses.

"Sorry..."

"Hey, don't worry about it. I like the rain and thunder, but big storms up close bother me too."

"I just…" began Kit, but she was cut off by the distant undulating wail of a tornado siren come to spinning life. Kit jumped for a radio, turning it on in the middle of a repeating weather bulletin warning. Kit went white. Skade listened intently to the announcement twice through.

"It's okay, Kit. The tornados are moving away from us. It's going to be loud and wet for a while, but we'll be okay."

Kit huddled, shaking, in a chair. Skade rubbed her back gently. "It's okay, Kit."

An apocalyptic crash of light and sound followed, and the lights went out. Kit let out a sound Skade had heard only once or twice in her life.

"Hey, hey…stop, stop, stop," said Skade in her most reassuring voice. "Kit, it's fine. We're fine…seriously. That was a big one. It probably took out the transformer. Listen, we're good. You've got enough candles in the place for two churches. Let me go light some for us. Come and sit with me on the couch in the front room with the puppets."

Skade pulled her Maglite from her bag. She gathered several candles onto the coffee table and lit them until the room was bathed in a flickering warmth.

"Kit. Come in here. I'll sit with you. We'll be safe."

Kit came hesitantly into the room, like a frightened cat. She had Janeyre Thinksquickly clutched in her arms. Skade put Kit in the corner of the couch and sat herself down next to her, hips touching. Outside, the world was coming to an end in wind and water.

"It's going to be fine, Kit. Don't worry. I'm sorry you're so afraid. I'm here," said Skade quietly.

Skade could tell Kit was fighting back sobs with a titanic effort. "I'm sorry…" she managed to say.

"Don't be sorry, Kit. It seems like you have astraphobia."

"What?"

"I know…when I first heard that I thought it meant fear of stars. It means fear of thunderstorms…a phobia…a really, really bad uncontrollable fear. Like some people have of snakes or spiders. Like panic."

"Yeah," muttered Kit. "My mom said we got caught in a tornado when I was about two. It's a miracle nobody died. I've seen the pictures. My sister was nine. My sister took me into the bathtub, and I guess that saved us. She held on to me."

The rain beat down and thunder rumbled, but it seemed farther away, and it had lost some of its intensity. Less personal now, more like it was just doing its job.

"When I got older, I would run to my sister whenever it felt like a storm was coming. We always slept in the same room, and if it started at night, she'd come over to my bed and curl up next to me and make sure I was okay. Sometimes it got real bad, especially those first days of summer where it feels like it's going to storm every afternoon. I used to follow her around trying to hold her hand. Once, when I was seven or eight, we had a tornado warning at school, and the teacher had to send for her to come sit with me because I was screaming."

Skade put an arm around Kit and pulled her closer. Kit held her breath for a moment, then the tears came, and the sobs.

"Two days after she died..." Kit choked on her spasms of anguish, her face pink and white and gray and wet. "Two days after she died, we had one of the worst thunderstorms I ever saw..." Kit buried her face in the back of her puppet.

"I was eleven...I...ran to her bed...I always did that—ran for my sister." Tears came as hard as the rain. "Some friends of mom...from church...had come and cleaned out her stuff. I was sleeping in Mom's... bed. I ran back into...our room...and...everything was gone...I..." And Kit, convulsed with sobbing, couldn't continue.

The storm got the last word with a last flash of blinding light and a whiplash cracking of thunder. The storm headed away.

Skade held on to Kit. "Hey, Kit. Look...see? The sky is still there."

And the rains poured.

And Skade pulled Kit to her shoulder and held her hard while she cried and thought of all those storms in all those years and this girl.

All alone.

25

*B*reathe, *two, three…*

Skade had gone back to the Skyline after Kit left for work.

Breathe, two, three…

It had been three days since her last drink. Skade felt different, clearer; but she felt all her bruises and aches—physical and emotional—a lot more clearly too. The thought of a drink and how good it would be was a constant companion.

So she went to the pool.

Breath, two, three…

The new Kensington Aquatic Center felt strange. The locker room was too new. The old one had been dark and dingy—the juniors and seniors used to try to scare the freshmen with yeast infections—but it had felt familiar. The pool, at least, was laid out mostly the same.

Breathe, two, three…

According to the signs posted in the locker room, the pool was laned off for the next couple of hours. It had been a while since Skade had swum in a competition pool. The splash-and-dash crowd was still several hours from showing up, and only the most serious tanners had come to stake out their sun spots. She cast a surreptitious glance at the girl in the lifeguard chair. Tan, athletic, bored out of her skull. God, they hire children now?

Breathe, two, three…

She found an open lane and dove in. It was cold, and that felt good. She did one lap to get warmed up. First lap went well, breathing every other stroke. Then she began to push, and that's when she started feeling it. She used to be an every-five-stroke breather, but now she couldn't move past three… *Breathe, two, three…* Her body wasn't cooperating, it just wouldn't shift into the rhythm. She fought every lap. She wore down.

Breathe, two, three…

She slowed her pace, feeling the mileage she'd put on her body. Her cardio was awful.

Breathe, two… Fuck this, I'm done.

She hadn't even gotten twenty lengths. Who had she become? Climbing out of the pool, she felt sore and rubbery-limbed. She could see the old pool complex in the distance as she toweled herself off. Was the woman who could do this effortlessly still over there someplace? Could she find her again?

Skade sat in a plastic chair, watching the pool through her sunglasses and empty, pissed-off mood. She caught sight of a little girl sitting on a chaise wearing a blue Cookie Monster hooded pool robe. She stared at the little girl for a moment. Something dawned on her. She grabbed her phone and did a quick search.

An hour before sunset, and the hot, hazy atmosphere felt like it was solidifying. Skade was inside her motel room, trying to work. Trying to do anything.

Going through hell.

Being alone she felt outnumbered. The entire concept of not drinking escaped her. Why not have a drink? It would feel so much better. Her thoughts turned off and she went for her car keys on autopilot. *Going to the liquor store. Right now.*

An email landed in her inbox, her laptop open in the window. Eileen.

Skade,
Just checking in. How's the work going? Hope you're finding some good material at the Fieldings site! Let me know if there's anything I can help you with. The people at Chancery are chomping at the bit to get going, so as soon as you're done, get it over. Can't wait!
Love,
Eileen

Skade rubbed her eyes and tears came. She sat down and went back to work as best she could.

Skade came out of the bucket full of sharp angles that had been her sleep. The day was already showing its August. Damned if this summer didn't feel like it was ever going to end. Like it wasn't a season anymore, but a thing all to itself. It had collected all the complaints about the heat that had been offered up as curses for the past several weeks and was wearing them like compliments. Her phone was ringing. It was Kit.

"I called Camille about coming out. She said whenever. You'll like her. You wanna go still?" Kit asked.

"Yeah," Skade mumbled. "Yeah, let me have some coffee and get dressed. Quit biting your nails." She yawned into the phone.

"I'm outside in the parking lot," said Kit sheepishly.

"What am I going to do with you, you big dork? Well, come in while I get ready." Skade built herself to standing and opened the door to let Kit in. Skade, her eyes half closed, shuffled off to the bathroom in her underwear and the tank top, a pair of army fatigues tossed over her shoulder. Kit sat in a chair on the other side of the room trying not to bite her nails and watched Skade's every movement.

Skade emerged feeling more human, pulling a comb through her heavy, wet obsidian hair. The fatigues were baggy on her and held above her hips by a battered embossed belt. She was still wearing the tank top she'd slept in.

"Aren't you hot?" asked Skade.

Kit was dressed in a faded flannel shirt, buttoned at the wrists and almost up to her neck. It hung like a deflated balloon over a pair of old jeans. Her green Humane Society trucker's hat was pulled low over her dry prairie hair.

"No," she replied quietly as she led them out the door to the truck.

The town dwindled behind them as if it were running out of fuel. They passed through the sputtering outskirts out into the farmland beyond. After a few miles Kit pulled the truck onto a long dirt driveway that led up a hill toward a large gray farmhouse.

A sign nailed to the mailbox advertised *Psychic Readings. Medium. Spiritual Advisor.*

"Really?" Skade asked. "I hope I'm not just going to have to pay for a palm reading and get a bullshit ghost story—"

"No, no. Camille isn't like that. You'll like her. And she doesn't do palm readings."

26

Bright summer flowers bloomed in hanging baskets across the front veranda of a well-kept house. Kit led the way up the steps as if she were about to show a secret treasure to someone new.

A striking woman opened the door. She had an ageless feeling to her, even though she had to be in her sixties. Her face was thin and fine boned, framed by silky silver hair that fell past her shoulders. Her eyes were bright and sharp, and her lips curved in an incandescent smile, revealing straight white teeth. She was wearing workout clothes and she glowed. Her figure would have been called statuesque fifty years ago.

"Kitten!" she said as she ushered Kit and Skade inside.

"Hey, Camille. This is my friend Skade, the one I told you was working on that book about roadside memorials?"

"Yes. Welcome, Skade." Camille took Skade by both hands and looked deeply into her eyes. Skade felt an uncomfortable sensation, as if someone were rummaging around inside her head. "I'm Camille Longday. Come on in and have a seat."

Camille settled lightly onto a sofa and pulled on a T-shirt from Alvin's Doughnuts and Bakery. Skade glanced up at the walls as she took a seat across from Camille. What she saw had her up and out of her chair again.

The wall behind Camille was covered in photographs, mostly of a younger Camille in various stages of undress—cheesecake and pin-up shots.

"That's Bunny Yeager!" Skade said, astonished, pointing at an image of attractive young women in sixties-era bikinis standing by a swimming pool, surrounding a taller blond woman holding a camera.

"Yes," said Camille from her seat. "I was a model. Men's magazines—that's what they called them then—and calendars, stuff like that. Bunny Yeager discovered me when I was a kid waiting tables."

"And now you're a medium?"

Camille smiled. "Yes. Now I'm a medium. I was then too, actually, but I made more money having my picture taken. It was tough enough to get taken seriously in the seventies. Especially walking around in a swimsuit or topless, so I didn't do the whole medium thing then. I was mostly just a model. Now I'm mostly just a medium."

"I love Bunny Yeager," said Skade, studying the photograph. "These are all great photographs… I don't get to see original Bunny Yeager shots much."

"Skade is an interesting name."

"Yeah, it's Scandinavian. Skade Felsdottir."

"You're working on a book? About roadside memorials?"

"Nearly finished."

"Kitten was telling me about meeting you, and I mentioned to her that I'd put up a memorial once. For a friend of mine. She said you might be interested in talking to me about it?"

"If you don't mind. I've got a lot of pictures of memorials, and I have the back-stories on many of them, but not many people want to sit down and talk about it. Especially if the loss is still fresh. They'll talk about their loved one all day, but they don't seem to have a lot of words for the descanso. Like why they put it up or why they did it the way they did."

Camille gave a soft laugh. "We've got something in common there. People come to see me to try and connect with someone who's died. But more often than not, they just want to talk about that person."

"Anyway, anything you could tell me might be helpful."

"Well, the loss certainly isn't fresh. This was decades ago." Camille slipped gracefully off the sofa and went to a bookshelf as she talked. "I was doing jobs all up and down the West Coast. Modeling, events, some bit-part acting…but you probably aren't interested in the background, are you?"

"It's all part of the story. You can tell me whatever you want to. I'll weed through it as I need to. Do you mind if I record you on my phone? I'll take notes too."

"No problem." Camille pulled a large green photo album off a shelf and returned to her seat on the sofa. "I was doing a job on the Oregon coast. Trophy girl. Christ, I hated that. Put on an uncomfortable swimsuit, smile a lot and do the whole shoulders-back-tits-out-show-everyone thing, hold a trophy, hand it to the winner, give him a kiss on the cheek, get a bunch of pictures taken, get doused with champagne, and spend the entire two days trying to convince the winning entourage that your vagina isn't part of the prize package.

"I was working this dune-buggy race. I met a guy there, a Vietnam vet, called Dale Farmington." Camille handed Skade the photo album. A tall, handsome young man in a blue-and-orange racing jacket and jeans was standing with a young Camille next to a converted VW Beetle.

"Quit biting your nails," Skade whispered as she passed the album to Kit.

"He was kind and quiet and really smart, and he didn't treat me or any of the other girls like meat or property. He was from around there, and I had several other jobs lined up within a day's drive, so we started going out a little bit.

"The summer stretched out, as it used to do. One thing led to another, and Dale and I started getting serious. He hired me onto his pit crew, and I spent a wonderful couple of months breaking down engines and suspensions, up to my elbows in oil and grease. I'd learned about engines from my dad and was pretty good with them.

"I moved into Dale's place on the dunes near Heceta Beach, but that September I got a call to do a job at a surfing competition back down in California, so off I went." Camille took the photo album from Kit and found a page and handed it to Skade. More pictures of Dale and Camille together, working on cars or at beach parties.

"I was just coming in off the beach after the event when the phone in my room rang. I knew what it was before I answered it. Tommy Davidson, who was Dale's best friend and team manager, was calling to tell me Dale had died in a one-car rollover just east of 101." Camille took the photo album from Kit again and turned to the back of it.

"There was never a clear idea of what had happened. Dale was a professional driver. The car was fine as far as the cops could tell, accident damage aside. There were no drugs or alcohol in his system, and Dale wasn't like that anyway. The road was good and the weather was clear. It happened early in the morning. Maybe he fell asleep, I don't know. *Accident* is all that was on the police report.

"That was a rough time for me. More so for Dale's close friends and family. He'd grown up with a group of people and they were a tight-knit tribe. His sister, especially, had a very hard time dealing with it. I stayed for a little while. But I had work calls again, back south in Las Vegas and LA and Palm Springs."

The last picture in the album depicted a grassy hillside in the setting sun, in the middle of which was a descanso.

"The service was nice, but they just didn't quite get at the point for me. So I decided to build an altar for Dale. He liked to surf. He wasn't very good at it, but he loved it. He was either racing or in the ocean or with me. About two weeks before I left for the surf competition, he broke a surfboard, so I used that. I guess it looks like a tombstone." The image showed the back half of a surfboard coming out of the ground, the fin visible. A red-painted tin sacred heart, about the size of a dinner plate, was attached to the board just below the fin. A burning candle had been set in a holder on top of the heart. Two odd-shaped metal bars were crossed like crossbones below the heart. A set of dog tags and a pink satin sash with the words *Sword Beach Dune Rally* embroidered on it hung from the fin.

"Dale had all kinds of Mexican art. That sacred heart was a *milagro* he had hanging on the bedroom wall. He was going to take me down there with him that October for Dia de los Muertos. I would go out to that hillside almost every sunset after I built that altar and do a shot of mescal for him and light that candle. Those are the shift arms from his racing buggy and the '57 Buick he'd been working on. The dog tags were from his tour in Vietnam. They used to give us those damn sashes after the trophy-girl jobs. I always threw those things away as I was leaving the parking lot. But for whatever reason, I held on to that one. That was where we met."

Skade looked at the image in the album. "Why did you make it? I mean what gave you the idea? Had you seen them before?"

"Dale had shown me pictures of the altars they make in Mexico for Dia de los Muertos. Those are just spectacular. I used to see those roadside crosses in the desert when I was little, driving with my dad. I always thought they were real grave markers—like people were really buried under them—until my dad explained it to me. I didn't give it a lot of thought after that. Until Dale died. It just sort of came to me then. It was just so Dale... What he'd have done. What he'd have wanted."

"How did it make you feel? To make the descanso?"

Camille thought for a minute. "I think it made me feel like I was getting a chance to sum up everything I wanted to say, but never did."

"Like some kind of closure?"

"God no." Camille laughed. "Closure? No. I think I was just experiencing the same thing a lot of the people who come to see me experience. Essentially, we all are terrible at communicating. There are things we want to tell people closest to us that we won't or don't. We're afraid that it will come out wrong or that it won't be taken the way we mean, or that when we say it, something will change in the relationship."

"You just needed to get that stuff out of yourself? Was it doing damage inside you? Or causing pain?"

"Sure, maybe. But more so he could know it and feel it."

"You think he somehow saw or experienced the memorial?" asked Skade, with a shade of sarcasm.

"Surely you've talked to other people who've made memorials? I talk to quite a few, and almost invariably they tell me they make them to try and communicate with the person for whom they made the marker. Look at what I do here, Skade."

"Yeah," said Skade. "I hear that a lot. Did you try to talk to Dale after the accident? As a medium?"

Camille didn't move a muscle. "Yes. Many times. I tried really hard. I still do every once in a while. I've never heard from him or felt him."

"Isn't that—what?—inconvenient?"

"I'm not sure I know what you mean. It makes me sad. But it's hardly unexpected. You can ask Kitten. Sometimes the people you most want to contact are the ones you never hear from. And the ones that want to talk are the ones you don't really want to talk with. Sort of like regular life, I guess."

"You don't think it's odd that *you* couldn't contact someone that close to you?"

Camille laughed again. "You don't understand how it really works. I don't have some kind of phonebook for the afterlife or whatever. And people don't come when they're called. You can reach out, but if they aren't there, or if they don't want to reach back, there's absolutely nothing you can do. I tried very hard to reach out for Dale, but I never felt him out there."

"But you think he saw it? How can you be sure?"

"I can't. But I think he has. Words are ephemeral. They disappear as soon as they're spoken. I know the memorial didn't last. One good Pacific storm probably destroyed most of it. But at least it existed. It had a longer dimension of time. I think he saw it."

"Any other reason you put it up? Besides sending him a message?"

"Memory aid."

"For you, or others?"

"Both maybe. Life is as ephemeral as words are. Especially if we're too scared to live it ourselves." Camille glanced at Kit with a kind but pointed look. "Objects can be like things frozen in time. They're less changeable than we are. So objects make better placeholders."

Skade looked out at the summer clouds. Probably not enough to generate any rain today, but maybe one would blow up and turn into a thunderhead. Her head felt full of static.

"Thanks, Camille. Could I make a copy of your photograph? The one of Dale's descanso? I might include it in the book if you're okay with it. I promise to run anything by you first."

"Of course, I'd be happy to have you use it. I'll make a copy and run it out to you. Are you staying with Kitten?"

"No. I'm at the Skyline."

Camille looked at Skade for a half a second longer than normal before replying. "Okay, I'll bring the copy out to you."

Skade and Kit rose to their feet, preparing to depart. Camille gathered Kit, who obligingly stooped, into a warm hug. Camille gazed into Skade's eyes—the intimacy of this exchange lingered with Skade in an odd way for a long time afterward.

"Let me have your cell number, Skade. I'll call you when I've got that copy and can bring it out to you."

Camille walked them out onto the veranda and watched as they drove back down the long dirt driveway.

"How'd you meet Camille?" asked Skade as they hit the road.

"I came to see her about my family," Kit said. Glancing over at her, Skade caught the flush of embarrassment that shaded Kit's cheeks. "I just…"

"I get it."

"I came to see if I could talk to my brother or sister or grandma… anybody." Kit's breath hitched and Skade reached out and squeezed her arm. "And 'cause I wanted to know what was going to happen to me, in the future, you know?" continued Kit. "But Camille never could find anybody. She told me that happens. Like she said to you. Did you like her?"

"She's really interesting. I don't dislike her. She's a little different. Intense. But I guess if you're a psychic, being different is to be expected, right?" Skade smiled. "She seems like a good person. I hope I look that good when I'm her age. She's pretty amazing right now, and she was incredible in some of those pictures."

"Yeah." Kit laughed. "I sometimes wish I had her boobs, but I get stared at enough."

"How much does she charge for a visit?" Skade asked.

"She charges what people can afford. I paid eighty dollars. You want to make an appointment with her?"

"No," said Skade. "How many times have you seen her?"

"About ten times. I haven't seen her in a while, though, not since she said it didn't seem like anything was working."

"Kit, that's eight hundred dollars!"

"No, I only paid for that first visit. Camille hasn't asked for any money after that. I offered to pay her, but she said no. She said if she wasn't helping, she wouldn't take any money. Skade, you don't trust her?"

"I don't know." Skade sighed. "That whole fortune-telling thing has a reputation. I don't want you to get taken advantage of."

"Thanks for looking out for me," Kit said, with a warm smile. "I'll be careful."

Shimmering waves of heat rose up from the surface of the road. Kit drove through a landscape of cornfields, then past brick ranch houses with concrete deer and flagpoles. Skade leaned out the window, feeling the rush of hot air. She pulled her head back inside and brushed her disheveled black mane out of her face.

"Kit, how old are you?" Skade asked.

"Twenty-three," said Kit.

"You've got a decent job with the highway right now, but what do you want to do beyond that? Probably not just hold a sign and put up with assholes for the rest of your life, right?"

"Yeah." Kit laughed.

"Okay. So when the average person thinks about puppets, what do you think they think about?"

"I don't know."

"I'm guessing they think about Kermit the Frog and Cookie Monster, right?"

"Sure. Sesame Street and the Muppets," said Kit, glancing sideways at Skade.

"Right. You remember that puppet show we were talking about?"

Kit turned to look at Skade quickly, a helpless smile crossing her face before turning back to look at the road. "I don't know, Skade…"

"I'm going to film it. I'm serious. You don't have to know a lot about puppets to see you're a unique talent. People should see your art. What you do is magical."

"Skade, stop it." Kit blushed with discomfort.

"No, you stop it. You're fucking talented, Kit. And you're wasting it, cooped up in your house playing around like you do."

Kit blanched, her hands tightening on the wheel.

"I'm sorry," Skade said. "I didn't mean it like that. I'm getting bitchy about it because I see your talent and the love you have for what you do, and I want you to be able to share that with people. I'm sorry."

Kit swallowed hard.

"Really, I'm sorry. I think you're amazing. But listen, I've got an idea. I know people at Jim Henson Studios and the Children's Television Workshop. Or rather, I know someone with CTW and I might know someone at Henson, and my agent knows lots of people. We can film your show and send it to them."

Kit looked at Skade, open-mouthed. "Skade, no way! No way am I going to do that! Come on!"

"You come on, Kit. Listen. I got a break after years of putting up with lots of bullshit to be able to do what I love for a living. I got lucky. You've put up with enough bullshit in your life already for ten people. Let me try to give you a break so you can do what you love? Please? After all, you're helping me get my book done. My agent will love you, believe me," Skade said with a grin.

Kit just looked at her for a long moment. "Just thinking about that makes me want to barf," Kit finally said. "What if everybody hates it or just laughs at it?"

"Then I'd say *Welcome to being an artist*… It happens. But you keep working and being persistent and patient about it and don't let a few rejections kill you. Right now, you're perfectly happy making puppets in your house. Getting turned down doesn't change that at all. You're doing puppetry because you love it, not because you want to be rich or famous. That's what's important."

"Skade—"

"You get whatever you need set up. One step at a time, okay?"

"Okay," Kit said nervously.

"Good!" Skade beamed. "And we're going to do it soon."

"I need some time—"

"Not long. And quit biting your fucking nails!"

27

The next morning, as Skade walked to the motel office to see about extending her stay another couple of weeks, she saw Kit's truck pull into the lot. They were going out early to see another descanso.

"Hey, got an extra coffee on my way in and thought you might want one," said Kit.

"Thanks for thinking of me. It's good to see you," said Skade, happy to see Kit. "Hang on a minute, I need to go down to the office. I'll be right back."

Skade spent a frustrating twenty minutes going around and around with the manager on duty, who didn't seem to want to extend her stay in the otherwise empty motel. Eventually, he relented after Skade paid up front. When she got back to her room, she found Kit sitting on the bed next to her memory box, the contents of which Skade had left strewn around. Kit was reading something she'd picked up. And she'd created a bird.

Skade had a pair of feathers in her box. A lovely long white and gray gull feather she'd found on a beach in Maine and a coal-black raven's feather bound on a leather cord. Kit had wrapped the cord through her fingers and slipped the gull feather into it. Now the feathers served as wings for the bird her hand had become. The effect was miraculous. The movements of hand and feathers completely captured the flight of a bird as it slowly dipped and rose and flew.

And those astonishing hands. Those hands were other things, accidentally attached to Kit's body, that went about their tasks and plans as best they could, given their strange situation—being attached to a body to which they didn't belong—and they were hypnotizing. Ineffable.

The bird-puppet, created from next to nothing, would have been stunning enough, but to watch Kit perform this magic while not paying any attention—while she was reading—was even more amazing.

The amazement was lost on Skade, however.

"What the hell are you doing?" Skade snapped. It came out sharp, even to Skade.

Kit had heard it too. "Sorry." Kit set the feathers down and rose to her feet.

Skade scooped everything back into her box, including the feathers, and glared up at Kit. "Don't go rooting through other people's stuff."

"Sorry," stammered Kit. "I was waiting—"

"Yeah? Well, so what? You don't go poking around like that." Kit looked frightened and worried. Skade felt herself soften. "Look, I'm sorry I yelled at you, but that stuff is personal."

"Those feathers are beautiful," said Kit timidly.

"Yeah." Skade laughed. "Yeah, they are. And they were probably happy to fly one more time."

"Did you really do a perfect score on your SATs?"

"What?"

"I saw that report sitting there when I sat down. You got a perfect score? There's a bunch of stuff here from when you were in high school. They thought you were a genius?"

"That's a stupid word. They should have known not to use it. Just ignore that crap," Skade said, her annoyance flaring again.

"And this is you?" asked Kit, gesturing toward the newspaper story about the Michael Pullman rescue. "This says you're Wonder Woman."

"Shit." Skade sighed. "Yeah, I know what it says. They made a big thing of it. Took my picture and everything. That was such a mess. I mean, yes, that is me. I was a lifeguard, and I pulled a little kid out of the pool. That happens more often than you'd think. I guess this one time was a little more serious."

"Yeah," said Kit. "It says the little kid was basically dead."

"Well, clearly he wasn't dead. He was very lucky. I was very lucky. I'm glad it worked out... But they made a lot more out of it than they should have," said Skade through the hornets in her head. "That whole Wonder Woman thing got out of hand."

Kit looked back down at the clipping and smiled, then looked at Skade again, still smiling. "Well, I think you're Wonder Woman."

"Don't. I'm not."

"Well, you do look just like her," Kit offered with a half grin as they climbed into Kit's truck.

"Okay, so what about this descanso we're going to? What is it?"

"I heard some people talking about it last year. I've never actually seen it, and I hope I can find it. I'm not even sure I know the story, except that it's about somebody's grandpa."

Kit slowed down along a long stretch of state highway bordered on either side by a broad bank sloping up to fences.

"It's supposed to be around here someplace," Kit said, scanning the right side of the road. "Up near the fence, I think they said."

"There," said Skade, pointing up the road. "Up the road a couple hundred yards in front of us. By the fence."

"Where? I still don't see—"

"Trust me. I see these damn things in my sleep. I think I have a sixth sense for them now. It's right there."

Kit stopped. "You're right. That's not easy to see."

They climbed up the bank, wading through knee-high grass to a small metal marker at the top of the rise. The metal had been treated with a dark-brown weatherproof coating, a five-digit number stamped on to its face. A small powder-blue vinyl suitcase, like one a little girl might carry, had been chained to the marker.

Skade got a couple of shots of the case and the marker and knelt down. The word *Open* had been painted on the top of suitcase. Kit slipped up next to her.

"Don't do it," said Kit as Skade began playing with the latch. "Some guy at work found a suitcase once on the side of the road. You don't even want to know what he said was inside it. I still have nightmares, and I never even saw it."

Skade popped the latch. Inside was an old yellow coffee can with a plastic lid, a battered envelope, and folded piece of faded cloth with what looked like lambs and flowers printed on it. Skade gently opened the unsealed envelope and took out three old photographs and a letter.

The black-and-white snapshots depicted a man, a woman, and a small girl standing in front of a '50s black Ford sedan. Another photo was a close-up shot of a young girl with a round face and sparkling eyes. The third shot, taken, it appeared, within an institution, revealed the face of an older man, looking dull and confused. He had lost most of his teeth and had the gaunt face of the nearly dead. Skade passed the photos to Kit. Then she unfolded the letter:

> My grandpa, Ed Foster, died here in a car crash. He worked for forty-eight years at the Menonqua sawmill and lumber yard. Right after he retired, my grandma passed and he was never the same. He always liked singing in church every Sunday. But then he took to sitting on a bench on Main St. in Menonqua and just singing and

singing at the top of his lungs. I guess that made people scared, singing for no reason, so they put him in Gardner. They drugged him and said he needed watching.

I used to visit him in Gardner. He lived in a little cement room with no windows. He was always confused, and unhappy, and scared. He didn't know who he was or who I was or who anybody was anymore. I brought pictures of his family to help him out, but he didn't know them.

He ran away from Gardner. He borrowed a truck from a man, said he was trying to find somebody. I don't know who. Maybe his kids or his grandkids. Maybe himself. He didn't know who he was. When the police got to the wreck, all he had was this suitcase, which used to be my mom's, and these pictures I'd given him, and my grandma's baby blanket—which he'd taken to Gardner with him because he said it smelled like somebody he loved, even if he couldn't say who it was. And he had a can of flowers he'd collected. He was always sad they wouldn't let him pick any flowers at Gardner.

I knew who he was, even if he didn't. He was the man who told me stories when I was a little girl. He was the man that taught me hymns. He knew the name of every flower and every tree in the county. He was so gentle and so kind and so happy. He was my grandpa. The people from Gardner claimed his body because he was a ward of the state. We don't know what happened to his body. We don't know where he's buried. They gave us his state burial marker, which they forgot to put on his grave. Pray for him. He had a hard life. I hope he's in a better place.

"What's Gardner?" asked Skade.

"Gardner Home for the Insane and the Feeble-Minded. That's what it used to be called. Just Gardner now. That's where they wanted to send my mom. That's a bad place," said Kit.

Skade handed the letter to Kit. "I've seen stories like that before."

Skade took a few shots of the inside of the case and its contents. Then she carefully peeled the lid off the coffee can. Several dried flowers rested inside. She resealed the can, put the photos and the letter back and closed the case, and moved on away from Ed Foster's life.

28

Condensation ran down the sides of the highball, the result of the clash between a three-in-the-afternoon August sun straining at its leash and a pair of heavy, quickly melting ice cubes.

Skade was in Lane's studio sitting on the edge of a table, watching him sort through bottles of ink. And she was watching a highball glass on the counter sweat worse than anyone coming into the studio. Lane had scheduled an appointment to fix the old tattoo he'd given her.

"Turn it up!" shouted Jerome from across the studio. Jerome had a TV set pulled up next to his workstation. He was working on the upper back of a good-looking guy resting on a massage chair. The guy and John Doe from the photo shoot were focused on the TV, and Jerome was paying as much attention to the screen as he could while he worked.

"This is that show! The one I was telling you about, Lane," he shouted across the room.

"The one about possession?" asked Lane.

"Yeah!"

John Doe turned up the volume. An announcer intoned in a deep important-sounding voice: "Deep in the swamps of south Louisiana…"

"Oh man, swamp monsters. How awesome?" said Jerome.

"What the hell are they watching?" Skade asked Lane quietly.

"A buddy of Jerome's is some kinda magical tech-hacker. He controls the world through his computer, if you believe Jerome's stories. What I do know is he's crazy good at hooking up a TV. I don't know what he ties it into; Jerome says he's figured out how to hack a signal off that giant military antenna way out in the woods in Jackson County, but whatever it is, he can get TV channels. Like, every TV channel. Jerome is exploring the world of wild backwoods pirate internet TV or whatever it is. This thing they're watching is some sort of twenty-four-hour supermarket tabloid channel. Freak shows and true crime and alien invasions and Elvis and Bigfoot have a love child."

"Honey Island Swamp Beast!" shouted Jerome. "I'm gonna go there on my boat!"

"What was it last week? True stories of demonic possession?" called out Lane.

"Oh yeah! There's demonic possession everywhere. Tons of it. Happens every day, especially in places like Mexico and Africa and Indonesia. They showed some guy in Africa who was possessed by a demon. He was chained by the neck to a tree in his front yard."

"That's horrible," said Skade loudly.

"Hey, he was attacking people, trying to bite their necks like a vampire. And he was casting spells," said Jerome. "They showed him. He was all crazy-eyed and barking and then he started mumbling and tossing dirt in the air. He was casting a spell at the film crew. They said one of the photographers got horrible cholera-level runs that night. Spells!"

Skade decided it was a losing battle.

"They were talking about how the Vatican has an exorcist school," put in John Doe.

"That's one of the Vatican's super-secret jobs—fighting demons," said Jerome.

"They followed that one young priest around as he learned to be an exorcist," said John Doe. "They got levels, I guess. New exorcists get easy demons to practice on. He had to go out and get a demon out of some old lady that stood at bus stops in Paterson, New Jersey, and shouted obscenities at people as they got on and off the buses. They showed it. She was pretty damn funny. But the priest got the demon out of her."

"How'd that work?" asked Lane.

"Priest snuck up on her at a bus stop while she was calling a bunch of third graders a pack of perverted crackheads. He tossed some Holy Water in her face and hit her with a special Bible."

"Hit her?"

"Right between the eyes. Stunned the fuck out of her, it looked like. Then he said a couple of hard-knuckle exorcist prayers and laid his hands on her. When she got up, she was free of the demon."

"So she quit shouting at people?" asked Lane.

"No," said John Doe. "She called the camera crew a bunch of fucking masturbators and told them to piss the hell off. But the demon was out of her at least."

"Pope's a super-exorcist," said Jerome. "It's one of those major Pope-skills."

"Oh shit, I almost forgot." Lane went over to one of the workstations and pulled open a drawer. "Here." He tossed her an amber-colored plastic pill bottle with a couple dozen pills inside it.

"What's this?" she asked.

"What you asked for."

"Percosets?"

"No. Something a little stronger. Only thing I could find easily, believe it or not. It's China Girl. Kitchen-sink Fentanyl. Be careful with that if you're not used to it."

"What's that?" she asked, pointing at the glass sweating on the counter.

"It's a perfectly good bourbon and ginger ale that will go to waste unless you drink it."

"Why go to waste?"

"I poured it before I remembered you had an appointment, but I don't drink if I'm going to work. So it'll sit and go stale now. You want it? It's a pretty decent local distillery."

Skade looked at the glass. "No," she said. The sound of the word in her mouth felt like steel wool.

Lane got her situated and she looked down at her arm as the buzz of the needle armature started up.

"What are you going to do?" she asked.

"I'm going to finish some touching up on the old piece, then I was thinking Puss in Boots next to it. But that isn't going to take the whole space. I'm going to think about something meaningful to put into the rest of it. Gimme some time on that."

An hour later, the feeling of the needle was past the point of being meditative and was now just annoying, like a hot ant biting under the skin.

Lane wiped her arm off. "That should do it for today. I can do some finishing touches on Mr. Boots later. I need to figure out what else to do in that spot, but otherwise I think it's good. Take a look."

Skade held her arm up and looked at the slightly inflamed image of Puss just beneath the roses. The roses themselves had also been touched up. It was all lovely and very colorful.

"I love it, thanks," she said wearily. "I'm feeling a little burnt, though. I think I'm going to head back. Get some more work in."

The heat had an elasticity as she fought her way through it. Skade folded in behind the wheel, fished out her keys, and turned the ignition. Nothing happened. She cranked the key again, and still nothing; the car was silent.

Skade cursed and wrenched open the hood of the Jeep. Her starter was dead. She slammed the hood down and cursed again, even louder than before, and leaned against the hood.

She took a deep breath of hot air and thought. Three options: wait for Lane to finish his work, wrestle with a Lyft, or call Kit. She called Kit's number and apologized, but Kit was more than delighted to come get her, if she could wait about half an hour or so. Skade said that was fine, and she stalked back to Lane's studio.

"Change your mind?" asked Lane.

"Fucking car is dead. Dead starter."

Lane laughed out loud. "I told you that thing looked like crap when I first saw it. I am hardly surprised."

"I can fix it, but not until tomorrow."

"You need a ride someplace?"

"No, I called a friend. She's coming to get me."

About forty minutes later, Skade was swiveling slowly back and forth on a rolling stool looking at a book on Hopi art when the door to the studio pushed open and Kit appeared. Lane, tattooing an elk skull on the thigh of a huge bearded guy, did a double take at the sight of Kit.

"Hey," said Kit.

"Hey, Kit. This is my friend Lane. Lane, this is Kit."

"Nice to meet you," said Lane.

"You too," said Kit, obviously a bit distracted by the sights and sounds of the studio. "Sorry about your car, Skade."

"It's a pain in the ass, but I can fix it tomorrow, I think."

Wide-eyed, Kit watched Lane working the needle on the bearded guy's leg.

"You want to stay and watch?" asked Lane.

"No. No thanks," said Kit, embarrassed. She turned back to Skade. "Should we go?"

"Sure. See you, Lane."

Skade climbed into the truck next to Kit and they pulled out.

"So was that your boyfriend?" asked Kit.

"A long time ago. Not now. Doesn't stop him from trying, though."

"You knew him from high school?"

"Yeah. A lot of things have changed. Me, mostly."

"What do you mean?" Kit asked as they passed sidewalks made vacant by the heat. The sun played hard games with the geometry of things, casting shadows as sharp as razors across buildings and making things feel two-dimensional.

"I've changed so much since I lived here. I'm not even sure I know who that girl was. She's a stranger to me now. I have some artifacts from her past—my past—but I don't feel like they're mine. It's hard to explain. Lane has changed a lot too. Now he seems a lot more cautious and serious. Everyone changes," said Skade finally, looking out the truck window as the town slipped by.

"I don't feel like I've changed much," said Kit.

"I'm sure you have."

There was a long silence between them.

"So you want me to take you to your motel?"

"That would be great. You want to go swimming?"

"Swimming?" Kit looked as if Skade had suggesting wrestling bears.

"Hell yes. It's hot and I could use the release."

"No. I don't swim."

Now it was Skade's turn to look shocked. "What do you mean, you don't swim? Everybody swims. I don't mean race a four-hundred-meter IM, even though I bet you'd be good at it. Being tall really helps in swimming. You look like a swimmer. But I mean just get in the water and play around."

Kit tightened her grip on the steering wheel a notch. "Yeah, I know. I don't swim, though. I don't like the water."

Skade snorted. "Well, we're just going to have to fix that. I'm not having any 'not liking the water.' No way."

"Not right now," said Kit with a painful smile.

"Okay, but soon. Even if I have to sneak up on you and push you in myself."

29

S kade spent the better part of the morning wrestling with her dead starter. At round eleven she tossed a socket wrench against the brick wall of one of the warehouses and dug her phone out of her hip pocket. Finding a place that had the part was not a problem; parts for old Jeep Waggoneers were easy to find. Finding a place that would do it fast, and for cheap, that was the bigger issue. By late afternoon the car had been towed and repaired, and Skade, sticky and irritable, was finally able to head to Kit's house.

The sun was slipping into its final act when Skade pulled up in Kit's driveway. Skade took a deep breath of sunlight and cut grass and dill weed and cricket-song on Kit's front landing before knocking.

"Sorry for just dropping by," said Skade.

"No," said Kit with a distracted but genuine smile. "Sorry, I'm working on something. Come on in. I'll be done soon." She returned to the kitchen, leaving Skade in the living room. The late-afternoon shadows from the front yard had begun their invasion of the house. Skade stood still, watching the last rays of sunlight creep up the outstretched leg of a large marionette: a frog in cutaway coat with a bouquet of roses clutched in his gloved hands. The light and the shadows played over the frog's face and a laundry list of thoughts and emotions appeared on it like clouds in the sky. Other than the inexorable movement of the sun, all was thick motionlessness. Dust floated in sunbeams. The whole house had the quality of the loneliness of dust.

Then there was something else. Something in the air felt wrong. All the air we breathe is made from the breath of other living things. Skade looked at the all faces in the room—cats and pumpkins and tin cans and spiders and people, all looking very not-alive in the encroaching twilight. What was the air inside Kit's house made of?

Skade left the slow-motion sunlight in the living room and found Kit at her kitchen table. A work lamp shone down on a piece of white modeling clay. Skade was riveted by her friend's long, elegant fingers—

they seemed to possess a will of their own, shaping the clay as if it were a religious ritual.

Kit looked up and smiled weakly. "Sorry. I had an idea while I was working. I left this undone this morning. I wanted to—"

"Don't worry about it," said Skade, putting a hand on her shoulder. Kit smiled again and sank back into her work.

Skade drifted into Kit's dining room, where each of six chairs, surrounding a honey-colored oak table, was occupied by a puppet propped up on pillows to their own individual place settings. The settings were odd. A delicately balanced ziggurat of different mismatched table objects sat on each placemat: a stacked tower of chargers and dinner plates, salad plates or dessert plates; there was a butter dish and a creamer, teacups and coffee mugs, plastic wine glasses and water glasses. A silver gravy boat. A brass candlestick.

A bouquet of paper flowers, dried flowers, plastic funeral flowers, and a few fresh flowers adorned the center of the table. An individual flower had been placed at the top of the tower that made up each place setting.

Skade stood, mesmerized. The scene bristled with meaning—she understood that—but she couldn't grasp it. It was the private language of Kit's amazing, star-crossed, slightly disturbed mind.

"Is that okay if I take a few more pictures?" she called.

"Sure," Kit muttered distractedly from the kitchen.

Skade framed the shot and snapped the picture. The notion that struck Skade first was reverence—a reverence like she'd seen in the congregation at Mass when she'd attended as a child. Something in the angle of the puppets' heads, and in the positions of their hands, that seemed to have the air of an Adoration. The diners, tucked up to the table like six silk pocket handkerchiefs, were expecting some sort of sudden and much-needed benediction. Answers and miracles. *So much wanting—or longing?—here. Who can sit in this much wanting?* She framed the shot and snapped another picture.

The puppet at the head of the table was an old woman with a gray bun, in a long ashen-colored dress. A stem of foxglove lay before her, and a small emerald-green hornet had been embroidered on the breast of her dress.

The next diner was a bug-eyed turtle holding a strange-looking woodwind instrument, a fantastic version of an oboe crossed with a saxophone made of bamboo. She framed the shot and snapped the picture. The turtle's expression seemed one of frightened bewilderment, as if he'd gotten off the bus at the wrong stop and found himself at the Mad Hatter's tea party by mistake.

The third member of the party was a lovely silk harlequin; the fourth, a gruff-looking brown bear in a red marching band jacket. Skade focused on the bear's paws. The bear, holding an artist's paintbrush and a small bicycle wheel, appeared to be in conversation with the turtle. Skade could feel it. The bear was trying to comfort the turtle in his confusion. *Don't worry*, the bear was saying, *the rain will come soon, and the pond will fill back up, and you can take your boat out under the full moon and play your new sonata.*

Skade framed the next puppet in her viewfinder, a circus acrobat in a fine pink satin leotard and a small black mask, then moved to her right, to the last puppet. And she stopped short.

The last puppet wore a short skirt and a strapless leotard of red, blue, and gold. She carried a sword and a shield and had a thick mane of black hair. Her arms and legs and chest had been skillfully painted to a very close approximation of the tattoos on Skade's own body—it was a Wonder Woman doll turned into Skade.

"We were having a dinner party," Kit murmured from behind.

"Is that supposed to be me?" Skade asked.

"Yeah. I have a big box of old toys and dolls. I find stuff at yard sales and Goodwill. I was going through it the other day, looking for some parts, and I found her in there. When I saw her, I just thought of you right away, I guess." Kit was searching Skade's face for approval. Her eyes darted back and forth, her face shifting like water in the wind. Hopeful. "I tried to make her look more like you? I think I got pretty close?"

Skade could hear the fear rising in Kit's voice. She could feel something rising up in herself as well. From the pit of her stomach.

"Sorry," Kit whispered.

In the long, stony silence, Kit's face went an unhealthy shade of pink with white stress points around her mouth and eyes. She shrank back into the kitchen.

Skade stayed in the dining room, her camera hanging loosely from its strap around her neck. The more she sat with the scene before her, the less sure she felt about anything. Except that she was sure how she felt about the puppet of her. She turned and went to the kitchen. Kit was sitting at the table, her head hanging down, her hair covering her face. Skade could tell she was trying very hard not to cry. Her hands were playing with a wooden ball that they probably meant to make into a puppet's head at some point. Skade stood in the doorway. Other than Kit's work light and the light in the dining room that was trying to creep around the edges of the kitchen doorway, no other lights were on in the house. Outside, the sounds of a million crickets starting in as the light left the sky could be heard. All the inside sounds had retreated to the background, as if they were clearing the stage. Nothing was present in the foreground but an echo. Kit's refrigerator kicked into a cycle. Kit sniffled in the silence.

"What you did in there, Kit, it makes me feel funny."

"I know. I'm sorry," Kit whispered.

"You know, but maybe you don't." Skade came into the room and pulled out a chair next to Kit and sat down. "This is crossing a bunch of boundaries. This really freaks me the fuck out." Her head was full of angry insects, buzzing and swarming. "I'm not Wonder Woman. I never was. I'm nobody's hero, do you understand?" Skade's voice had teeth and claws now, and she knew it.

Kit didn't move or make a sound. She stopped rolling her ball and held it delicately.

"What made you think that was okay? How the fuck do you get away with thinking you know who I actually am enough to make me into Wonder Woman?" she shouted. "Do you take me out and play with me at night? Make me do tricks? Do I hang out with your damn Barbies?" Skade closed her eyes and turned away. She knew she was hurting Kit, and she hated herself for it, but another part of her didn't care and needed to bleed it all out. Kit shrank further under her hair.

"Look at me, Kit," Skade seethed. "I said *look at me*, damn it. You had to look at me enough to paint me. I see you looking at me all the time. Look at me now." Kit quivered and raised her head enough that Skade caught the gleam of a wet eye in the shadows of her fallen hair. "I'm not a doll. I'm not a toy. I'm not a puppet. You don't know who I am. You don't know where I've been or what I've done. Don't make me up in your damn head. I'm not twelve inches high."

But then she found some kindness she didn't know was there. The broken bottles and flame died in her voice and she calmed.

"I'm not Wonder Woman, Kit."

They sat there in a silence in the kitchen. The refrigerator kicked into another cycle. The crickets kept on. The atmosphere was different.

"When I was a kid that comic book stuff was cool. I guess I look a little like Wonder Woman. Or maybe I used to. Anyway, everyone called me that. It made me feel special. It was part of my armor or whatever. Somebody has pictures of me dressed up like Wonder Woman for Halloween, I'm sure." Skade looked over at Kit. "After the accident at the pool with Michael Pullman, somebody told a reporter about my nickname, and oh my God did they light that up. It got bad. Uncomfortable. Then..." Skade stopped and took a long breath. "I started to hit that identity projection crap. It was so hard to figure out and inhabit who I really was. It is for most women that age. The way men talk to me and look at me like I'm not there. Or that only my body is there. Treat me like I'm a dumbshit. I was seventeen, for fuck's sake—what the fuck am I supposed to do with that? And my relationship with my dad was pretty horrible. Not abusive or anything, but it was like we were roommates who hardly spoke. That did not help at all. I just felt so used. People started to treat me like I was something I wasn't. That's part of the reason I started getting all these tattoos. I figured if all I was was some sort of canvas for people to project their shit on, their judgments and sick fantasies and whatever the fuck their problems were, then I might as well start doing it too. Less blank space for them to fuck with. Force them to see me."

"I'm sorry," Kit whispered again.

"No, I'm sorry. I'm sorry I lashed out at you. It's just this place is getting to me. Carleton. I have a lot of bad stuff tied up here. I know you tried to include me in there, Kit, and I appreciate the sentiment. I'm not good at being included. But I know you didn't mean any harm."

They sat quietly together for a few heartbeats.

"I don't..." Kit began unsteadily. "People..." She took a long, wet breath, gulping for air as if she were surfacing from a lake.

"I live in this house all by myself, and I gotta keep to myself because I feel like a freak. Not just this," she said quietly, brushing a hand over her chest. "Not just a freak because I'm so much taller than anybody...I feel like a freak in here." She pointed at her head with one long index finger. She struggled and clouded over again, then dropped her head again.

"Nothing moves here unless I move it," she whispered through her hair. Then she raised her head and locked eyes with Skade. The impact was visceral. "Nothing. Do you know what that's like? To live in a dead place where nothing moves…" She was like a building coming down in a demolition implosion. "Doll bones. I live on a pile of doll bones. My puppets are all just things I use to keep in contact with dead people."

"Sometimes…" Kit started laughing and tears came. "Sometimes I really…really…really wish I would go crazy. I mean, most people think I already am. I probably am. But I mean like real crazy-crazy so that the stuff in here would move. Just once, I'd like to see one of these puppets I make move without me doing it. It'd be worth losing my mind to have that, I think sometimes."

For the first time, Skade could see the wounds—they had always been there, but Skade hadn't been able to see them through her own self-absorbed crap until now.

"My dad left. My sister and brother got killed. My mom…" Tears streaked down her cheeks. "I've got no family. Nobody. Sometimes I go on the internet and meet guys. There's stuff you do, you know, when you're really alone, and really lonely. You talk yourself into stuff and get all twisted up inside like it's all good and okay and everything." Kit glanced at Skade, her eyes red-rimmed. "It makes me feel sick and awful, so I don't do that anymore. I can pretend to be somebody else, like you do with all the tattoos. I can be somebody different, something somebody wants. I don't want to be a puppet, either. Puppets are made of things no one wants. They're freaks that scare people. I'm just a puppet like everything else in this house."

They were both silent for a couple of heartbeats.

"I'm so lonely. I shouldn't have made that puppet. I'm sorry." Kit dropped her head back down again. "Do you want her? The puppet? Or should I burn her?"

Skade reached out and took Kit's hand in her own. They sat quietly again. "Hey…"

"You're just about done." Kit's voice sounded small and far away from under her hair.

"What?"

"With your book. You're almost done, right?" Kit whispered.

"Done? I don't know. I feel like I've got forever to go with it yet."

"But with the pictures. You've got all those now."

"Maybe. I hope so. Thanks to you. You've been such a huge help to me, Kit. Thank you."

"So you're going away, aren't you?"

"Yeah. Probably. I'm going to be leaving soon. A week, maybe."

Kit didn't say anything, Skade looked at her sitting hunched and alone at her table.

"Kit, you're my friend. Christ, right now maybe my only friend. I'm sorry I went off on you like that, but that puppet made me feel scared and angry. You know that? You need people. You need close. I suck at close. That puppet felt close, and it surprised me." Skade smiled.

"Yeah."

"I'm sorry for what I said." Skade took a deep breath and felt as if she were diving into water she knew was ice-cold. "I'm going to be here for a while longer. I need to finish some things up, and here is as good a place as any to do it. I need to get back into the totem poles at least one more time, right? I need to talk to a couple of people. I need to get that stuff from Camille Longday. I've got a shitload to do actually, so I might be here longer than that. We will see what happens."

Kit looked up at her and the accent of a smile crossed her face.

"But listen, no more games." The hues of anger colored the edges of Skade's voice again. "And no more Skade puppets. I'm coming back here with my equipment. We are going to film that puppet show. No more screwing around. You better be ready, okay?"

"Okay. But can you still hang out with my Barbies?" There was a gleam in the eyes under the straw-blond hair and maybe a sly smile.

It wasn't just the puppet, Skade mused as she drove back to the Skyline. *That whole damn dinner party. There's something in that that I can't get. It's what's missing from my pictures. That whole thing felt like a descanso. Kit understands a descanso better than I do...*

30

Skade made another adjustment to her lights and checked her focus. "For someone who says she doesn't do puppet shows, you sure as hell have a big and seriously complicated stage set up here, Kit."

"Is it too—?"

"Stop it. No. It's perfect and I'm sure you need every inch of it and I'm sure it's going to be breathtaking. Quit being nervous."

The speed with which Kit had managed the setup was a little shocking. One entire bedroom in Kit's house had been converted into a fully functioning puppet theater. The only way Skade could film the stage was to set up her camera in the doorway.

"Wonder Woman's not in this, is she?" asked Skade from behind the camera with a smile.

"No," said Kit, her arms full of puppets.

"Okay," said Skade. "I think we're ready. You ready?"

"Yeah," said Kit with a surprising amount of confidence.

"Good. So I want you to introduce yourself. Just say your name and how long you've been doing puppetry. Then give us the name of the play—"

"I don't think it's got a name," said Kit, looking suddenly terrified.

"Don't worry. It doesn't have to have a name. Just tell us that you created it and what it is. I'm guessing it's a fairy tale, right?"

"Yeah."

"Okay, just say this is a fairy tale that you created. Then introduce us to the characters. Not too much, because we don't want to be here into tomorrow."

"Sorry. There's a lot of them, I know."

"Don't worry, Kit. Just say their names or who they are, and then we will do the show. Ready? Okay. Go."

Kit stood before the camera. Skade had to pan upward to get her face. She looked a little nervous, but not so much as Skade had expected.

"I'm Kitten Dyer. And this is a fairy tale puppet show that I created. It doesn't really have a name. Oh, and I made all these puppets too."

The lights went down. Skade started recording. Magic happened.

❧

"I have never seen anything like that bird and that lion, Kit," said Skade as she uploaded the video. "Those two alone will get you noticed. My God!"

"Yeah, Pierre—that's the lion—I'm still having trouble with him. He doesn't move exactly like I want him to move. He's kinda stiff and jerky. But Garuda is pretty cool."

"What's he made of?"

"Honestly, he's mostly clothespins and coat hangers." Kit picked up two control bars for the huge wooden bird, and it rose to an elegant standing pose and flapped its wings loudly.

Skade turned to fully face Kit, who was busily packing up her puppets and breaking down the stage set. "Kit, I have to tell you. What you just did was extraordinary. I'm serious. That was just spectacular. After seeing that, there is no way I'm letting you not share that skill and talent with the world. You are a serious, serious artist."

Kit's face raced through several emotions, as it was wont to do, and she blushed but didn't say anything. She dove into her work with a glow.

❧

That night Skade packaged up the video and sent it along with a letter of introduction to her contacts. Then she stared at the Tower of Babel that her own project had become.

Skade stood and stretched. The clock, half buried under a tossed-in-frustration pillow by her disheveled bed, said she'd been working for hours. She'd lost patience with herself and the bed and the dark and the motel room and the fucking annoying clock and her pillow and God, and she'd gotten up to work, since she couldn't sleep—again—at around four in the morning. She worked until one in the afternoon, picked at some leftover pizza, napped like a hungry lioness, went for an unsatisfying swim, and sat back down to work. Now it was after eight. Her eyes felt like cotton balls and her spine felt like a splintered tree limb. She eyed her laptop and the piles of photos and notes scattered on the bed next to it.

The idea that she "might be close to done" had been nagging at her.

She opened the master file on her laptop to check her progress. Page after page. Photo after photo. Checklists. Everything.

She wasn't almost done. She was done.

The pictures were good enough, even if many of them still felt hollow. She had enough essays, too many; that was done too. Her vision for the book was more or less in place. All she needed now was a conclusion, and she had that outlined. The book was done. She picked up the cornhusk puppet and clung to it.

And she still had time. *Holy crap, what do I do now?*

She sat on the bed as the room shrank around her. A vacuum opened and peace and panic rushed in together to fill it. *Time to recalibrate. Put everything together and seal the cracks. Finish the edit I started on these three images. I need the conclusion... I need to celebrate. I need a drink.*

Clean days had helped, but now she both needed and deserved a drink. The hard part was over.

Drink first.

Skade flowed out to her Jeep. She found the bottle of pills Lane had gotten for her when she dug out her car keys. She tossed them onto the seat next to her. Liquor store. Vodka. Two. Back in the car. She went toward town and let the dark warm air wash over her as she watched the passage of things. She felt more like herself now. She breathed it all in deeply, just like the night inhaled her.

She drove the liquid-dark streets out to the empty parking lot at the aquatic center at Kensington Park. She turned off her Jeep and opened a bottle. Thoughts floated past like ghosts—about the book, about what would happen next, about...*too many thoughts.* She took another long pull from the bottle and tossed down one of Lane's pills. *I need to move.* She started the car and pulled out of the parking lot and drove.

Darkness fell.

Notes from
American Still Life

From the files of
Skade Felsdottir

There's another reason for our strangely dissonant attraction to these thin spaces between life and death marked by descansos: the intersection of intense feelings they generate. The volcanic eruptions of other people's grief give us feelings of empathy and sympathy and deep sadness and fear and shift our perspectives and our points of view. They jolt us lightly into a new space, spinning us back through ourselves, making us become audiences of our own existence. These new feelings generated by the impact of a descanso, even one put up for someone we never knew, are visceral and psychological and spiritual all at the same time. They serve as reminders, however briefly, that we are here, and we are alive, and we have some connection to something.

Jung said, "I must communicate my answers for if not I am dependent on the world's answer." Maybe that's all I have. The world's answer to the question "Who am I?"

~~What if I don't like that answer? I try to define myself. I try to make my own identity.~~

Identity is often anchored by location. We often say, "I am of this place." For me, "who I am" and "where I am" begin to merge. And because I never sit still for very long, I cannot say anything other than I am in a state of constant change. My identity is me, it is the vehicle through which I move through the world. My identity is ultimately the only thing I actually own. But I don't own it. I cannot control it. Invariably my identity winds up in the hands or hearts or minds of others—every "other"—not in mine. I cannot choose it. I cannot change it.

~~I'm losing my mind.~~

I see my reflection and I don't know who that thing is. ~~God, I hate mirrors now! Why am I losing my shit?~~ I don't even know if it's real. It shifts and twists like it doesn't want to be seen. My identity is developing a sort of camouflage, like a seahorse in a bed of kelp. It hides in the contours of that ~~strange unfamiliar~~ familiar face and peeks out at me furtively. But the image itself is an illusion. It's a lie. That thing in the glass isn't me. I look at a descanso and I'm not an audience to my own existence. I'm an audience to a stranger. A stranger that points at me and asks who I am, and I don't have the slightest fucking clue.

~~Yeah, I do. I'm not of this place. I am of that event. I am what happened. What happened left and took me with it. I left and part of me—the better part—stayed at that event. I am empty and guilty and unfinished and incomplete and undeserving.~~

I take photographs for a living. There exist, perhaps, six photographs of me. Actually, not me. Just parts of me. I'm anonymous. But those parts, are they me? Even if they weren't fuzzy out-of-focus images of various parts of me, can any picture actually be taken of me? Of anyone? What does that mean?

~~Is a photograph really a representation of a person? A self? Is a mirror? Is it possible to take a picture of "someone"?~~

In this age of social media, it seems that the value or intensity or physicality of existence is more or less defined by the total number of images of oneself. This seems, on the surface, vapid and narcissistic. But how the hell do I know that's not true? It at least means there are people out there that care enough about you to take your picture. The more pictures of you means the more you're loved, and the Skin Horse tells us that love is what makes you real. Even if you're just taking six million fucking selfies, at least you like yourself enough to do it. Of the six images that actually exist of me, I own four of them. Two of them were taken by a man I couldn't stand, one was taken by an ex-boyfriend I had to escape from, and one was taken by someone I don't even know.

A photograph of me is supposed to be an answer to the question, "Who am I?" But I spread out the images of me in existence on my bed and I look at them and I get no fucking answers. I just get a cascade of more fucking questions. A scrambled deck of hows and whens and whos and whys.

~~I am a mistake. A deleted image. I am less than. I am a walking photograph, not real. And I shouldn't be.~~

~~I take pictures of these memorials to the dead. Someone cares enough to go out and perform this act: to sum up the identity of a person who has died and to bind their own identity to that dead person's. An act of mourning and an act of love. If I were to miss a turn on the~~

~~road one night and slam into a tree and go through the windshield, if~~
~~there were someone out there that gave enough of a fuck to put up a~~
~~descanso for me—and there isn't—what would there be to center the~~
~~memorial around? A fixing my identity to a place like that would be~~
~~like nailing water to a fence post. And there would be nothing to bind~~
~~anyone else's identity with. And no one should.~~

This project is driving me fucking crazy. I should just quit.

- S. Felsdottir

31

Night brought Skade in its long, thin arms, and laid her indelicately on the doorstep of Day. Whether she was glad—or safe—was her business. Neither Night, who'd passed her off, nor Day, who'd begrudgingly received her, cared, and both looked away.

The first things that registered were the smells. Her personal quiver of smells was there now, because she was there now, but everything else was different. She'd become accustomed—inured—to the smells of waking up in the Skyline, but the cheap caustic detergent, ammonia, fried food, and old cigarette smoke that haunted the background of her room had been replaced by coffee, and the unmistakable collection of smells of a man and of sex. All of it drifted through her brain without really eliciting a reaction.

She became aware of tactile sensations next. She was lying down. She was warm. Sheets. A bed. Much more comfortable than the Skyline. These felt soft and inviting, not the poor cousin of sackcloth and shrouds at the motel.

She did an automatic audit. She felt on the bad end of the bad-morning scale. Bad enough to not want to move, but because she couldn't figure out where she was without looking around, she got enough of the levers and pulleys to work to raise her head and open her eyes. Light streamed in and it hurt. She slammed her eyelids shut. A body audit revealed something else as well: she'd had sex. And she couldn't place it.

She tried her eyes again. She was in a room she didn't immediately recognize. But the feeling of the room told her it had to be Lane's. She tried to retrace her steps.

She remembered...going...out? The book was finished. She had to celebrate. She went out. And? It became murky and empty after that. A party? Doing shots? Vomiting in a parking lot? The parking lot at the Skyline? Music? But beyond that was just a blank. A long, dark blank.

Skade pushed herself up onto her elbows. She was naked. The lack of a memory of the night before made her feel as if she were in a dark free fall. She gathered the sheets around herself and sat up tentatively. The door to the bedroom was ajar, and for the first time Skade realized she heard sounds of movement coming from down the hall. She'd lost nights before, and she'd woken up in a strange bed with an unfamiliar bedmate before, so this feeling, though frightening and disconcerting, wasn't entirely new to her, but what if she'd lost more than a night? It wouldn't be the first time.

Her clothes lay in a pile on a chair. She stepped onto the floor as though she wasn't completely sure she'd woken up in her real body. All the bones and muscles seemed to be present and accounted for, and in more or less decent working order, so she retrieved her jeans and dug into the pocket to feel for her phone. She turned it on. Only one night. Relief. A glance out the window confirmed what she already knew—Lane's apartment.

She pulled on her jeans and stuffed her underwear, which she found on the floor by the bed, in her pocket. The only shirt she could find was a paint-stained gray-and-yellow T-shirt that was several sizes too big for her. Skade looked around the room, holding the shirt in her hand, not wanting to put it on. Maybe hers was lying someplace else? What had she been wearing, anyway? She couldn't remember. She saw nothing in the bedroom, so she reluctantly pulled the T-shirt on over her head.

She pulled her boots on and sat for a moment. What had happened last night? At a base level she knew what had happened. It hadn't happened for a long time, but it had happened again. The thundering sound of an emotional tidal wave began vibrating in her mind: fear, pain, grief, fury, disgust, self-loathing, disappointment, shame, and engulfing sadness. Quickly, before she was overwhelmed by it and swept out to sea, Skade erected a succession of walls and barriers in her mind, a kind of grand emotional public engineering project that re-routed the thoughts and feelings backward and sideways and in convoluted loops and ultimately down into the deep gaping hole inside her. A hole that strangely seemed to get bigger the more crap and pain she dumped into it. But despite her architectural talent for emotional waste management, Skade's wet effluent of shame, rage, and fear overflowed the channels she'd built and soaked into her bones.

She forcibly distanced herself from the moment, as if she were retreating into her own echo and looking the other way. She was familiar with this state; she'd been in it before. It gave her the ability to walk through the wreckage of her present and her past.

She watched herself walk down the long hallway toward the sounds in the kitchen. Slivers of the missing past night reappeared. She'd been wearing her Detroit Cobras T-shirt while drinking with two guys whose names she couldn't remember. Then she was in Lane's car, head hanging out the window, the hot night air blowing over her face and through her hair, the city rushing by.

She turned the corner into the kitchen and stood in the threshold, feeling the smooth texture of the lid she was using to hold her emotions down. Lane stood over the stove, his back to her, the redolent aroma of pancakes filling the air. He wore a pair of gray sweatpants, the intricate tattoo of a flight of Japanese cranes spread across the muscles of his back. She hovered in the entryway of the kitchen, suspended like one of Kit's mismatched scrap-heap marionettes. He turned and caught sight of her.

"Hey, you're up. Want some coffee?" His demeanor was light and happy. Just the sound of it sent searing sparks through her body. He poured her a cup and handed it to her. "You look a little worse for wear. Need some ibuprofen? Look in the bathroom—"

"What happened?" she interrupted.

A slow smile slipped across his face. "You don't remember?"

"No." Her spring was coiling.

"Guess I shouldn't be surprised. It was pretty epic, start to finish. I hope that's not a normal Tuesday night for you."

"What happened, Lane?" she shot out. Her angry confusion made him smile again.

"Fine. What's the last thing you remember?" he asked, turning off the fire on the range and leaning back against the counter, folding his arms across his bare chest, and taking a sip of coffee, not releasing her from his bemused gaze.

She snarled inside her head, where a massive colorless dust storm raged. She tried to breathe through it but she wasn't getting anywhere. "I don't know. Yesterday afternoon maybe..."

"And?"

She felt an eruption coming. "And nothing much after that," she seethed.

Lane took a long drink of his coffee and paused again, smiling at her.

"Fuck, Lane!" she hissed.

"Well, I can only give you a bunch of educated guesses between whenever that was and about one in the morning. You remember the guys in the unit down from you at the Skyline?"

"No," she ground out, feeling a rising panic.

"I guess you wanted to make some new friends. I met you out in the parking lot at the Skyline about one. You were chemically enhanced, to say the least. You were in a pretty colorful shouting match with these three guys. Seems you were all having a nice cozy little party until somebody suggested a show-us-your-ink tattoo contest. I was coming by to see if you had looked at those tattoo ideas I'd given you. It was actually a little tense when I got there."

Skade felt herself beginning to turn to glass. A spot between her shoulder blades began to tighten and ache. The dust storm in Skade's head didn't clear, but it moved enough to tell her Lane was telling the truth.

"You thought you'd won the contest, but they wanted more evidence. Your pants, I'm guessing. But you had enough left in your head to put a stop to it, and you were arguing the point in the parking lot when I got there."

Skade could hardly breathe. "Did I—?"

"What?"

"Shit, Lane… You know…"

"Were you screwing them? No. I'm pretty sure about that."

Skade felt a small measure of relief, which narrowed down the options. She knew she'd had sex last night.

"Some nightshift person from the Skyline showed up. I suspect they called the cops, too, so I thought it best, between the angry dudes and the cops and the pissed-off management and your general condition, to take you back here for the night. You were sliding up and down the scale at a hundred miles an hour: laughing, cursing, screaming, pawing at me. Like I say, I'm not surprised you don't remember much."

There was a pause.

"Where's my shirt?" Skade asked quietly.

"No idea. That's the packaging you came in. If you were wearing something different, it's probably with those guys now. Maybe you traded it," Lane said with caustic dryness.

Another long rumbling pause.

"What happened then?" she asked, truly focusing on him for the first time.

"What do you mean?" he asked obliquely.

"After we got back here. Then what?"

Lane's look became opaque, and he took another long pull from his coffee cup. Skade felt a violent angry heat building behind her glass insides. "You don't remember any of that either?"

Skade drew herself up in a series of jagged angles. "No, Lane. Obviously, I don't. But something sure as hell happened. I know that much."

"Like I said, Skade, you were all hands and tongue after I got you out of that trouble. You were all fired up and ready to go. It was all I could do to keep you in your seat on the way over here. When we got back I guess you talked me into it."

"You guess?"

"I mean, yeah, Skade. Sure. I could hardly get the door open you were so turned on. You wanted it in the stairwell, for Christ's sake."

They locked eyes and the eruption Skade had been feeling build inside her began to come to a head.

"Ever since I saw you in the liquor store..." continued Lane. "Shit, Skade, we can still fix it—"

"That's sexual assault, Lane. I was out of my mind. How could you—?"

"You were the best thing in my life. Look, I will always have this." He touched the tattoo of the tiger and the lotus on his chest.

"Rape, Lane—"

"We can make this work. I felt it in you last night—"

"Fuck, Lane! You raped me!" Tears of rage came, and Skade felt her emotions eject from her body and take most of her insides with them, as if she were turning herself inside out.

Lane's head snapped back from the force of it. "I didn't rape you, Skade. Don't be stupid. You wanted it so bad, you refused to take no for an answer. Get real—"

"God...damn...it!" she screamed, her throat scoured raw. "You self-obsessed little boy! I was always just part of your stuff—your pussy. Of course a narcissistic asshole like you would want that back. I'm sure I fucking diminished your ego when I left. Asshole! You walk around like the fucking poster boy of solipsistic male dickheads! Fuck me! I swore this wouldn't happen to me again! And here it is, I put my own ass into the fire again! I saw it coming and did it to myself anyway!"

Skade vibrated inside with pain and anger, everything pouring out in a flood of furious emotion. She closed the gap between herself and Lane and tried to tear the skin from his body with her words.

"Let me tell you what fucking happened twelve years ago. We had that big party out at Colleen's house. Remember that? Those two guys that were in from someplace like New Zealand or something and…" Skade began laughing. "What were their names? Gary and Don, right? Yeah, I'm sure of it. You know why I'm sure of it? Because they fucking had names, Lane! I didn't. You always introduced me as your girlfriend, and right then I realized, I had the possessive pronoun *my* stapled to my ass. Half the school actually thought my name was *Lane's girlfriend*—I was losing any sense of self I ever had. I was like a fucking shadow.

"Yeah, well, all that shit hit me suddenly. So I was standing out in the back yard that night and Mike and I got to talking. He treated me like a human being. We left the party and hung out just the two of us. You probably fucking didn't even notice. We talked about the idea of ipseity and identity. He was smart, and thoughtful and gentle, and he gave a damn about me as a person.

"Mike and I had been sleeping together for six months before I just couldn't take it anymore with you. And everyone knew it, too, except you. You had your head crammed so far up your ass that you couldn't envision that your little private possession wouldn't want to be with you. Everyone was laughing at you, and you were so consumed with yourself that you never noticed. And you want to know the best part?" Skade reached out and put her hand on his chest, right on the tiger and the lotus and the words *Love rises from the mud and blooms towards heaven. Love stalks the night with silent strength* tattooed directly over his heart.

"The best part, Lane, is that you went and did this. This is just spectacular. You took that card that I had made—that I had spent days creating by hand—that I didn't give to you, and you fucking inked it over your heart." Skade doubled over, laughing, as Lane stood by in growing confusion.

"Do you remember what happened? You were looking for a lighter in my bag, and you dug that envelope out, and you opened it. I pretended it was a surprise for you—a bullshit story I made up on the spot. I was so fucking weak! Christ!

"That card was a birthday present for Mike. I let you keep it. That was what finally told me I had to just cut you off like a rotting limb. And I did. And look, you pathetic fucker, you went and tattooed my admission of love for someone else on your own chest. Another man's love letter. Perfect."

Skade set her coffee cup down on the counter. "Fuck you, Lane. You deserved that."

And she rushed out of the apartment like a dark wind.

32

Along walk. A bus ride. Another long walk. The adrenaline had worn off, replaced by a brush fire of shame and self-recrimination that burned through the dry tinder and cane fields inside her.

She tried to focus on her breath and the rhythm of her footsteps, her body feeling disjointed and achy and nauseous. The night before came back in shards—the motel room with the three guys; drinking from a bottle of whiskey; smoking and dancing; shirts coming off and the scent of sweaty bodies. The memories kept playing, over and over again, like a disintegrating tape loop.

She remembered nothing of Lane. She despised herself.

She cautiously approached the parking lot of the Skyline, skirting the side of the building up by the fence. Her car was still in its place. Nothing moved, no sign of life. She got to her door and pushed her way inside into an oppressive gloom. She cringed at the empty vodka bottles. Smells of herself shifted in and out like ghosts as she locked the door behind her.

The afternoon became an endless well of heat, a black hole that trapped time and energy and let nothing go. The numbers passing by on the clock didn't have any meaning. Everything felt heavy and dead. And where was her camera and her bag? Her wallet, phone, and keys had been in her jeans when she left Lane's, and she'd just assumed her camera was at the Skyline. But it wasn't. If she'd left them in Lane's apartment, retrieving them would be painful. At least she hoped that's where they were.

Skade stared out her window. The heat rose off the pavement in glistening waves distorting reality. The crows—the ever-present guardians of the parking lot—seemed involved in some sort of ritual of their own: casting spells and invocations and making magic. She looked over her shoulder at her motel room, a room of abandoned things. Her work—now finished—lay spread out over much of the bed and the floor around it. It was all meaningless. Any connection she had to it had left to join the crows. She opened the door and stepped onto the walkway. Outside, she found only heat and bad thoughts and herself, the air corrupted by the smells of garbage and car exhaust. The heat clung to her and made her skin itch. She sank into her bad mood and headed back into her room. *Another shower.*

As she got undressed her phone rang. She glanced at it but didn't recognize the number, so she ignored it and stepped into the bathroom.

The water felt good; she began to feel lighter. She'd found a half-full bottle of vodka under the bed and had taken it into the shower with her. She wanted nothing more than to get this damn project over with, to get the fuck out of town; to take the manuscript to New York in person and tell Eileen to shove it up her ass.

Skade shut the water off and stood naked in the shower stall, letting the water stream and drip off her body. Eventually she dried off and realized she had begun playing with her cornhusk puppet. She'd set it on the sink before she showered.

She pulled on her jeans and glowered down at the phone on the bed—she was looking for reasons to be angry now—she had a voice-mail.

"Skade, it's Camille Longday. Sorry I missed you. I've got a copy of those photos you wanted. I'm over near the Skyline now. I'll stop by and drop them off. If you're not there, I'll leave them with the manager. If the manager isn't around, I'll try again later, or you can give me a call and come get them. Hope you're doing well. See you."

Skade glanced through the parted curtains into the parking lot as she unwrapped her hair and began combing it out. A vintage midnight-blue Plymouth pulled in, and Camille rose gracefully from the driver's seat, a manila envelope in her hand.

There was a soft knock on the door.

Skade carefully set the half-full vodka bottle in the trash can, dropped her towel over it, and opened the door.

Camille stood smiling on the threshold in jeans, a loose linen shirt, and sandals, a pair of aviators on her head pulling her silver-gray hair out of her face.

"Oh, sorry, Skade. Did I get you out of the shower?" she asked brightly.

"No," said Skade flatly.

"So," said Camille, holding up the envelope. "I brought those photos you wanted."

"Yeah, thanks," Skade replied, holding out a hand.

Camille pulled the envelope back. "Can I come in and talk to you for a minute?"

Skade narrowed her eyes a fraction, then stepped aside and waved her in. "Sure. Welcome to my…whatever this is."

Camille took the room in quickly and efficiently, her smile fixed and unwavering. Skade folded onto the rumpled bed, pulled her legs into a half-lotus, and stared at Camille. Camille remained standing. Outside the crows started to make a fuss, with a cacophony of loud cawing and a fluttering of wings. Camille looked out through the parted drapes. "Crows are the loudest angels," she said.

"They've been out there bullying the parking lot since I got here. That's the first I've heard from them, though."

"Wonder why that is?" Camille said with a cryptic smile.

"What would you like to talk about?" asked Skade, her voice taking on the quality of a sword sliding out of a sheath.

Camille's gaze swept the room again, then settled on Skade. "I'd like to talk to you about Kitten."

"She prefers Kit."

"I know."

"What about her?"

Camille took a long slow breath and let it out. "When Kitten first came to see if she could connect with her relatives, I asked her about any dreams she was having—"

Skade cocked her head. "So, how long have you been"—she gave a dismissive wave of her hand—"'gifted' like this, anyway?"

"All my life," Camille said. "But you don't really care—"

"Oh no! No! I care. I'm a journalist, remember. It's my job to be curious. And you sure are…curious."

"Anyway," continued Camille evenly, "I asked Kitten about her dreams and she told me about one that was very clear and strong for her. She has nightmares. Vivid ones, about dead bodies."

"What about it?"

"You've been to her house?"

"Yep."

Camille looked at Skade sitting on the bed. Skade twitched and shifted, unable to sit still, playing restlessly with the cornhusk doll that Kit had given her.

"I'm worried about Kitten," said Camille.

"What are you? Her mom or something?"

"I'm her friend, Skade," said Camille quietly. "Kitten desperately needs friends."

"So I've noticed, yeah. Well, I'm her friend too."

"Yes, you are," said Camille. "I think you're the most important friend Kitten has, Skade."

Skade felt her anger sharpen into an arrowhead. "What the fuck is that supposed to mean?" she blurted out.

Camille looked down at her impassively.

"I mean, seriously?" continued Skade, sliding off the bed and standing up. "What is that? It sounds like fortune-telling con-game bullshit, Camille. Are you setting me up now? Because that's not going to work. She sure as hell seems to do okay on her own. Do you have any idea how talented she is?"

"Yes. She's extraordinary."

"Fuck yes, she is. She's a savant. And she is perfectly fine on her own."

"Skade, I think you know that's not true."

"She's lonely. She's had a hard time. It's sad, but stuff like that happens. But, you know, maybe you are a psychic priestess." Skade locked eyes with Camille again. Camille was soft and impassive, but she had polished steel behind her eyes. Skade felt tears coming to her own eyes and it only made her angrier. "I got a video of her doing a puppet show. It was incredible. And I know people at the Children's Television Workshop and *Sesame Street*. I sent that video to them. So maybe I just brought Kit her golden ticket. So, yeah, maybe I am important to her. Probably better than somebody bleeding her for eighty a week and leading her around by her nose with a bunch of magic con-game fortune-telling shit, right?" Skade spat bitterly.

"I'm sure Kitten told you she doesn't pay me anymore—"

"Whatever." Skade waved at the air angrily.

"That's wonderful, Skade. I'm glad you did that for her. That makes me so happy," Camille said gently. "But I think it's deeper than that."

"What?"

"I don't know, Skade."

"Well, shouldn't you know? I mean you're a fortune-teller, right? Shouldn't you be able to say for sure? *Sees all, knows all, reveals all,* right?"

Camille sighed. "I don't know."

"You don't know? Well, shit, Camille. Let's find out, right? If you're so damn good—so gifted or whatever you call it—tell my fortune then." Skade cocked her head defiantly. "You want me to tell you about my dreams? 'Cause I got some good ones."

"Only if you want to—"

"No, I don't. Just do your magic and look into my future."

"Want me to go get my crystal ball and fly around the room on my broomstick?"

"Something like that. Might as well give me and Kit our money's worth, right?"

"Okay, but you're going to be disappointed. I don't own a crystal ball, and I've never gotten a broom to work." With a grin, Camille dropped her bag and went back out to her car. She came back in with a small paper box about the size of a coffee mug. "Clear of the papers off that table," said Camille, motioning toward a round café table in the corner. With a violent swipe of her hand, Skade swept her work to the floor and brought the table over to Camille.

"Here," said Camille, handing the box to Skade. "Open the box."

Skade opened the box to find it full of needles and straight pins.

"Pour the pins out in a circle on the table. Make it fairly large. Keep going around until the box is empty."

Skade slowly poured the pins and needles out into a circle. They slithered and bounced randomly. Skade then stepped back and looked expectantly at Camille.

"Well?" asked Skade impatiently.

Camille looked up with a pained expression. "Skade, I don't know what happened to you, but something did. I'm so sorry. And this project you're working on, it's so full of pain. That's a lot to carry. Where are you in all this? What happened to you?"

"Leave me the hell alone! I'm right fucking here!" Skade lunged across the room to get the backup camera she had and her memory box. "You want to know where I am? Take a look at these fucking pictures…" Skade dumped the contents of the box out onto the bed. "Here I am. I'm in this box. Here's a shitload of pictures, old ones, pretty much every picture of me growing up that exists. Plus, all these shots for the book. I've got several thousand images for that. Where am I in all that? Nowhere, Camille. I'm nowhere. I'm behind the fucking camera. Nowhere to be seen. I don't exist."

"Yes, you do, Skade," said Camille quietly. "But this place is so full of trauma for you, I can tell. Why did you come back?"

"Oh my god! You can read minds!" Skade said, sarcasm heavy in her voice. "I was just asking myself that very same question in the shower. This, Camille, is why I came back." She waved her camera at Camille.

"To take pictures. Yes, I know," Camille said, her expression sympathetic.

"No! Not to take fucking pictures. I can take pictures anywhere on the planet. I don't have to come…here…to take pictures." Skade tossed the camera strap over her head and held the camera out in front of her. "I have this little black box full of grief around my neck, like a noose." Skade gestured at the pictures of descansos scattered across the floor. Her voice was losing steam and tears were welling up in her eyes like a crowd at a bad traffic accident. "Every time I take another picture, that box gets heavier, as if adding another stone to a bag dragging me down into a cesspool. And this is the bottom of the well. This place. This place is hell. Every day I get up out of this bed and get my camera and go out into the parking lot, and it's like crawling out of my own grave." Skade looked around the room as if she suddenly didn't recognize any of it.

"What did you see in those pins?" she asked, sinking to the bed. The fire of her anger had been doused by despair. "You saw an accident, didn't you? But you didn't see a future. You didn't see a fortune. I know you didn't. Here's my fortune. Standing here. I'm a dead end. There is no fortune to tell."

"I saw a lot, actually. It's very sad and very complicated—"

"Yeah, well, I've got my own circle of pins and needles. Here." Skade dove into the pile of herself on the bed and pulled out two envelopes. "Here's my fortune. Let me read it to you."

Dear Ms. Felsdottir. We are pleased to offer you admission into the incoming Princeton University freshman class. Your record of academic achievement and your accomplishments both in and out of the classroom indicate that you would be a valuable and successful addition to the Princeton family. Because of your outstanding work in astronomy and related sciences, we are also pleased to award you the Dauchenburg Scholarship for Women in Science, along with need-based financial aid. Details attached…

"They gave me a full ride, Camille. A full ride to study astronomy at Princeton. And look." She brandished the other letter. "Same thing at Stanford. Full ride. I got six offers. I wasn't going to have to pay or even borrow a dime in five of them. And look at me." She dropped the letters onto the bed and picked up the cornhusk doll that had fallen on the floor. One of its arms had begun to come untwisted.

"I was supposed to go to college. I was all set. But then..." Skade ran her hand through the photographs on the bed. "I died here, Camille. I died here twelve years ago. There's no descanso for me. I have no marker. I shouldn't have one. I don't deserve one. I should be buried in a shallow grave by the side of the road. I'm erased. I should be."

Skade wrapped her arms around her body and hugged herself, tears running down her face.

Camille reached a hand toward Skade. "You and Kitten are in the same place; you both just got there from different directions. She doesn't understand why she's alone and she doesn't want to be. She wants to live so very desperately."

Skade shook her head.

"I started doing this book, where I'd go and talk to loved ones or survivors or whatever. It was like a flaming arrow shot through my chest to do that. Then after a while it got easier, all this stuff, it was more like putting a cigarette out on my arm or something. I think I came back to Carleton because a few weeks ago I quit feeling anything. I felt dead inside. And I should damn well be *feeling* the pain... People died... A boy I liked died and took... I don't deserve to feel any redemption. I don't even deserve to be here."

"Maybe here is where you have to be? I can help, if you want me to," Camille said in a soft whisper.

"No. I'm sorry," said Skade quietly through more tears. "I'm not doing real well right now. I'm sorry I got bitchy and mean." She wiped her face. "I'm sorry I got all sloppy and maudlin, Camille. Thanks for bringing me your pictures. And thanks for trying to help. I'm fine. I just need to get this damn thing over with and take a break for a little while."

"Sometimes I think people are like birds nesting in drainpipes, forgetting the last time it rained. People hear the dead speaking all the time, Skade," said Camille gently. "They just don't know that's what they're hearing. You need to be really careful. You're being led into a very dark place."

"I've been there for a while."

"Yes, I know. But it's getting darker."

The leveling rays of the sun came in sideways now, blinding drivers in westbound lanes. Camille and Skade stood quietly as the sun set the eastern wall of the motel room on fire.

"Skade, promise me you'll call me or come see me if things get scary or out of control?" Camille said.

Skade took a big breath, threw her head back, and exhaled at the ceiling. "You mean like they already are? No. I probably won't," she said. "But I'll keep it in mind anyway. Don't worry about me. Or Kit either. I'll keep an eye on her."

Camille gathered up her pins and her bag. "Be careful," she said before the door closed behind her.

Skade stood at the window and watched the slow darkening in the sky. She didn't move for a long time and the night rushed in like ink. *I don't deserve. I don't deserve.*

She couldn't stay here, in this room, in the motel, even in this town anymore. She went out to her car. Sitting behind the wheel, a wave of self-loathing hit her without warning. It was only going to get worse unless she had company. She jumped out of the car and gathered up her camping gear and headed out toward Kit's house.

Kit was home and happy to see her. Skade was struck by both the familiarity of the puppets and the changes. Puppets had moved, and new vignettes and stories were being played out in silent pantomime.

"I need to do something," Skade said. "And I need to get out of this town for a couple of days. I don't know what your schedule is like—"

"To do what?"

"Want to go on an overnight camping trip? There's a place I want to photograph. It's a long drive. We could leave before light tomorrow morning, get there, take pictures, look around, camp out, then turn around and head back here the next morning. Or take another day, depending on what you can do?"

Kit looked at her with a sparkling brightness. "Yeah. I could do that. That sounds like fun."

Skade felt a knot loosen in her solar plexus.

"Where are we going?" asked Kit.

"Nebraska. Come here, I'll show you on the map." Skade waved a battered road atlas in front of her. "One thing, though, can we take your truck? My car's been acting up lately, and I'm not sure it's big enough..."

"For me?"

"Well, you've got long legs—"

"I've got long everything, Skade." Kit smiled. "Yeah, let's take the truck. I'll pay for the gas."

"We'll split it."

33

So, tell me about this place?" Kit asked, with a yawn. The sun had come up behind them—the truck mirrors were set on fire by the rising sun—and the day ahead promised to be bright and clear.

"Don't really know," said Skade from behind her sunglasses. "It's a stretch of road with a lot of descansos. Guess we'll see. A guy I met told me about it and circled it on the map, but he didn't seem dead sure where it was. Hopefully, we're not on some kind of snipe hunt."

Driving west, the land began opening up. Skade watched the unfolding from the passenger-side window. She'd brought her shoebox and tucked it on the floor under her feet—why, she had no idea. She opened it and found the cornhusk puppet sitting on top of a photograph of herself as a teenager being awarded a science scholarship. She dropped the photo in her lap and looked out the window.

"Do you ever wonder how many times you show up in other people's photographs?" she asked.

"What?"

"Take a look at a picture of you at a picnic or the fair or something. There will be people in the background. You're the one whoever took the picture wanted to capture in that moment, but they captured other people too. I've gotten that a lot, taking pictures of people at concerts or wherever. Sometimes you get their backs, or their asses—"

Kit snorted with laughter.

"Yeah, I know," continued Skade, "but sometimes you get pretty clear and interesting shots of people."

"Sure. My cousins and stuff."

"Yeah, but a lot of times it's complete strangers. Think about it. How many times are you the complete stranger in the background of other people's pictures. Probably a lot, right? I'd bet nearly as many as there are of you as the subject. Unless you're some kind of celebrity or supermodel. And the thing is, those shots where you're the stranger? Those are closer to being the real person you are than the ones where you're the subject."

"Like how?"

"We're all like those Russian nesting dolls—"

"I've got some of those at home someplace—"

"Yeah. We hide personalities inside other personalities like that. So when I point a camera at you to take your picture—" Skade pointed her camera at Kit and started snapping images.

"Stop!" Kit said, laughing as she held up a hand. "Stop it, Skade! I hate having my picture taken!"

"Oh, you stop it, Kit," Skade scolded. "But when I take your picture, a personality pops out. The biggest nesting doll, the biggest fake of all. It's us pretending to be something we think we're supposed to be. And we hide our other personalities inside there, one inside another, inside another, inside another. Think of the personality you are at work. Or with your family. Or the one you are when you're all alone—"

A strange emotion swam in the depths under the surface of Kit's face.

"But when a camera catches you unaware—in the background... Well then, maybe it captures the smallest nesting doll. The one that is really you."

Skade took a deep breath and frowned and looked down at the photograph again.

"I mean, I look at a picture like this one"—she held the photo up, and Kit took a quick glance—"and I have no idea who that is. I don't recognize anything about that person. It's as if I've been handed a box of someone else's things."

"Well, I mean you look a lot different now," offered Kit.

"Yeah, but it's not just that... It's like the image in this photograph— and sometimes even when I look in the mirror lately, it feels like—it's just an image. Like a façade. It isn't real. None of it is me. Images are questions—who is this? Not the answer to that question everyone thinks it is. Anyway, who we are is so much determined by external things. Carl Jung said—"

"Who?"

"Carl Jung? Famous psychoanalyst and philosopher. Anyway, Jung said something about how if we don't define ourselves, then we are subject to having the world define us. Much of the time, who we are is at the mercy of how other people define us or label us. I mean, I can say I'm one thing, but a bunch of other people say I'm something else. Who's right?

"I have these memories, and they are like my little autobiography in my head, and they add up to something, right? They add up to an image of me that I have. But maybe that image is wrong. Maybe what other people believe is what really is me.

"I feel like I was a different person in every place I've lived. Like where I was and who I was were tangled up. You've never lived anyplace else, but I've moved around so much that I feel like I've lost touch with parts of me. Stuff got lost in the moving. I'm a box of images. What if I started unpacking my nesting dolls and find out that I don't have one at the center? That I've lost the thing that I am?"

"The puppets have that," said Kit.

"What do you mean?"

"The puppets. They have that thing-that-I-am in them. They all do."

"How?"

"I don't know," said Kit. "But they do. That's how I know their names and their stories. It's like the puppets come into being. They get made and then that thing that they are, it comes trailing along behind them like a shadow. Your shadow is there, you just can't always find it. It will come when it's ready. Don't overthink it."

Skade smiled at Kit. "Don't overthink it? You're telling me to not overthink something? Talk about robbing me of my essential nature. Jeez, Kit." She laughed.

They drove into the afternoon and the sun got angry. Then it got furious. They'd hit the edge of the Big Sky, and Skade was beginning to do more in the way of navigation than just waving her hand westward and saying, "Go that way."

They pulled into a gas station. Flinching in response to the welding torch of the summer afternoon, Skade began pumping gas and Kit went inside to use the bathroom.

The pump kicked off in Skade's hand and Kit hadn't reappeared, so Skade walked out from under the shelter of the pump canopy across the pressed gravel and dirt toward a tent that covered a produce stand. She pulled out her phone. The loss of her camera had been gnawing at her, and she'd resisted contacting Lane about it; but she couldn't stand being without it any longer. She punched in Lane's number, hoping he wouldn't pick up. He didn't. She left a voicemail:

"Lane, it's me. I think my camera and bag are in your apartment someplace. Find them and give them back to me, please. I'm out of town for a couple of days."

Skade walked back across the scalding tarmac with a paper bag, the flowery scent of peaches wrapping around her. She leaned against the side of the truck in the shade of the canopy and ate one. The skin slipped off like a silk dress, the flavor and aroma pungent and intoxicating. Still no Kit.

Putting her bag in the truck and wiping her mouth off with the back of her hand, Skade went inside the general store to find Kit. A friendly old man was behind the counter, and when Skade didn't immediately see Kit, she got her map and asked him about their destination. He seemed to know exactly what she was talking about and pointed to the spot about forty-five minutes up the road. Skade heard the sound of children's laughter and followed it to the back of the store where she found Kit.

Kit was on her knees in front of three children There was a spinning rack of toys, including a few sad, dusty hand puppets, on the rack behind her. Kit had a cream-colored lion on one hand and a fluffy white bunny on the other, and the two animals might have been the most alive things in the entire store.

Skade watched from a distance as Kit improvised a story that seemed to involve stolen carrots and a crown. The children laughed with glee at the lively personalities and realistic movements of the two puppets, and the voices Kit gave them. Kit was completely wrapped up in her puppet performance, but when she caught sight of Skade, she slipped back into herself.

"I gotta go now," she said to the kids, placing the now-inanimate puppets back on the rack.

The kids ran back toward the front of the store and Kit unfolded herself back to her looming height. "Sorry," she said bashfully. "I kind of got carried away with that."

"No," said Skade. "No worries. Seriously. That was fun to see. Wish I could have seen the whole performance."

"Yeah. It was fun. But we should go, right?" Kit flashed Skade a quick smile, then brushed past, down the aisle, and out the door.

They climbed back into the truck. "What's that smell?" asked Kit in wonder. The entire cab of the truck had the smell of nectar and confection and spiced flowers.

"Peaches. They're great. Want one?" Skade offered one to Kit.

And they covered the last few miles in a private covenant of sticky sweetness and flowers.

34

They stopped again briefly to wash up; peaches made it impossible to tolerate doing anything without getting clean, and Skade took over behind the wheel. The sky was a clear and clean resonating blue, and the heat shimmered in the air.

"I see why they call this Big Sky country now," said Kit nervously. "It seems so much bigger here. I feel small."

"It does take some getting used to. I remember feeling sort of vulnerable the first time I saw it too," Skade said, realizing this was probably as far from her home as Kit had ever been. "I think we're only about twenty miles out now. Weather looks good."

"Hey, Kit," she began, after a few minutes of silence. "Listen, when I was taking your picture before? Don't hate having your picture taken."

"I do hate it. I hate the way I look."

"Christ, Kit! Why? I mean, yeah, you are maybe, what—?"

"What?"

"Maybe unconventional? But when I look through my camera, I see you, Kit. That's beautiful. And you've got a beautiful smile."

"I don't," Kit said turning away, embarrassed.

"You do. It's a very honest, wonderful smile."

Kit looked out the window. "It's not just that I don't like the way I look—not liking my picture taken, I mean. It's like what you said about celebrities not knowing what it's like to be in the background of a picture? I'm like that. I'm never in the background of a picture. A couple of times a month, probably, I get people pointing cameras at me out of the blue. They stop when I'm working on the highway, like I'm some kind of freaky roadside attraction, and they take my picture. Most times they don't even ask me…just point and shoot, you know? One time, I had a family come up to me and want to take a picture of me standing with their kids, like I'm a giraffe in the zoo, or something. I'm like a freak. I hate that."

"Kit, shut up, okay? You are in no way a freak. You're just tall."

"Not just tall," said Kit. "I'm odd-tall. I'm strange-tall. I'm out of normal proportion—"

Skade made a noise and a dismissive gesture, but Kit cut her short.

"No, it's true. I know it. I'm used to it, you know? I'm like one of the puppets. The puppets are strange, out of proportion. Maybe that's why I like them. I recognize them. They're made of things that get left behind. Things that are lost. And they're waiting for someone to give them life. Then the life gets stripped away from them when you put them down. I get so sad for a puppet when I put it down. It's not like it has any needs, really…but it does. It needs life. It needs someone to pick it up and turn it into what it really is.

"I live in a world where literally anything can come to life. I wouldn't eat, sometimes—used to drive my mom crazy. I'd just sit at the dinner table and bring forks and knives and broccoli and bread to life. My mom said I'd starve to death to bring things to life, like I was dumping my life into other things."

Kit went silent for a minute and looked out the window again. Skade glanced at her.

"And that's kind of funny." Kit picked up again with a deep sigh, sounding a little more relaxed. "'Cause in some places—Asia mostly—they think puppets are containers for the souls of people that have died."

"Repositories," said Skade.

"Yeah. Repositories for dead souls. That's how they fix it when someone dies. They make a puppet, and the soul goes there; or just a part of it maybe. I never did get how that worked. So it's like my mom was saying, I was trying to get my soul into the puppets or something, I guess. Maybe I am, I don't know."

"What does it feel like to make something come alive like that?" Skade asked. "I mean, I've watched you do it, Kit. Even back with those kids. I've seen puppet shows before on TV. Street theater, carnivals. There was a guy that used to do a puppet theater on the street in Portland, Maine. He had a theater he'd set up and he had a rabbit puppet that he would bring outside the booth, and it would play a violin with him when he played his violin. Some kind of set up with fishing line or wires or something—"

"Yeah, I've seen that before. It's pretty cool the way it works, and it's not as complicated as you think."

"I never could figure it out. But as good as he was, he wasn't as good as you are. I'm not a puppet expert or anything, but I've never seen anything like what you can do. How does that feel?"

Kit sighed and a strange, awkward smile came across her face. "I honestly don't know how to answer that. It feels good. It feels natural… which is kinda different from everything else, 'cause nothing else really feels all that natural to me, you know? When I'm working with the puppets, time sort of slips away…and I sort of slip away."

"I get that when I'm deep into taking pictures."

"I can get into playing with the puppets or making new ones, and I look up and, like, four hours will have disappeared. It's weird how that happens. But the biggest thing is that part about me not being there anymore. That's the best thing, I guess. I'm not there… Or only a part of me is there, just a little part, you know? Outside myself. Watching. There's someone new there…and the puppet feels real, I guess. That part is crazy, I know."

"No, it's not. I can tell, because the puppets sure as hell seem real to me when you're working with them."

"When I can get that out of them, they become more real, and people become less real. That feels better."

They hit the outskirts of Fury, Nebraska, a town seemingly devoid of people. A skinny yellow dog trotted slowly along the sidewalk. They passed a church, then a laundromat, then a series of long-vacant storefronts. Then a bar. Then another bar. Then a liquor store, and another bar, and a general store, then another liquor store and another bar. And then, the edge of town and back out into the dusty prairie.

Almost as soon as they left Fury, they began to see the crosses on the roadside. At first, one at a time, then in groups of two or four. They drove on in silence for a few more minutes up a slight rise in the land. At the crest of the rise a railroad track ran into infinity in either direction, perpendicular to the road they were on. The rise was the built-up bed for the tracks. Another road ran parallel to the railroad. Skade stopped. No other vehicles could be seen. They got out of the truck and stepped into the intersection and looked slowly north and south. They had found their destination.

"Oh my god," said Kit.

"Shit," said Skade.

South from where they stood on top of the rise, the road went arrow-straight into the haze of the horizon, where they could just make out the bare outline of a small town. North from where they stood, the road went off on its surveyor line into an unending distance. As far as the eye could see in either direction, the road was lined with stark white crosses—sometimes grouped together in two or fours, and in other places just one alone. It seemed the road couldn't go a hundred yards without a cross sprouting up on one side or the other.

Skade unpacked her camera and began lining up long-distance establishing shots, trying to capture the eerie grandeur and strangeness of the spectacle. Kit shaded her eyes, counting under her breath.

"Forty-one. I count forty-one that I can see," she said. "Are they all—?"

"Descansos? Yeah, I'm pretty sure they are," said Skade from behind her camera.

"Why so many?"

Skade stood and looked off down the road to the south. "That way," she said, pointing into the distance at the mirage of the town they'd left, "is the town of Fury, Nebraska. Population one hundred forty-three. That way," she said, pointing off into the vague distance to the north, "are four big reservations. Native American homelands. This is the main road into town from those reservation lands. These descansos"—Skade waved her arm back and forth down the road—"are fifteen years of road deaths."

"But the road is so straight."

"Road is, driver, not so much. You saw all the bars and liquor stores? Capitalism."

"Drunk driving?"

"Yep."

"God, that's terrible."

Skade didn't say anything and dove back in behind her camera, snapping off dozens of images.

Skade shook herself loose from the viewfinder long enough to grab the map out of the truck, make a few notes, and show Kit the location of the campsite—about twenty-five miles down the road. Kit left to go set up, and Skade stayed behind, hunting images like a cat stalking its prey. She walked down the empty sun-blasted road and stopped at each descanso she encountered to take a series of close detail shots. Most of the crosses were identical: white PVC slats with a name and date painted in black paint on the crossarm. Many names appeared to be related, deaths. Some of the markers had offerings: hats, keys, feathers, small leather bags, shoes (Nike high-tops, mostly); others had horses or the rodeo: bits, bridals, spurs, stirrups, rope. Some of the markers were inscribed in a language Skade could only guess at, clearly tribal. Some were completely blank.

Frustration. Skade couldn't get the image she knew was there. An iconic shot was hiding in plain sight, and she couldn't find it. She needed a better vantage point. Telephone poles ran along the side of the highway. She approached one, the scent of creosote hanging in the air. Linemen used climbing spikes on their boots and a climbing belt to get up to the wires.

Skade had done work in trees before and had done enough climbing to know ropes. From her gear bag she retrieved a climbing harness, rope, and hardware, and before long she'd fashioned a competent rig that could get her up the pole.

She clambered up, careful to avoid the wires. They didn't look like live high-voltage wires, but better safe than sorry. She found her shot. From forty feet in the air there was an uninterrupted view of the timeline of grief stretching to the horizon.

Skade was only vaguely aware of the dusty rooster tail kicked up by Kit's truck. Kit slowly got out of the cab, staring intently at her phone. She walked slowly to the base of the pole without looking up.

"Hey," Skade called down from her perch. "Did you find that campsite?"

Kit pulled herself out of her phone and looked up at Skade, shading her eyes. "Yeah. It's nice. What are you doing up there?"

"I got a great set of pictures from up here. I'll be done in a second. Everything okay?"

"Huh?" Kit had sunk back into her phone. "Oh yeah. But can you come down here a second and look at something?"

Kit seemed worried, so Skade took one more long shot, and hitched back down the pole.

"What's up?" asked Skade, dusting her jeans off and setting her gear down.

"I'm not sure. Here." Kit held out her phone.

Skade took it and read the email open on the screen:

Dear Kit,

Thanks for sending us your puppetry. I'm sure you can understand that we receive hundreds of submissions every year from wonderfully talented people, and we rarely have openings on our team. It isn't often that we're able to give much more than a cursory review of such submissions, but Skade Felsdottir was pretty insistent that we look at your work, and a member of our team trusts her recommendations explicitly.

As such, our creative staff has reviewed your file, and we are very glad we did!

Our team can be pretty jaded when it comes to these things, but words like "extraordinary" and "amazing" were used to describe what they saw. As one creative staff member put it: "The level of skill and artistry on display in this (submission) is so intuitive and natural and emotive. I haven't seen anything like this in decades. I'd love to see it live."

And so would the rest of us.

I'd love to set up a time for you to come to New York and talk with us and our creative team. Show us some more of your work. We understand you design and make puppets as well? We'd really love for you to bring some with you. We are able to set something up for the rest of the summer, but we get pretty busy in early September. Please contact me either by this email address or on the attached phone number as soon as you can.

Looking forward to meeting you!

Sincerely,

Jane Carpenter
Administrative director
Children's Television Workshop

"Holy shit, Kit!" Skade exclaimed with a laugh. "This is fantastic!"

Kit looked slightly bewildered. "I don't..." she stammered.

"This is amazing!" Skade grabbed Kit and hugged her. "Don't worry. It will be great. We can talk about what you should do next. First, let's go back into town and buy something to celebrate with. Tequila or something. Then let's head to the campsite. Is it nice? I hope so. Damn, Kit! Congratulations!"

Skade grabbed the keys and ushered Kit to the truck.

"You sure?" asked Kit, glancing at the nearest cross, leaning at an off-angle just beyond where she'd parked. A little plastic palomino horse sat at its base.

"Hell yes!" said Skade, pushing her along. "And it looks like starweather tonight!"

35

Starweather," said Skade. "It's what we used to call nights like we're going to have tonight. Clear, low humidity, and no moon. Perfect conditions for watching the stars. Starweather."

She and Kit were driving into the setting sun. Skade had first taken them back into Fury and ducked into a liquor store. At Kit's pleading, she'd skipped the tequila and gone with a bottle of champagne (the package store in Middle-of-Nowhere, Nebraska, actually had a decent selection, much to Skade's surprise), and a pint of vodka to go with it. Now they were headed to their campsite.

"Who's *we?*" asked Kit.

"Friends from high school. We'd load into somebody's car with a telescope or binoculars and get high. I was an astronomy nerd back when I was a kid. Really, I think that term—starweather—came from my dad. He used to tell me it was starweather when I was little, and he'd take me out on his boat or out to the docks. I guess I carried that with me."

"That sounds nice."

"Sometimes it was. But it wore off. I used to have starweather parties. A lot of the time I was the only one that attended, so I don't know how much of a party it was, but it was fun anyway."

"So we can have a starweather party now?"

"That's exactly what we'll have!"

Skade pulled past a State DNR sign. The road wound through an encroachment of small pines and sage until it opened up on a bluff overlooking the Platte River, shimmering and glistening in the sharp narrow sunlight.

Kit led them to the campsite, with a beat-up picnic table, a dirty iron grill, and a great uninterrupted view of the sky. Kit went to go fetch water from the pump. When she returned with the full water bottles, Skade was standing in the bed of the truck with her hands on her hips.

"Too hot for the tent," she said, looking around. "I think we ought to just sleep in the truck bed tonight. That'll be the most comfortable.

Breeze is up, so the bugs won't be too much of a problem, and it will give us the best sky view."

"Sure, I've done that before," said Kit, putting the bottles on the table. "But we'll need to let the tailgate down. Leg room."

Soon Skade and Kit had the truck bed set up. Skade sat with cross-legged ease and watched with empathy as Kit folded her long, unruly legs with a self-conscious lack of grace, like some kind of tall wading bird settling into a nest.

"Okay, now for the important stuff," said Skade as she twisted the cork off the champagne with a muffled pop.

"I thought you were supposed to shoot the cork across the room?" said Kit, slightly disappointed.

"Only idiots and in the movies," said Skade. "It's dangerous and a waste. Here." She poured champagne into a pair of plastic cups. "Not as elegant as it should be, but here it is… Here's to you, Kit. And to your amazing big break. Now grab it by the horns and make something of it! Congratulations!"

Skade downed hers; Kit took a big sip and made a face. "That's real fizzy," she said, her eyes watering.

"You get used to it. Here, have some more."

"Skade," said Kit, "I'm not so sure about all this—"

"All what?"

"You know…all this New York and *Sesame Street* and going in to meet a bunch of people and do puppets and stuff—"

"Kit, seriously," Skade sputtered through another gulp of champagne. "Don't be afraid!"

"But, Skade, I've never been to New York! These people are professionals. I'm just some girl from some small town in the middle of nowhere who barely got through high school and works on some stupid road crew who makes puppets out of junk and old toys—"

"You read the email, right?"

"Yeah, but—"

"But what?"

"I mean…I'm not that good, Skade. I'll just make a fool of myself in front of these important people. They'll just laugh at me."

"Kit, listen. I know how you feel. That's really normal. I know it's scary. But you are that good."

"Skade!"

"Stop it, you are that good. These people saw it. You're absolutely right. They are professionals. They look at puppets and puppetry all day. They've been doing it for years. You won't fool them. You can't. They see it. It's the same thing I saw when you first made my cornhusk puppet. You're very, very good, Kit. You're gifted. They're genuinely excited to see you. Now maybe it won't work out. Maybe it won't be a good fit or whatever. But you won't fail, and they won't laugh at you. I promise."

Kit looked exactly like her namesake: a frightened kitten.

"Listen," continued Skade, "don't be afraid. Part of it is being female. Society tells you you can't, or you shouldn't do this or that. And everybody gets that imposter's syndrome crap—"

"What?"

"Imposter's syndrome. It's where you feel like a fraud. Like you're just fooling people and you don't know what you're doing or what you're talking about, and you can't keep it up forever."

"Yeah. That—"

"Yeah. I know. Its normal. I still get it. You don't know how often I feel like that with this book I'm doing. I think: *This is such crap. I have no idea what I'm doing*, or I think I sound utterly pretentious, or I'm so derivative, or naïve or amateurish or stupid. The worst is when I start in with the *I'm just fooling myself. I can't do this* bullshit.

"I've won awards, Kit. People tell me I know what I'm doing. I have an agent. And I still get all that stuff. I know what that's like. And it's a billion times worse for someone like you who doesn't have any of that. It was for me. I was so self-conscious that I felt as if I needed to apologize for *daring to try* to submit something. I was sure they would just laugh at me. But when they see you in person, and they see what you can do, they will fall in love with you. You're extraordinary. And…I will go with you, if you want."

"What?" Kit looked shocked and hopeful.

"Yeah. I'll go with you if you want. I have to go to New York anyway, to talk to my agent and the publishers. So tell them that you'll come, and that you're bringing your personal assistant and spiritual advisor or something. We can go together. And I can show you around New York."

Kit looked like she was going to burst, then melt. Skade wasn't sure she'd seen anything quite like the look that played across her face in that clear light from the sinking Big Sky sun.

"Really?"

"Yes, really." Skade laughed, poking Kit with her foot. "But that means you have to do your best, and not be afraid, and not get too worked up over what happens. This is just a first step. It might take a while for something to catch. So don't start spending money you haven't made yet. These things can be tricky. People say stuff, then reality hits and it's very different. But I have a good feeling. About you and about this offer. So let's just enjoy the moment, okay?" Skade filled up Kit's cup and drained her own again.

"I promise!" Kit seemed to settle onto a cloud of excited happiness.

The sun had gone down, but the western afterglow still daubed the sky, and shadows gently draped themselves over everything in veils of black and dark blues and purples.

The champagne was gone. Kit was looking a bit unsteady, and Skade had relaxed a notch. But the animal in her chest was awake now and prowling, and her mind was never very far from the bottle of vodka on the floor of the truck.

"*Entre le chien et le loup*," said Skade.

"What?" said Kit slightly hazily.

"Entre le chien et le loup," Skade repeated. "That's what the French call this time of day: twilight. It means between the dog and the wolf. This is the time between the dog and the wolf. I love that. It's so beautiful."

"You know French?" Kit asked, fishing inside an old canvas sack.

"Some. Enough to be stupid in Paris," replied Skade.

Kit produced two hand-puppets—a dog and a wolf—then slipped her hands inside and suddenly they came to life. Emotions were suddenly discernible on the faces of the puppet, and Kit herself seemed in beatitude. Skade pulled up her camera and snapped off a series of shots, hoping to have enough light to capture something of what she was seeing, and to not disturb Kit in her reverie.

The dog and the wolf seemed to be deep in conversation, with the wolf pointing out various aspects of the truck and the landscape and the sky to the dog, who seemed rapt in wonder at it all.

"Kit," said Skade quietly. "Show me."

Kit came back like she was rising from a warm bath. "Show you?"

"Show me how you do that. Show me how it works?"

Skade reached out and gently pulled the dog puppet off Kit's right hand; it came free with a whispering sigh. Kit's long fingers hummed with something Skade would describe thereafter as a kind of grace, and she felt it deep inside her body. Skade slipped the dog, still warm from Kit's hand, onto her own hand. The puppet felt slightly alive—or perhaps it was the afterglow of life? Skade folded her fingers in, and the dog woodenly closed its arms in a stiff clapping motion. Kit and Skade both laughed.

"Damn it," said Skade. "How do you make these things work?"

"I don't."

"What do you mean? I've watched you bring these things to life over and over again, and when I try it, it's just a dead piece of cloth on my hand. Are you saying they just come to life on their own or something?"

"No." Kit laughed. "I'm saying I don't make *them* work." She sighed and looked around at the dissolving light. "It's really complicated, and I'm no good at explaining it. I've been asked that same thing since I was about fourteen. It doesn't make a lot of sense, and when I say it, it sounds like a...what's the word, where you are saying *yes* and *no* at the same time?"

"A contradiction?"

"Yeah, that...a contradiction. It sounds like I'm saying a contradiction when I explain it."

Skade rolled halfway over to better look at Kit's face. "Well, try telling me, and let me see if I can make heads or tails of it. I'm pretty good at contradictions. I wrestle about six of them into submission every morning before I put my pants on."

"Okay, I'll try. So I know they're not real like you or me or a dog or a cat or something. I'm not that crazy yet," continued Kit seriously. "It's different. The puppet is just something my hands are wearing. Or just something my hands are touching or controlling, like rods or strings. The puppet doesn't really work. Your hands work."

Kit picked up a dark-blue bandanna and twisted the plastic lid off one of the water bottles. She held the bandanna loosely between her index and middle fingers of her right hand. She pushed the index finger of her left hand into the bottle lid, so it looked like her index finger was wearing a hat. And suddenly, a dance began.

As Skade watched, the bandanna transformed into a graceful dancer, and the hand with the hat became her dashing dance partner. Kit used the smallest and strangest little movements of her fingers to convey a complicated and artful pas de deux. The emotions in the two dancers were obvious and enthralling. It was magical.

Kit stopped. "It's not here," she said, indicating the lid and the bandanna. "It's here." She put the two objects down and waved her hands in the air, and again Skade was stuck by the beauty in the motions of her hands. "The puppet is just the skin. The hands are where the life really is. You were focusing on making the puppet *work*, that's not how it's done. Focus on your hands. Think about it. When anybody works with a puppet, what they're doing is trying to get you to recognize something. This, for example." She held up the dog puppet. "If I use this as a dog, I'm trying to do things with it that you recognize as dog." She popped the dog on her hand and instantly Skade saw a tiny dog, sniffing around at the air and making recognizably dog-like movements.

"Or I could play the dog against itself—a contradiction, right?—and make it do things you'd recognize as something else. Like this." And suddenly the dog became a distinguished gentleman taking in the evening air.

"But I think that's only half of it," she continued. "Because we all can do that, right? More or less? Imitate things?"

"Easy for you to say, master artist." Skade laughed.

"Stop. I'm not. Okay, I've had more practice. But anyway, we can imitate like that. But think about what else the hands can do, right? We use five languages."

"Okay, wait. Stop. Now you're going deep."

"Sorry," Kit said, looking a little embarrassed. "But we do. You do a lot."

"What five languages are those?"

"Well, the obvious one is our spoken language, right? When I say 'language' that's the first thing anyone thinks of. But we also have the language in our faces. Looks and expressions. Those say a lot, right? And then there's body language. Everybody knows that one, so that's three. And then the fourth one is the vibe people give off. I'm no good at that one. But you are." A strange look passed between them as she and Skade locked eyes for a moment.

"The fifth language is our hands. They have a language all their own. We can give somebody the finger or beckon to them. Think of all the gestures and things we say with our hands—promise, pray, request, defend, prop up, put down, show exasperation or excitement. Give up or cheer on." Kit went through a fast array of hand gestures to match her examples, all of which Skade recognized. "And then there are hand gestures that you know but can't easily put a label on." Kit's hands told a short story, of grief and guilt and hope and redemption. All without words. All completely understandable to Skade. Skade gasped at its clarity and beauty.

"We communicate so much with our hands," said Kit, picking up her dog puppet again. "The real cool thing to do is to combine that imitation-language with hand-language. Then you can do so much with a puppet." Kit put her hand back inside the dog and began an evocative performance of hope and fear. A solo dance. "That's how we tell stories. That's how it comes to life," said Kit, slipping the puppet off and holding up her bare hands.

"This is the Lady Rafaella of the Prairie Kingdoms. And this is her lover, Lord Castigillian. They can only see each other on a single night each year because of the plagues of war and jealousy and a magic curse. This is their one night." And again Kit created a love-ballet for two hands. Her hands became the Lady Rafaella and the Lord Castigillian, and an entire seduction and rapture and leaving played out in front of Skade, in the darkling evening in the back of a truck bed.

36

As the sky deepened and the bravest stars began to come out and show themselves, Skade lit a kerosene lantern. "We may as well have some light," she said. "The stars won't be really good for a while yet, and I gotta go pee. Be right back." She hopped over the wall of the truck bed.

Everywhere the roar of insects broke. When she came out of the bathroom, she found a visitor: an enormous yellow and pink moth as big as her hand had landed on her lantern. Carefully she lifted lantern and moth and gingerly carried both back to the truck.

"Kit, check it out," she whispered as she reached the truck.

Kit came over and looked down at the light. Skade ever so gently moved her hand under the moth and lifted it for Kit to look at. She could feel it tremble on her fingertips.

"Wow. That's beautiful," said Kit quietly.

"It's an imperial moth. A male. You can tell by the color. Females are more all-over yellow," Skade said, slowly turning her hand to look closely at its wings.

"It doesn't seem afraid."

"It's probably dying. They don't live very long once they come out of their cocoon. They don't even eat. No mouth."

"What?" said Kit, grimacing.

"Yeah. A lot of moths are like that. Their only job is to mate and lay eggs. This guy probably just did his job. One big fuck, then it's time to die."

Kit snorted a laugh. Skade carefully reached up and placed the moth in her hair, and it clung there firmly.

"Ew! Don't put bugs in your hair!" said Kit.

"Relax. He's beautiful. And he's clean. Given that we're about to sleep in the bed of a truck, we'll probably both have worse than this by morning."

"Gross! Don't say that!"

"Calm down." Skade laughed, climbing back into the truck with her new hair ornament and her lantern. "This guy was attracted to the lights.

Light pollution has created huge areas where moths like these don't exist anymore. We hardly ever get real honest darkness and real night. Especially people who live in cities. There are people who've never seen more than a couple of stars in their lives. People who will have lived and died without seeing the stars. That just kills me."

"We get stars back home," said Kit.

"Yeah. More than people in Chicago do for sure. But have you ever seen the Milky Way?"

"Only the candy bar."

"Just you wait, little girl!" said Skade with a smile. "Just you wait! Tonight, I suspect you'll see something amazing. Once it gets truly dark enough, you'll really see stars for the first time."

"Okay." Kit yawned.

"But obviously, I have to keep you awake long enough," said Skade, and she picked the lantern up and held it up to her chest. "The moth in my hair is related to this guy." She pointed at a tattoo on her chest of a beautiful moth with huge owl-like eye spots under a sliver of a moon and three stars. "This is a cecropia moth, another one of the giant silk moths, like this imperial."

"What's this?" Kit pointed at a simple line tattoo of a large rectangle broken into smaller rectangles with a spiral describing the inside of the breakdown.

"That is the golden ratio. Actually, that's the golden rectangle, but it represents the golden ratio," said Skade. "The golden ratio is math. It's a way of dividing up a line or a figure that shows up in nature and art all the time. Here, like this." Skade pulled out her notebook and drew a pentagon using an index card as a straight edge. Then she drew a pentagram inside her pentagon, joining the five angles in the figure into a perfect five-pointed star.

"Okay, so these lines that make up my star, they are all in the golden ratio. Basically, that means the ratio of the smallest part to the largest part is the same as the largest part to the whole. That's shown as phi." Skade drew the Greek letter next to her drawing.

Kit looked lost.

"The number is 1.6180339887 and on and on. It shows up in geometry a lot, and it seems to be the basis for how nature organizes itself. Flowers and shells and the way trees set out branches and cells and crystals. Even in the stars. Water, DNA, the proportions of most living things. It's an important, almost magical number."

Kit still looked completely confused, and Skade laughed out loud, squeezing Kit's hand. "It's just math, but it's really pretty math. Meaningful math."

"I hated math." Kit grinned.

"I've always loved it."

"And what's this? Did you write this one?" asked Kit, pointing to five lines of poetry on Skade's thigh.

"This? No: *My candle burns at both ends/ It will not last the night;/ But ah, my foes, and oh, my/ friends / It gives a lovely light!* That's Edna St. Vincent Millay. I love that little poem. I love her too."

"And this?" Kit traced a line of words over Skade's knee with her fingertip. The touch felt vibrant.

"Schopenhauer. A German philosopher. That's one of his quotes: *We forfeit three-quarters of ourselves to be like other people.* I have one on my other knee." Skade shifted so Kit could see in the lamplight. "*Every person is born as many people, but dies as a single person.* That's Heidegger notion. Another German philosopher."

Kit delicately traced the outline of a flying fish on Skade's forearm with one of her long fingers. "Does it hurt, getting tattoos?"

"Depends. Stuff like this," she said, pointing to the gray and pink cascade of Chinese fans rolling down the back of her arm, "didn't hurt at all. In fact, once I got used to it, I liked the feeling."

Kit's eyes sparkled and a faint smile traced her lips.

"But this kind of stuff," she pointed to a cascade of ivy that wrapped under her armpit, "hurts like fuck. It depends on where it is on your body and how long you have to sit for it. It gets annoying after a while, and you want to take a break. Feels like a bad sunburn."

"And what about this crazy stuff?" She pointed to a set of ochre figures running around Skade's wrist.

"That is a copy of a set of petroglyphs on a wall in a canyon in Bears Ears in Utah. Probably ancient ancestral Puebloan people made them a couple of thousand years ago. There are a lot of different styles of art in Utah. It gets really hard to date them. And this"—she pointed to an intricate design wrapping around her other wrist—"is called *The Breath of the Compassionate.* It's a pattern from the Maghrib: Algeria and Morocco. Islamic art is a wonderfully complex geometry. This is formed by a base pattern of squares and octagons. You join every third corner of the octagons to form a star in what's called a khatam…"

"How do you know so much?" said Kit in a burst of annoyance and reverence.

"What?"

"How are you so smart, Skade? I mean, you know more than anybody I know. Stars and photography and books and philosophy and art and history and music and math…and everything! How do you know all this stuff?"

Skade stared up at Kit with a slightly bemused smile on her face, unsure of what to say. "Well, I…Hell, Kit, I read a lot as a kid. I still read a lot. I guess I'm compulsively curious. But I am not real smart."

"You know more than anyone I know. The school said you were a genius."

"There's a huge difference between knowing a lot of stuff and being smart."

"How?"

"If I were smart, I wouldn't be where I am. Living in some crappy motel or in the back of my car. Scraping by. There's times, Kit, when I'm maybe the dumbest person you know. It depends on how you look at it. Enough of that, I think it's dark enough now. Let's kill the lantern and see what's going on in the sky." Skade shut off the lantern, and Kit gasped.

Above her, above the truck, above the campground, above the entire world, the night sky had exploded. The sun had passed far enough out of the curve of the earth that there was little residual light, so all the stars in the sky were plainly visible, and the spectacle of the Milky Way was on full display. Kit craned her neck to look up, her mouth agape.

"Yeah. This is good. I thought it would be. You've never seen that, have you?' asked Skade with a grin.

"No," Kit whispered, without taking her eyes off the sky.

"So that's the Milky Way. You can't see it in a lot of the country because of light pollution. But out here, you can."

"What is it?" asked Kit.

"Our galaxy," said Skade. "Think of our galaxy as a Frisbee. It's round and flat. We're not in the center of it, but we aren't on the edge of it either. The Milky Way is us seeing into the Frisbee, sort of looking across it. It's a huge collection of stars that are closer together than they are in the rest of the night sky."

"It's amazing," said Kit quietly.

"Yeah. Come down here by me; you're going to hurt your neck." Skade moved over, creating space in the bed of the truck. The two of them spread out their bedding next to each other and lay back down.

Skade pointed up into the vastness. "It has other names besides Milky Way. It's the Straw Thief's Path or the Straw Road in Africa. It's the Silver River in Vietnam. It's the Heavenly Ganges in India. It's associated with Saint James and Saint Anne. In Scandinavia, where my ancestors are from, it's called the Winter Way. And many cultures call it the Bird's Path or the Way of the Grey Goose."

"It's so beautiful. If feels weird to say this, but it feels like a 3D movie."

"Yeah. You can get that feeling sometimes. That feels great—"

"Look!" shouted Kit, pointing. "Is that a shooting star?"

"Nope. Satellite. You'll know a shooting star when you see one; it will just be a flash and a streak and it will disappear. It won't track continuously across the sky like that…unless it's a really special meteor or something."

"Meteors? We can see meteors?"

"If they show up, we sure will, but they aren't super common. Shooting stars are meteorites that burn up in the atmosphere. Do you know any constellations?"

"The Big Dipper?"

"Yep, that's the one most people know really well. Can you find it?"

Kit scanned the sky for a moment and laughed. "It's hard because there are too many stars. That's crazy." She went on scanning.

"Try over here," said Skade, pointing over to a part of the sky to their right.

Kit shifted her scan. "There?" she said, pointing in the vicinity of where Skade was pointing.

"Yeah, that's it. Ursa Major. And now you can find Polaris, the North Star. Know how?"

"No?"

"Draw a line up from the outside lip of the Big Dipper. Those two stars are Merak and Dubhe. Polaris is in a straight line up from them. Right there." Skade pointed. "Now you can always find the North Star and so now you can never get lost."

Kit shifted a tiny bit closer. "Once you find that, then you can find a bunch of other constellations. Draco is right above Ursa Major, and

Ursa Minor—the little bear—is where Polaris is. Those are called cir-cumpolar because they stay in the sky year-round in the northern hemi-sphere; they circle Polaris, which stays put in the sky, which is why it's a great star to use in navigation." Skade pointed out the constellations.

"The best one, though, is Sagittarius. It's right there; it's pretty com-plicated to trace."

"Why is it the best one?"

"Besides the fact that I'm a Sagittarius, you mean? Well, if we had a telescope, I could show you. Sagittarius sits in a line that goes directly into the heart of the Milky Way. So there's a ton of stuff to see in-side it. There was a French astronomer named Charles Messier in the eighteenth century who created a catalog of important objects in deep space: nebulae and star clusters. There are either 103 or 110, depending on how you define it. Now, of course, we know of thousands more, but those 110 Messier Objects are what most amateur astronomers try to see. Anyway, in Sagittarius, that one constellation, you can find fifteen Messier objects. Over ten percent of the entire list in one spot. So it's really important and beautiful."

"Can you show me one of those Messier things?"

"Not without a telescope, no."

Kit rolled over on her side to look directly at Skade, lying next to her on her back. "You remind me of my sister."

"Why is that?" asked Skade.

"Lots of reasons. But right now it's because she always wanted a telescope. I remember her driving Mom crazy asking for a telescope every birthday and Christmas. It got to be a family joke." Kit breathed deeply for a second, and a sadness passed over her face in the shade and darkness. "She never got one."

They stayed in the bed of the truck looking up at the sky, Skade point-ing out important stars and constellations. Kit got to see her shooting star. Then they fell together into a meditative quiet under the vault of infinity. Kit yawned deeply again.

"Probably ought to try and get some sleep," Skade said to her in a quiet jewel-box voice.

"Gotta pee first," whispered Kit.

"Well go. Take the lantern. Just back up the road that way."

Kit hesitated, looking at Skade.

"You're scared," Skade said.

Kit nodded.

"Okay, you big goofball. I'll go with you. Come on." They walked together up the path toward the wash house, the scent of sweet grass and dirt and night swirling around them. About halfway between the truck and the bathrooms, Kit reached out a tentative hand and took Skade's.

Skade waited in the dark outside, her mind spinning out into the stars and space. Then they walked quietly back to the truck, hand in hand again.

Skade was in a tank top and denim cutoffs, and she was too hot. The night hadn't completely dissipated the heat that had built up over the long day. Kit was still in her flannel shirt.

"Christ, Kit. You cannot be comfortable. Tell me you're not sleeping like that."

Kit smiled, but it was full of fear, her lip trembling slightly in the lantern light.

"Hey, Kit. What's the matter?" asked Skade, touching Kit's sleeve.

Kit buried her head into her knees for a moment, then looked at Skade again. "I need to tell you something. Show you something," she said, unbuttoning her shirt. "But please don't hate me."

Kit's chest and arms from her shoulders to her wrists were covered with scars. Not burn scars or injury scars but cuts. Deep, fierce, deliberate cuts into her flesh.

"Kit," said Skade quietly, "did somebody do this to you?"

"I did it," said Kit quietly, without looking up at Skade. "I do it."

Skade looked again, holding up the lantern to see better while Kit sat with her head down and her hair falling over her face. Kit's upper body and arms were a mass of red tiger stripes, most just a couple of inches long, some healed, and some shockingly fresh. In places, especially on her upper arms, the stripes were cross-hatched, and the epidural damage was frightening. On her chest, the scars and cuts were longer and curved in delicate traces of her ribs. The upper part of her small breasts were covered in small patches of cross-hatched scars.

"Why are you doing this, Kit?"

Kit didn't lift her head. The emotion had drained from her voice. "I don't know. I start getting uncomfortable sometimes, when I'm alone. Like my body isn't right. And my head gets kinda squirrelly and I can't hold thoughts real well…except bad thoughts. Bad memories. I start thinking about how much of a piece of shit I am. And those thoughts won't go away. And I start thinking about doing bad things. And I get this sort of tingly feeling in my neck, down between my shoulders. It heats up, and it starts running up my neck to my head, and I know the headaches are coming. I get real bad headaches sometimes."

Kit paused for a breath.

"I'm really scared. Of the headaches and the bad thoughts and bad feelings and everything. I'm just so…scared…sometimes. Getting out my X-Acto knife makes me calm down. It makes the headaches go away. It makes things slow down, and I can concentrate better. It makes things make more sense."

"It started…I started…when I was eighteen or so. School was over, and my family was all gone, and I didn't really have any friends. It was just me and Mom. And Mom was—" Kit broke into sobs; she pulled her shirt up and covered her chest, clinging to it like a blanket.

"God…" she wept. "I was so lonely and scared. Doing this stuff with the knife…I hate it. It makes me feel so sick and ugly and afraid. But I can't stop doing. I cannot stop it. It's too hard."

Skade scooted over as close to Kit as she could get and put her arm around her, her hand falling on the waxy scar tissue that covered Kit's shoulder.

"Kit…I'm so sorry. I know those feelings you're talking about. I know that place you wind up going to. Thank you for telling me about it. That took so much. That was really, really brave. You are incredibly brave. And, no, I could never hate you. I love you. You're my friend."

Kit let out a strange little sound under her hair.

"Come on, put your shirt back on if you want. You'll probably be more comfortable, right? Was this why you said you didn't want to go swimming with me?"

"Yeah," said Kit from under her emotions.

"Yeah. Well, now I know. So now just you and me, we can go swimming together. We can go where nobody else is if you want, or we can just tell everyone to fuck off and go to the most crowded pool we can find and let everyone stare at us. You're beautiful. Now come here and lie down with me."

And Kit lay down next to Skade in the bed of the truck and looked up at the stars through her tear-filled eyes. Skade pulled her close and whispered to her. And they looked into the never-ending above them and at some point, the stars began to fall on all the damage done.

37

They woke up when the sun became insistent on their presence and began the trip home.

"You should work up a few things to show the people in New York," said Skade.

"Yeah. I'm not sure what though. It's hard to think about."

"But you have to. It's important. Not a lot, maybe just a couple of puppets, and don't expect to show them everything you bring. Expect minimal, hope maximal."

"Thinking about it still makes me want to barf. I'm not sure I can go to New York."

"Yes, Kit," said Skade, putting her hand on Kit's shoulder. "Yes, you can. You should and you will. Don't worry. I'm going with you, remember? You can always tell them you'll think it over, and you can always say no… Hell, you don't even have an offer yet. Let's not get ahead of ourselves here." She laughed.

Skade continued to dance the dance of assuaging Kit's fears and stroking her self-esteem for the next four hundred miles.

They said their goodbyes in the Skyline parking lot. It was well past dark and both of them were washed out by road fatigue. Skade watched Kit drive away, then took a long, slow walk in the residual heat to stretch her legs.

She noticed a few new cars in the lot, and car smells—oil, antifreeze, exhaust—seeped out of the pavement under her feet. On top of the industrial aroma, she could smell the green smells of cut grass and weeds and the sumac on the hillside. The whine of cars and trucks on the bypass mixed with the incessant buzzing of the security lights and the intermittent electric not-quite-animal sound of a nighthawk hunting insects.

She thought about Kit. And then tried to squeeze between the noise and the pieces of the stonewall in her mind to think about her book. That thing she couldn't quite grasp was still missing. And she thought about Kit again, and it began to quiet in her mind. Maybe she'd found something rare that had been missing in her world for the last twelve years. Maybe for all her years.

Her relationships had been mostly edgy, transactional affairs at the best of times, and emotional versions of capture the flag played with knives and clubs at the worst of times. Friends, if she even knew what that meant, were arms-length and need-to-know only. But now the armor might be coming down.

She noticed a large sign on the fence surrounding the pool. *Closed for cleaning and repairs. Sorry for the inconvenience.* The pool was now an empty cement hole in the ground that smelled simultaneously of chlorine and mildew.

"Shit," said Skade under her breath. She thought about the pool at the apartment complex, and the Kensington Aquatic Center, and her old dead pool sitting in the dark, and the lake.

The road.

Christ. Mike.

The thought of the lake and the accident and Mike took her by surprise, and she felt her stomach tighten and her mind race. She needed a drink.

Skade turned on her heels and jogged over to her room and wrestled the key into the lock. The meager light that spilled in ahead of her revealed half a bottle of vodka on the table by her bed. Half-empty bottles were a rarity. They tended to go from full to dry quickly and without pause. She opened it and began taking long-suffering pulls from it as she shed her clothes and fought her way to the shower. She'd need to get more vodka, but this would do until she felt clean again.

She pulled a pair of jeans from the neat stack in her laundry basket, yanked on a T-shirt, and grabbed her keys to head out to the drugstore for more to drink. When she looked down at her phone, she had a voicemail from Kit—and she sounded terrified.

Skade rushed to her Jeep and tore off toward Kit's house. Someone had broken into her house while they'd been starwatching in Nebraska.

All the lights were blazing inside Kit's house when Skade got there. She came through the front door without knocking.

"Kit?" she called, looking around. Kit came rushing in from the back of the house and ran to Skade, grabbing her in a trembling hug. Skade guided her to the couch and sat holding her.

"What happened?"

"I don't know. Somebody broke in..." Kit was beside herself.

"Take a deep breath. Calm down. Tell me what happened when you got home."

Kit sat quietly and breathed deeply, her eyes closed.

"I came home after I dropped you off," Kit said in a small quavering voice. "The side door from the garage to the kitchen was open."

"Wide open?"

"No, just a little bit open. But I locked it before we left."

"Is anything missing? Is anything damaged?"

"Some stuff has been moved around, knocked over. In the kitchen and in the den. The den was stirred up. My room was messed with too." Kit's breath hitched, and she began to cry. "I can't find Janeyre."

"Anything else? Do you have anything valuable here? Computer? TV? Any cash or jewelry or anything like that? Guns?"

Kit shook her head. "No, nothing at all. I have a couple of puppets that are valuable, but they're still here. Janeyre isn't worth anything. Wait—"Kit jumped up, wiping her eyes as she dashed off and came back with an antique black silk purse.

"I had some cash in here," she said, opening it to reveal a roll of money. "It's still here."

"It must have been some stupid kids or something," said Skade putting her arm around Kit. "I'm glad it's not worse. You should call the police right now."

Two officers showed up soon thereafter and asked a lot of questions and took a lot of notes. If they were taken aback by the strangeness of Kit's house, they didn't show it. They seemed to take all the puppets in stride.

While Kit led the two officers through the property, Skade stayed out of the way and looked to see if she could notice anything. Puppets were on the floor, which was unusual. Kit's puppets had always been set up on tables or shelves or hanging, but never on the floor. Pillows had been tossed around and chairs moved. Everything looked handled by someone else. How awful and violated that must make Kit feel, Skade realized, given how deeply her house was her sanctuary.

The cops left, promising to let Kit know if anything turned up. They agreed with Skade that since nothing of any real value was taken and no real appreciable damage was done, it was probably some kids, and that Kit ought to look into getting a security system.

"You okay?" asked Skade as they watched the police drive away.

"I'm worried about Janeyre," said Kit quietly as she chewed her nails. "I want her back."

"Don't bite your nails. I bet the cops find her. Give them a couple of days. Janeyre kinda stands out. Someone will see something and report it."

"I hope so."

"But are you okay?"

"I guess so."

"You okay being alone here?"

Kit didn't respond but started picking up puppets that had been misplaced or moved.

"Kit?" asked Skade.

"I don't know," said Kit, without looking at her.

Skade put a hand on Kit's arm. "Hey, want me to come stay for a while? Would that make you feel better?"

Kit looked at Skade and smiled a little, then looked away. "Yeah."

Skade squeezed Kit's arm. "Okay, let me run back to my place and grab some stuff. I'll be back. Are you going to be okay here, or do you want to come with me?"

"I think I'll be okay," said Kit in a small voice. "Hurry."

"I will." Skade bolted out the door.

She gathered up her writing and her cameras and enough clothes for a couple of days and her stuff from the bathroom. She wanted to call Kit to see if she needed anything from the store, but she'd left her phone in her car in the rush. When she found it she had another voicemail. It was Lane.

38

Skade looked at the voicemail notification. Lane was the last person she wanted to have anything to do with right now, but maybe he'd found her camera and her bag. She pressed the play button and listened:

> Hey, Skade. Listen, I was a piece of shit for what happened. That never should have occurred, and it's my fault. And I'm incredibly sorry. You probably don't want to talk to me, and I couldn't blame you. But I did find your camera and your bag.
>
> I'd like to have the chance to apologize to you in person and give you back your stuff, so you can make sure it's all there. Gimme a call and let me know if you want to come meet me at the studio or something.

She angrily shoved her phone in her pocket. On the way back to Kit's she pulled into a liquor store.

❧

Kit had changed her sheets and made up a bed for Skade on the couch; now she was in the living room, absently chewing her nails and looking at a row of puppets—all sitting shoulder to shoulder like obedient schoolchildren waiting for the teacher to begin a lesson.

"Quit biting your nails," said Skade, dropping her bags next to the couch.

"I'm trying to decide what puppets to take to New York."

Skade took her bag from the liquor store and dug out her bathroom kit and headed back to the bathroom. She stood over the sink and poured a strong drink into a plastic cup. She wandered back into the living room. Kit had lined up ten puppets on the table.

"My advice?" said Skade, settling down on the couch. "That's way too many. I've never done anything with puppets, but when I've shown my photographs to people like this, I usually don't have a lot of time for a big show. I would winnow that down to maybe four or five and expect to not even be able to show all of them."

Kit made a face and reflexively started chewing her nails again as she stared back at the table with a worried look.

"Quit biting your nails," said Skade.

Skade tried to nurse her drink slowly. Kit needed her. A part of her was seriously upset with herself for drinking at all right now—a surprisingly large part, which felt different. But her mind kept being pulled back to Lane and his voicemail.

"I'm worried about Janeyre," said Kit, without turning around. "I wish she was here."

"I know. Like I said, I'm sure she'll turn up. She's not the kind of thing somebody could easily sell or get rid of. Someone is going to notice her, and the cops will find out. Don't worry, you'll get her back."

Kit was down to six puppets now and seemed to be deciding between a comical-looking turtle with a top hat and big eyes and a thin, faceless woman draped in a collection of gray and white gauzy veils. Skade's thoughts shifted back to Lane and her camera and bag like a fly caught behind her eyes.

"Hey, Kit. I need to go out and make a quick phone call," said Skade, standing up. The abrupt motion made her head swim. The drink was hitting unexpectedly hard. "Remember, you're going to talk to people who specialize in kids' shows. I'd go with the turtle over the ghost if that's what you're trying to decide between."

"She's not a ghost," said Kit as she turned to watch Skade slip out the front door.

Skade walked out to the end of Kit's driveway and stood looking up at a streetlight. An endless cloud of insects swarmed and dove in and out in the glow. The heat had a presence like the spirits of the dead. She looked in the other direction and saw the lights of farm machinery in the field across the road. The sounds of insects and frogs came from everywhere. It was getting harder to focus on her thoughts. She finished her drink, her anger building. She stood and quietly raged by the side of the road in the hot darkness. She pulled up Lane's voicemail again.

She typed out two long texts, then deleted both before sending. The wave of anger crashed and subsided as she did so, and she began feeling weaker and smaller and less well. Finally, she settled on:

I'll come by the studio and get my stuff tomorrow afternoon

She sent it and stared at the screen. Then she typed a new message:

Thanks for finding it

She sent that, too, then turned off her phone and shoved it back into her pocket. Almost instantly, she felt a different tide rising inside her. Her mouth began to water uncontrollably, and she felt her jaw and throat hitch. She was going to be sick. Right now. She barely had time to drop to the side of the drainage ditch that ran alongside the road before she started retching. Her insides kept contracting and she began to feel the acidity in her throat. Her eyes watered and a headache broke loose at her temples, and she threw up again.

She felt a gentle touch on her back and someone gathered up her hair and held it back behind her. She endured two more sets of vomiting contractions and coughed for a moment, then felt slightly better. She sat down on her knees in the grass beside the road and looked up, wiping her mouth with the back of her arm. Kit was kneeling next to her in the dark. She looked sad and worried.

"Thanks," Skade managed, sounding stronger than she felt.

"You okay?" asked Kit.

"Yeah, I think I am now. Sorry." Skade stood up, trying to pull off okay. "I haven't eaten a lot lately, and all the stress of everything finally caught me, I guess."

"Let's go back inside if you feel like it," said Kit, taking her arm. "It reeks out here."

"I grabbed something to drink before I came back," Skade admitted as they made their way back to the house. "I needed to steady my nerves. I guess that was a mistake."

"Yeah," said Kit. "I guess."

Skade sat wearily back down on the couch. "Listen, Kit. Something bad happened with that guy Lane who works at that tattoo shop. That whole thing sort of got to me. Sorry for my bad display out there. Between that and everything that happened to you and the nerves and the not eating, I probably shouldn't have had anything to drink. Sorry. But I'm better now." Kit still looked sad and worried. "I'm okay, Kit."

"Okay," Kit said and smiled.

Kit started sorting through her puppets again; she'd narrowed them down to five—a hedgehog with a bow tie; a ballerina with a pink tutu; a long-legged frog marionette; a tall soldier in a red jacket with a cat's head; and the faceless woman in the veils. Kit seemed agitated and over-busy.

"Hey, Kit," said Skade, standing up and taking her arm. She managed to hold Kit's eyes with hers. "I'm sorry I've made you worried. Please don't be. I'm okay and we're going to be okay. I won't let you down."

Several things seemed to be moving around behind Kit's eyes, like animals sheltering within the shade of a forest. But Skade felt her soften, and Kit relaxed into a smile.

"I'm going to go wash up." Skade went back toward the bathroom. "Don't start biting your nails while I'm gone."

Skade took a long while in the bathroom, getting a better grip on herself, and willing the swimmy rush of the alcohol out of her brain as best she could. When she came out, she found Kit sitting on the chair, wearing a faded blue XXL T-shirt from a radio station in Louisiana and a pair of gray cotton athletic shorts as pajamas. Her arms were bare for the first time since Skade had met her and the scars were ugly and vivid. Kit shifted nervously in her seat, looking more vulnerable and uncomfortable than she usually did, pulling up her legs, then stretching them out in front of her and crossing and uncrossing her arms and glancing around. Skade realized that the T-shirt was an effort and a gift she was offering up.

Skade sat near Kit on the couch-turned-bed. "Hey," she said, "don't be uncomfortable. You look fine. Thanks for relaxing. That has to feel a little better, right?"

"A little," said Kit with a weak smile, her hair falling across her face.

"Yeah. One less thing you gotta worry about. We're only as sick as the secrets we keep. One less secret, and one less burden you have to carry. You don't have to hide from me anymore. But don't you ever pick up a knife to yourself in my presence. Or out of my presence, Kit. Don't. I'm dead serious. If you cut yourself, you're cutting me. And I'll come find you and kick your ass. I don't care if you're bigger than me. I'll still kick your ass." Skade reached up and brushed the hair out of Kit's face. "And thanks for holding my hair out there. That's how you know who your friends are. If they hold your hair while you're puking in a drainage ditch by the side of the road. Thanks."

Kit snorted. "Yeah, well," she mumbled, "don't start puking in ditches like that anymore, or I'll come find you and kick your ass, Skade. Remember, I am bigger than you. Take better care of yourself. I don't have a lot of friends."

"I know. I don't either," said Skade and held Kit's hand. "Tomorrow I need to go get my camera and the rest of my shit from Lane, then I need to put the last bow on my manuscript, and we can get ready to head east."

39

At four thirty the next afternoon Skade parked her car a block from Lane's studio. The sun was shining brightly but there was no movement in the air. A strange sense of anticipation waited on everything, as though a misplaced cough could send the world into an avalanche.

The studio was nice and cool compared to the grimy heat of the street. A young woman with long lavender-colored hair was lounging at the counter. She regarded Skade with a slightly haughty, unfriendly look. Lane's voice came up from the back of the studio: "Hey, Andrea. You wanna take a break for about twenty minutes? Maybe go across to the Pins and Needles and grab a beer?"

The young woman slid off the stool behind the counter with an attitude like she was being asked to go clean the toilets. "Sure," she said in a dark voice.

"And grab a couple of Old Milwaukees to bring back, would you? Take some cash from the drawer," said Lane, coming into the light of the waiting area.

Andrea popped open the cash drawer and took a twenty. She slunk out the door and Skade felt the rush of the hot air flow in and then cut off as the door closed behind her.

"She seems nice," said Skade.

"She's young and insecure. It's a defense mechanism. She thinks she's supposed to act like that. Give her a few years. She might make it all the way to tolerable." Lane smiled, trying to break the tension.

Skade didn't return the smile. She stood with her arms wrapped around her body.

"Hey, listen," began Lane. "I meant what I said. I understand I was a piece of shit—"

"Worse," interrupted Skade before Lane could say any more. "Way worse. I would call the fucking cops on you if I thought they'd do anything. Or if I thought it would make a damn difference to you or the universe."

"I get that. I'm sorry," he said, and they let that sit in the air for a while.

Skade rolled her shoulders back and took a deep breath. "You got my camera?" She felt fatigue and resignation beginning to take the place of hatred and vitriol.

"Yeah," said Lane, clearly relieved for the change of subject. "Hang on. I'll go grab it." He disappeared into the back and returned holding Skade's bag.

Skade rifled through it—everything seemed to be there. Her camera, her notebooks, some camera gear, all present and accounted for. Skade powered up her camera and checked the files. All the images were there.

"Where'd you find it?"

"Your camera was in the back of my car. Your bag wasn't there. I took a chance and went back to a convenience store we'd stopped at because you needed the bathroom. You'd left it there and they had it behind the counter."

That was more than she expected from Lane, but she wasn't giving him any brownie points for it. "Thanks."

"I wanted to tell you that I'm leaving. I mean, I'm leaving town."

"Really?"

"Yeah," he said, letting her hostility wash by. "It came together the day before yesterday. I've committed. I've told my landlord. I started packing. I'll be gone by the start of next week."

"Well, I guess I should say good luck."

"You don't have to say anything, Skade. I get it. But listen, before I go... Let me finish that piece on your arm. If nothing else, as some offering of respect to you."

Skade stared at him and started to seethe again. "That's a funny word coming from you."

"Yeah, I know. That's why I wanted to say it, and to do that. Finish that piece, I mean. It wouldn't surprise me if you decide to have it covered up. But at least let me put top effort into finishing it first. A gesture. I'm sorry. And you and I both hate leaving something like that unfinished. Maybe finishing that piece is a fitting end to everything."

Skade stared at him, then squeezed her eyes shut in frustration. "I'm not sitting in your fucking chair for more than half an hour, Lane. You've done enough damage to me. Can you do it in thirty minutes?"

"Yeah. We can do it right now, then you can tell me to fuck off or whatever you want, and we're done with no loose ends."

"Then let's go." Skade brushed past him back to the studio.

Skade settled into the chair, her camera resting in her lap; having it made her feel a little safer and more grounded. Lane began working quietly and quickly.

"So, it must be weird hanging out with somebody with that kind of story," he said after a little while.

"What?"

"That girl you're hanging with. I mean she's crazy enough, right? Nine feet tall and so strange and everything? But her story? Man—"

"What do you mean *her story*?"

"She's like some weird local celebrity."

"What the hell are you talking about?"

"Wait." Lane stopped his work and smiled. "You don't know who she is?"

"I know who she is. She's my friend and she's the nicest and most talented person I've run into in a very long time. What more is there to it?"

"You really don't know? I mean, I guess it makes sense. I probably wouldn't talk much about that sort of thing myself, right?"

"Lane, fuck off. What are you trying to say?"

Lane started up the needles again and got back to work. "Now that I think about it, all this might have gone down after you ran off. There was a girl who got killed that summer. Out by the lake. Do you remember that?"

Skade's insides tensed up. She didn't answer.

"Hit and run on Fairfax," continued Lane as he finished up. He wiped down Skade's arm and wrapped it in a bandage and cling-wrap. "Turns out, Mike hit her. He took off right about the same time you did, and no one could figure out why. Something about the army? Some people thought you guys went together, actually. But then Mike showed up a couple of years later and confessed to the whole thing. He'd hit the girl and run away rather than go to jail. And then Mike killed himself. It really had eaten at him for a while, I guess. Did you know that?"

Skade couldn't breathe.

"Her name was Chastity Wilkes. That girl you're hanging with is Kitten Dyer, right? That's Chastity's little sister. Different fathers, maybe? Different names, but that's her sister."

Skade convulsed out of the chair and wheeled on Lane. Her camera flew out of her lap and hit the polished concrete and exploded. The lens shattered and glass sprayed out into a glittering fan. Parts skittering across the floor. She stood in shock, looking at Lane.

"What?" A smile played around his lips.

It took her a moment to find her words. "You knew? You knew who she was the whole time and didn't say anything?"

"What are you talking about?" he asked. He wasn't even trying to hide it now..

"You know," said Skade, on the verge of hyperventilating in a panic attack.

"Know what? Is there some secret, Skade?"

Skade grabbed the largest piece of her destroyed and shattered camera and her bag and she ran from the studio into the excruciating light of the sun.

40

She had no idea how long she'd been driving, or how fast. She'd been traveling in a direction that wasn't on any compass. She pulled off to the side of the road and tried to calm herself. Eventually she managed to get one thought in front of the other, her hands clutching the steering wheel in a death grip.

Lane knew.

Skade climbed out of the car. The sun had started to sink in the sky, casting cattails and reeds in a bright orange hue. Fireflies rose from the understory. She lifted her head and felt the wind flitting past her. A whistling note to her left drew her attention; the wind had turned the reeds and willows along the creek bed into an aeolian harp. She felt hollow and the wind pushed her easily back to her car as it became night.

Skade sat in her car in the growing darkness, feeling as if her body had begun to atomize into the velvet black. She wrapped her mind in a coarse wool burial shroud and succumbed to the long, engaging silence of the dead and to her own tears.

Skade surfaced. Kit. Something needed to be done. Instinctively she went back to the Skyline. Lane might be lying, but it felt like the truth. The walls of the motel room began to converge on her. She couldn't stay in her room. She needed to find Kit. She grabbed her keys again.

As she walked out the door again, someone grabbed her by her wrist and whirled her around. Lane's face was all shadows and deep wells of dark, a backpack slung across one shoulder.

Skade shouted a curse at him and tried to rip her hand from his grasp, but he held harder, twisting his grip until a sharp pain shot up Skade's arm and she stifled a shriek.

"Hold still," he growled. "I've got some things for you. Before you disappear again."

"You knew?" she demanded. "You knew this entire time? Before I got here? And you didn't say anything?" The pain had quelled her rage for a moment, bringing fear and shock in its wake.

Lane laughed. "Of course I knew, Skade. Dear god, for someone who's supposed to be a fucking genius, you can be such a moron. You think you and Mike killing some girl was going to go unknown forever? Especially after you vanish suddenly into thin air? Fuck, Mike told."

Skade felt like she'd been slapped.

"Don't give me that dumb look. He was almost as big a drunk as you are. He ran his mouth to a couple of those morons he hung out with when he came back. There's about fifty people that know now, probably eight or ten still in town. I'm just the only one you know."

"And you didn't tell me?" Skade whispered, horrified.

"Fuck no. I wanted to watch. I should have bought popcorn. You show up in classic portfolio ink, better than ever, standing on the edge of an alcoholic junkie collapse, and I get to watch. And to put a cherry on top, you accidentally cozy up to your victim's little sister. Anyway, before you slink off to whatever drunken hole you're running for, I need to give you some parting gifts." From his backpack, Lane pulled out a small jar filled with gray powder. "I've actually already given you one. That thing on your arm? Take a quick look."

Skade looked at her arm in the dim light coming from the open door of her motel room. Puss in Boots now had a long silver rope in his clenched hand. The rope coiled into a knot under his feet, with the words *Always Remember.*

"See that rope in his hand? That's a forget-me-knot. That rope was done with some very special ink." Lane shook the baby food jar at her. "This," he continued, "is Chastity Wilkes."

Skade was paralyzed by what he was saying now.

"See, I'm an idiot and always have been when it came to you. I thought right up to the moment you had your little rage-fit at my place that we could be together again, Skade. I really wanted that. But then, well, after you told me about my tattoo and what it meant, I needed to get even. After you hit me with your little number about the ink on my chest, and then took off for parts unknown with your new pal, I went to Kit's house and borrowed some of her sister. You probably didn't even bother to read that story about me in the magazine, did you? I got highlighted for memorial tattoos. Mixing crematory ashes with the ink base to make special memorial tattoos for the bereaved. That's what you've got there, Skade. A little memorial and a little bit of Chastity Wilkes inside you. Forever. You can cover it if you want. But that ink is always going to be there. Always. And you won't forget that, I'm sure."

Skade felt her consciousness thinning. Blood pounded in her ears, and she felt her equilibrium shift. She fell back against the wall of the motel and sank heavily to the ground. She was unable to speak or take her eyes off Lane.

"So here," said Lane, tossing the baby food jar in Skade's lap. "Give Kit back her sister. I didn't need much. And I've got this too." Lane reached inside his backpack and pulled out Janeyre. "I took this creepy thing, just in case you called bullshit on my story about the ink. It's real. You can see I was there. You can give this back to her with her sister. Or you can do what I know you're going to do. Run away. Whatever, Skade. I don't care. And if you get the idea to come after me with the cops, I'll just deny it all and say you probably concocted the whole story to get back at me for a mistaken sexual encounter you were pissed about."

Lane walked away into the darkness of the parking lot, got in his car, and drove away.

Shaking uncontrollably, Skade crawled to the edge of the lot and vomited in the weeds by the fence, then sat back on her heels, coughing and crying. Overhead the stars came out. It was going to be a lovely night.

41

Her mind had locked her out and it was slipping little notes of nonsense under the doorjamb. Skade reached for Janeyre, who had fallen face down on the concrete; then she searched for the jar. She could barely pick it up. Her hand refused to grasp it.

She stuffed the puppet and the jar into her bag that Lane had discarded and stumbled back inside her room. She grabbed her shoebox and her keys. She recognized her Jeep after a moment of staring at it dumbly. She got inside, somehow. Turned the ignition, somehow. Drove away, somehow.

She watched herself drive to the Kensington Aquatic Center, get out of the Jeep with her box and her bag, and move with real intention; she watched herself melt into the darkness of the trees, skirting around the fence surrounding the old pool, and enter through the break behind the signboard.

Once she was on the pool deck her movements slowed again. She slipped into the empty blue shell and slowly drifted down the slope into the darkness of the deep end, where no light reached.

Sliding to the floor of the pool, she reached into her bag and pulled out Janeyre, breathing in the puppet's scent. Kit was there. There was a slightly acrid note that she assigned to Lane, but it was mostly Kit. She watched her hands caress the puppet. A single long tear rolled down her face.

She set Janeyre down gently, then reached back into the bag and pulled out a bottle of vodka, resting it gently against her thigh. Then she pulled the broken pieces of her beloved camera out of the bag—it had served as her eyes, her voice, her thoughts, her companion, her shield and armor.

A peal of thunder.

Next she brought out the cornhusk puppet that Kit had given her, partly unraveled now, one leg frayed to threads. She felt her muscles tense and watched in horror as she slowly crushed the cornhusk puppet and tossed it into the blackness.

She pulled the small jar of ashes from inside her bag. The tiny jar was too heavy. It weighed as much as a girl lying dead and bleeding in her hands. She dropped it as if it had scorched her.

Then, lastly, the amber pill bottle, the one Lane had given her, half full of fentanyl.

For Skade, being in her own head was like being trapped inside a dark slaughterhouse, bumping blindly into the bloody carcasses of memories. She went quiet, her mind still like February's horses, and lay down and waited for it all to end.

Gathering the shoebox of silk and joy and horror, and Janeyre, and the useless Odradek of her camera, and the jar of dead girl, and the vodka, and the bottle of pills, Skade made a neat little stack of it all. This was the answer to everything. This little pile in front of her on the bottom of a soon-to-be-demolished pool was the final answer to the ultimate question—Who am I? What is the meaning of it all? Is there a plan? All of it was answered by this small pile of grief and shame and lies and faulty memory. The facts were all here, and now it all made sense. She popped open the pill bottle, poured a handful of pills into her palm, and dropped them into her mouth. She opened the vodka and washed the bitterness down.

And closed her eyes.

And opened her eyes.

And crawled over to the remains of the cornhusk puppet she'd tossed into the dark to add it to her final act.

And it started to rain.

42

Kit listened to a far-off siren. Police or an ambulance? Maybe a fire truck? Why did it always seem like there were sirens every time it started raining? The thunder and lightning hadn't been too bad this time, and now there was just rain—a soft summer rain like cubs following along behind their ferocious thunderstorm mother.

A tired fan swung a slow lazy arc in the corner of the kitchen and Kit sat back down to her sewing. She was working on a new puppet and was almost finished. It was a chimera—the body of a human woman covered in dark sable fur and topped with rabbit's ears that lay flat against her head. Thickly lashed green eyes provided a provocative expression. She was strong, confident, and alert. And she had wings.

The wings had taken Kit considerable time to get right; they were beautiful and intricate and dark as a raven's. She'd worked out a complicated articulation system inside the puppet that allowed the rabbit to open and close and rotate her wings just like a bird. Kit was especially happy with the wing-motion, which carried a lot of emotion with it. The puppet was dressed in a pair of loose green pants with a leather belt, and Kit was finishing her midnight-blue short-sleeved tailored shirt.

Another siren sounded from farther away—unmistakably an ambulance.

Kit pulled the final stitches on the rabbit's shirt and carefully fit it onto the body. She looked deeply into the rabbit's face and frowned. Something wasn't quite the way it should be. She used a seam ripper to open up some stiches on either side of the rabbit's face and carefully went back to work with her long fingers to restitch the expression. Finally, she got it right. Provocative still, but now kinder and wiser.

She stood the rabbit up on the table with a puppet stand and carefully articulated her wings to open in an expression of power. It was pure Skade. Kit hoped she'd get away with this one; she wasn't Wonder Woman—this puppet was a little more personal. Maybe she could hide it and Skade wouldn't see. Or maybe she wouldn't notice. Kit smiled.

But something else wasn't right. Something deeper. Kit had assembled her puppets for New York and had been working on preparing for the interview. She was nervous about everything and had been feeling particularly small lately. But this feeling she had now was something else. There was something wrong with the night. Something was off in her heart, and she couldn't explain it. Something was coming.

She heard a knock at her door.

43

This was going to be the worst part of the worst time. The door that opened on the other end of the tunnel through hell was filled with light, and Kit stood on the threshold.

Skade was an open wound on Kit's doorstep. She was soaking wet, battered, and defeated. She felt worse—far, far worse—than she looked. She clutched her bag to her chest with both arms and she couldn't bring herself to look Kit in the eyes.

"Skade?" said Kit. "You look terrible." Kit stepped out of the doorway. Skade came no further than the threshold. "What happened? Did you get your stuff?"

Skade pried the bag from her chest and reached inside. She pulled out Janeyre and held her out to Kit. She was wet too.

"Oh god! You found her!" Kit was overjoyed. "Where did you find her?"

Skade could not speak and was unable to meet Kit's eyes. She gathered her bag back up against her chest and squeezed it harder.

Kit inspected Janeyre closely. As soon as she slipped her hand inside the puppet's mechanism, Janeyre reached out and wrapped her arms around Kit's neck and clung there. Kit looked up again at Skade.

"Skade, tell me what happened."

"Who was your sister?" A broken voice.

"What?"

Skade finally managed to look up to Kit's face. "I don't know how to do this."

Getting from the bottom of the empty swimming pool to Kit's door had been the hardest thing Skade had ever done. A large part of her didn't want to be here. Some of her wanted to go back and try death again. Another part of her wanted to find a convenient lie and run. But now a part of her she'd never really met before, or couldn't remember, was holding her to a task she had no concept of how to complete.

Kit and Janeyre went into the dark living room. Kit sat down and looked at Skade. "Come and sit down and tell me what's going on."

"I'm not..." She stood frozen to her spot.

"Skade, you're starting to scare me. Come and sit down."

Skade looked up at Kit for a brief moment, then slid to her knees on the worn carpet next to the coffee table. "Who was your sister?" she asked again.

"Her name was Chastity. She hated that name." Kit laughed at the memory. "We all called her Chass. She got hit by a car when we lived in Decker. She was just a girl. Where did you find Janeyre?"

There was a gigantic knot inside Skade's head, and she had no idea how to untie it or even where to begin. But she did. With shaking hands, she pulled her bag open and took out her shoebox and her broken camera and placed them on the floor between her and Kit. She pulled the vodka bottle out and put it next to the box. Last, she pulled out the baby food jar and the crumpled cornhusk puppet.

"This pile of crap is me," Skade said. "This is the best, deepest, most perfect image of me that exists. Right here on your floor. It's better than any picture." She paused for a moment. "There was this time, once—when everything was okay." Skade took a ragged breath. "Things were beginning to work out in their broken, fucked-up ways. I was sort of happy. I had gotten into the colleges I really wanted to get into. Really good schools. I was going to be free of my horrible father. It was going to be good." Skade scowled, then hit herself hard on her forehead with her fist.

"Skade!" shouted Kit and she came half off the couch toward her.

"No!" shouted Skade back at her. "No! That's not it. This isn't some poor-little-sad-gifted-girl bullshit. No way. I'm just an alcoholic, Kit. I'm no better than that. I'm just a waste. That's all I've really ever been. Useless, afraid and pathetic. I was then too."

"Stop it."

"So don't pity me or feel bad for me at all. I fucking don't deserve a moment of it. I've run away from everything in my life. I don't deserve any of it. I tried to run away twice tonight. Same old, same old. I tried to run away first by killing myself." Skade dug into her bag angrily and pulled out the pill bottle. "I took about a dozen of these in one gulp. Enough to kill half the people in this godforsaken town." She tossed the bottle into a corner.

Kit's face went pale. "Skade...no..."

"Yeah. Right after I did it, I changed my mind. I guess. I'm not sure what happened. For whatever reason I stuck my fingers down my throat and puked the whole thing up. Ran away from that too. Then I started over here and for all the world I wanted to just turn my car around and run as far away as I could. Leave town, leave the country. Leave the planet if I could figure out a way. I think I was just too tired. It takes a lot of energy to be that cowardly. So, here I am. Just me and my shame and disgrace."

Kit was crying now. "Skade?"

Skade looked up at her.

"I killed your sister, Kit."

They sat in an electric silence for a long time. All the puppets around the room sat very still, listening for the sound of their own heartbeats.

"No, you didn't," said Kit finally. "Some guy did it. He confessed."

"Yeah," said Skade. "Mike Curtis. I guess you could say Mike was my boyfriend at that moment."

"But he was alone—"

"No, he wasn't." The silence rushed in again like the tide coming into a stormy bay.

"Twelve years ago. April 27th. The hottest spring anyone could remember," began Skade quietly. "There was a big party out at Lake St. Vincent. Not that anybody needed a reason for a party—at least the people I hung out with—but some of us had gotten our acceptance letters for school, and pretty much everyone was feeling the chance for something new to happen. So there was this big party. Mike and I were there. I was high—we were both high. Totally. And just stupid drunk too. Like I told you, Kit, I've always just been a pathetic useless alcoholic, probably. I just never realized it before now. Anyway, we both had to leave the party early. It was only really getting started, but Mike and I both had to go to work the next morning, so we left at right about eleven."

Kit sat silently; her face had the vacancy of fluorescent lights on a subway platform.

"We were coming back on Fairfax. Both of us were wasted, but Mike was doing okay with the driving. Except for me. I was trying to get into his lap and stuff. I had no idea what I was doing, except I was trying to get attention, I guess.

"We hit something. At first I thought it was a trash can or a deer." Skade hitched and pain ran through her body.

"Mike stopped the car, and we got out and looked but we didn't see anything. There was nothing in the road at all. Everything was so quiet. I remember how strange the quiet felt. We were heading back to the car when I saw her lying in the ditch by the side of the road."

Kit put her head down toward her knees.

"I climbed down into the weeds and lifted her out, both of us covered in blood. I needed to get her onto some kind of stable level surface. I started CPR. Mike kept screaming that we needed to get out of there before someone came by, that your sister was dead and we needed to run. We were going to wind up in jail.

"I don't know how long I sat with her. How long I spent trying to resuscitate her. Mike threatened to leave me there. Finally…" Skade felt herself contract inside.

"I remember walking back toward the car. All the blood. Mike said we had to hide her. Get her off the road. He said we needed to buy ourselves some time. But he wouldn't touch her." Skade stopped again. Kit was still.

"I picked her up and carried her into the field, and we buried her. Mike had a plan. We were going to grab as much money as we could and meet up in an hour and we'd run together. Mexico or something. I can't really remember. But I couldn't. There are not words in any language to describe what I felt. I packed a bag, got in my car, and left. Alone. That's how I ran away twelve years ago. That's why I left. I've wanted to die every day since that happened. I've never tried until tonight. God, I wish it had worked. I didn't know Mike had come back and confessed. I don't know why he lied about it. I was there. I was screwing around in the car. It's as much my fault as it was his. More, probably."

Another long blast of silence. The puppets decided to play the game of being someone else, to keep each other company forever.

Then Kit silently rose to her full height, hair hanging over her face. She stood for a moment, neither looking at anything nor saying a word. The only thing that moved were her hands. She clutched Janeyre in both hands and they began to work in a dancing caress over the puppet, a sort of intimate communication that got faster and more frantic with each moment. Then, suddenly, Kit threw Janeyre with shocking violence against the wall where Skade knelt. Janeyre shattered into several pieces. Skade flinched. Kit turned silently and disappeared into the back of the house.

Skade sat stunned. The scattered pieces of the broken puppet rooted her to the floor. She could barely breathe. She coughed finally, and gagged, and scrambled to her feet, trying to escape the circle of tiny carnage of which she was the center. She staggered toward the door, avoiding stepping on a little arm.

"Wait."

Kit stood in the doorway, holding a new puppet.

"We used to live down in Decker," Kit began. "It's a little nothing town down near the lake. Mom was born there, and she grew up there. That's where I was born too. Fairfax Road cuts right through the edge of it." Kit looked at her hands, as if she were surprised by their presence, and she paused for a moment more.

"Eddie died eight days before. Well, really, I think he died a couple of weeks before, but we got word he'd died eight days before. It's funny how that works, isn't it? It's not actually when they die, it's when you find out.

"I was in our bedroom, and it was late. I was in the bedroom because Mom was getting up again. That's what Chass used to call it: *Mom's getting up again.* She'd start out by crying, a soft crying. Soft crying was good. I used to get a crocheted afghan and the pink pillow, and I'd wrap up with Mom while she cried. It was like watching it rain in spring. I felt like a cat in her lap. Or maybe she felt like a cat in my lap. Both. I don't think Mom was really sad. It was just all coming out of her, like she used to say. She said she had too much inside her sometimes, and it just had to come out. When it came out in soft crying, that was okay.

"But just before dinner, she started hard-crying. Wailing. Then she started shouting. I hated the shouting. She'd shout at the people upstairs. We didn't have an upstairs, or even an attic, but Mom would shout at the people upstairs to be quiet and stop talking about her like that. Or she'd shout at Chass, call her wicked and a devil and all kinds of things. Or she'd shout at nothing and say nothing, just sounds and funny half-words. She'd always shout during thunderstorms. Always. That was when it got worst. She'd shout back at the thunder and the lightning. Sometimes she'd shout for a while, then she'd stop and she'd cut out all the lights. All the lights in the house, except for one flashlight she had; then she'd go around in her nightgown with her face all screwed up, poking into every room real quiet until she found something—like a coat or a book or a mirror or me or Chass—and then she'd start shouting again. She'd get right up in my face when she found me under the bed or in the closet, and she looked terrible—all purple around her eyes and her face all messed up, and she smelled like something chemical. It was like a nightmare hide-and-seek. I hate hide-and-seek.

"Mom started walking back and forth down the hallway, and that's a bad sign too. So Chass got me and took me to the bedroom and sat with me and read me a story and we talked about horses and the fair. And I could hear Mom walking outside the door, but it was okay because Chass was there."

Kit stopped and seemed lost in thought, Skade wasn't sure she was going to be able to get back on her own. Then Kit started again.

"After a while we didn't hear Mom walking anymore. She usually wore herself out between the walking and the shouting, or when she started throwing stuff or when she started her shakings. But we didn't hear anything, so Chass got up really quietly and went to the door to check. She went out into the hall and the house was all dark. After a few minutes Chass came back and told me it was going to be okay. Mom was asleep on the couch by the front door. Chass said she needed to go make a phone call. She needed to call the doctor about Mom. We didn't have a phone then, because we couldn't pay the bill. But the Watersons that lived down Fairfax would let us use their phone if we needed to. So Chass said she was going to walk down to the Watersons' to use the phone. Mom thought she'd run away. The next day, when Chass didn't come home, Mom said she'd run away. We went down to the Watersons' to see if Chass was there, but they hadn't seen her at all. She was just gone.

"The governor came down and they had the big thing for Eddie, and I kept looking around, looking for Chass. I kept thinking she was going to come out of that crowd or something. The whole time Mom was saying over and over again, *She's gone, she's gone, she's run away.* But I knew that wasn't true. I knew Chass wouldn't run away. She'd promised never to leave unless she took me too. And things were hard after Dad left. Chass kept things together. She held Mom together and she held me together and she held us together as a family. Running away like that just wasn't her. Even though she probably thought about it.

"Even the police thought she'd run away. I had to go down to the police station myself. I was eleven years old. I went into the police station, and I made them listen to me. I told them she didn't run away, that something bad must have happened to her. Finally, they did listen. I told them Chass was in charge of the house and that she was trying to go to college, and she was looking forward to summer and the fair and everything. That's when they started looking. And then they found her. She'd been hit by a car, they said. Somebody had buried her in a field."

Kit looked at the broken puppet scattered across the floor. "Janeyre was hers. She always sat on Chass's dresser next to her books. Janeyyre was her favorite. She was the only thing they let me keep. She's the only thing I have left that Chass touched."

Skade curled into herself while Kit was talking, sinking down to the floor again, and she began crying. Loudly. Through all of it—all the pain and all the self-hatred and all the bad things that had happened to her over the last twelve years—she had never felt so despairing. Kit raised her head finally and looked down at Skade crumpled on the floor.

"I hated you," she said quietly as she slowly began gathering the parts of Janeyre. "I hated you for years. I had a picture of the person who had hit Chass in my mind and I hated him. I would scream at you at night when I was alone. Then that guy showed up and confessed. And I hated him for a while, but then it sort of started to go away. Then he killed himself. But I still hated you. I still, even after he killed himself, hated the made-up person I had in my head. You. Except it wasn't you. It was some guy who didn't care. Some guy who was mean. That was the you I had in my head."

They sat. The puppets sat too. Traps for dreams. Traps for dreamers.

Skade began to feel a strange, painful clarity. She stopped crying but still sat hunched over on the floor.

"Where did you find Janeyre? You still haven't told me," asked Kit softly.

"I went to Lane's studio to get my camera back. Last week, right before we went to Nebraska, I had too much to drink and he raped me. I lost it with him, and I told him something bad that he never knew. I got back at him a little bit. I won't explain it, but it was bad. Anyway, like an idiot I listened to him apologize and I let him finish some ink he'd started. He said he was leaving town, and I wanted to be as cleanly rid of him as I could have it, so I let him finish it. It turns out he had Janeyre."

Kit looked at Skade quizzically. Skade hugged herself and made a face. "Jesus, Kit. If it wasn't all so bad enough. You know, I get all these images on my skin—all this ink. And I keep hoping one of them will just catch fire and kill me one day. Now one of them has really done it."

Skade picked up the jar and looked at it. "I guess Lane was the one who broke into your house. I told him where you lived once, but I'm sure he could have found out even without me telling him. He knew about your sister and the accident. He knew before I even got to town. He's always known. He broke in and he took Janeyre. He gave her back to me when I saw him tonight."

"Why?" asked Kit.

"To get back at me. To get back at me for dumping him when we were kids and to get back at me for what I told him."

"He took Janeyre to get back at you?"

"No. He took Janeyre to prove he'd been here. He took this to get back at me." She held up the ashes in the jar. "These are some of your sister's ashes, Kit. He mixed them into the ink he used to do my tattoo. He did a piece that says *Always Remember* out of your sister's ashes and put it on my arm. Your sister, the girl I killed, is part of my body now. I can erase the image, but I can't change that. That's why I tried to kill myself tonight." Skade held out her forearm for Kit to see.

Kit was still silent, but the expression on her face had changed. Skade couldn't read it. She'd never seen anything like it before.

"And this," Skade continued, picking up the remains of the cornhusk puppet Kit had made for her, so long ago now, "is why I couldn't kill myself tonight. I picked this up and it wouldn't let me do it. There's not much left of it now. But it helped. I should give it back to you." Skade held the damp crumpled husk out to Kit.

Kit took it and looked at it for a minute. Then she got up slowly went back into the kitchen. She came back with a shallow dish and a bottle of lighter fluid and a book of matches. She put the cornhusk puppet in the dish, doused it with the lighter fluid, and handed the matches to Skade.

"It's done its job. Set it free. It will take some of you with it."

Skade struck a match and held it to the puppet, which went up in dark, smoky flames. Skade and Kit watched it come to ashes together. Kit retrieved her new puppet and sat down on the floor with Skade.

"I said I hated you for years. But then I met you. And I don't hate you. Everyone walked away from my grief, away from me. Always. But you didn't." Kit took Skade's arm gently in her hands and ran a long spidery finger along the rope and the words *Always Remember*. "Chass is in here. So I'm in here too." Kit squeezed her hand. "It's okay, Skade. I don't hate you. I love you. I'm sorry." Kit handed Skade the new puppet. "This is for you now. To replace the one you just set free."

Skade wiped her eyes and took the puppet and held it gently. "She's wearing my clothes?"

"She's you, Skade," Kit continued. "She isn't Wonder Woman. She is different. She is you. I didn't tell you this, but right after you first met her at the totems, Janeyre gave you a new name. I told you she does that. She gives everyone a new name. The name she gave you was Corphael the Crow-Angel, angel with the blackest wings. So, this puppet is Corphael, and she is you. She's complex. Really hard to work. But when you get her figured out, she's an amazing puppet. I'm not going to show you how to work her. You'll have to figure that out. You have to show me once you do."

The two of them sat in the darkness on the floor of Kit's living room, surrounded by every kind of strange creature imaginable. The final echo of all the sins of a long-ago summer night.

An excerpt from the Conclusion to
American Still Life

by Skade Felsdottir

I've tried to distill what I've found in these lonely powerful places into words and images and present them to you, the reader. But something is missing. There is something else there that is not present on these pages. My words and my camera cannot capture what it is. I cannot describe it. Perhaps it requires loss. Fishermen, after all, know more about the sea than any scientist that studies the waves.

I think there is a stubbornness inherent in descansos to be mysterious. To be truly enigmatic. When I talked to the survivors that put up descansos, the idea of closure was strange. No one was seeking closure. I think that's what we-as-society want them to want. A punctuation mark and on to the next sentence. But the survivors want a continuation, not an end. So, these descansos flaunt their detextualized reality. They are trying to deny the viewer the comfort of making sense. When they do this, they bring us closer to the reality that death is not just a noun that can be kept at a distance and will sit still for us. Death is also a verb. It moves and has an energy, and this is what we are meant to understand. And that is hard and uncomfortable. But there is a type of closure here that might be closer to what the survivors are trying to do. In the world of comic books and graphic novels, the word closure refers to the mental process of creating a unified reality out of a series of still images. There is closure for all of us if we let it come.

Grief is the base level, the water table. That is why it can feel so chthonic. It sinks below our modern rational existence and connects to something spiritual, a place of superstition and the unsaid. Descansos are a kind of Ur-language. A non-linguistic message is formed in the viewers' mind as they try to comprehend what is there before them. All we can do is cobble together our own experience and our own filters and lexicon to come up with a translation into a linguistic message, and it is imperfect. Then we send that cobbled-together representation of the original, made from our individual minds, across the greatest gulf between our reality and the reality of the person with whom we want to communicate. They then take our pieces and try to reconstruct the original using their own subjective lexicon and metaphors and understanding. We may be sending a dachshund and what arrives is a carrot. That is why these roadside markers exist in the first place. They are each tiny cathedrals, trying to form a representation of the ineffable.

I was helped toward an understanding of this, and a realization of what I was missing, by a friend. She is truly what the French call a *bricolateur*, a rag and bone man. She collects things discarded and makes a powerful new language from all of it, a language she exists entirely within. A language she finally willed me to understand.

Ultimately then, descansos are epistles. They begin as communications from the remaining to the specific departed. But then they reflect. They become something of a communication back to the wider audience from those that are gone, perhaps as messages written in bottles and tossed out into the sea of coincidence or opportunity. Or perhaps as cairns at a crossroads, markers along the road for any of us who will listen. And perhaps their message is as simple as *All of it having led to this, and this is okay*. They are themselves the final point. And paying attention at least to them is our propitiation to the dead.

During the process of creating this book a lot of things happened to me. I went into this one thing and came out of it another. I've been asked multiple times why I went back to that place. Part of it was not my choice. But also, I think that this might have been the last place where I knew who I was. The last place I saw myself before I became lost. Maybe that's where I needed to start looking. And it was.

I was involved in a terrible accident as a teenager where a young woman was killed. And the accident was largely my fault. I spent over a decade shackled to that accident. It was the origin of the thing I became; my soul belonged to that accident. And I felt I deserved nothing—not relief, not kindness, not compassion, and certainly not forgiveness. But by retracing my steps toward myself, I found the one person in the world who could and would offer me a piece of that forgiveness. Half of it.

Forgiveness is something most of us get wrong. We get the idea of it largely from the Bible, but the original word for forgiveness was mistranslated from the Greek. Jesus didn't mean forgiveness as a sort of *that's okay, let's forget about it. You are fine and we are all good.* The original word was closer to *Unbinding*. When we become engaged with a wrongdoing, we become bound to that action. To the action and to the other people involved in that action, however far removed. We become knotted together, unable to escape the essence of it. When we forgive someone, what we really mean is that we cut the cord that binds us to that event or that person. We free ourselves from that thing having power over us. I do not forgive for someone else. I forgive for myself. I was forgiven by the person still alive, to whom I had caused the most pain and damage—and that pain and damage was considerable. But she then left me with the task of forgiving myself. I still need to unbind myself from the event. Until I can do that, I can only glimpse a world from which I am absent through a camera lens. Everywhere I go is a haunted house because I bring the ghosts with me. They are a part of me. Unbinding myself and setting myself free is a work in progress. Also a work in progress is my dealing with my own demons and my own defects. My journey now is to re-establish a relationship with myself. This will be the path for the rest of my life, I'm sure.

But however far I get down that path, and however bright the sun might shine along the way, whatever strength or wisdom I may gain, I also know something else. There is, in the thorny forests that always are nearby in me, a dark black lake. It is frightening and it calls quietly to me. And I so want to swim in it in my times of strife. And I will forever know exactly where it is and how to get to it. And so, the work.

And so there it is.

A stranger's death is always someone else's business. Yet a marker sits beside a highway as the rest of us roar past without noticing. Created by the tears and grief of someone unknown to us. Draped in meaning with indecipherable material objects. It is the very definition of a metaphor, a thing symbolic of something else. A communication back at us from the dead. This then is a truly American still life: the stuff of the minutia of life become meaning, become metaphor, and stare blankly back at us in our hubris of immortality and forever-youth.

Through these things, the dead communicate with us again.

-S. Felsdottir

44

Late afternoon had been married to the heat all summer, but now there was movement in the air. The sky was the color of a guess and Skade smelled the scent of pine pitch and the wind as she climbed out of her Jeep and walked down a wide dirt track leading to the edge of Stevens Creek, a fat and sluggish tributary of Black River. The sight that confronted her as she made her way down to the waterside made her smile.

It looked like an island made of refuse, like a place in the creek where a tree had long ago fallen and acted like a net, catching all the floating debris that the flow of the water offered to it and creating its own slowly shifting collage of detritus. Standing in the middle of it all was Jerome in a pair of battered cutoff jeans and wearing his ridiculously small captain's hat. His upper body, bared to the sun, was a mosaic of tattoos. As Skade got closer she realized that this pile of chaos, this debris beneath his feet, was actually Jerome's boat. John Doe waited on the bank, listlessly holding one end of a long rope, the other end of which was tied off somewhere in the disorder of Jerome's craft.

"Skade! Damn, you showed up!" shouted Jerome when he saw her making her way toward the boat.

"Of course I did, Jerome. I couldn't miss this."

Jerome disappeared into one of the packing crates that served as a cabin on his pile and quickly reappeared with a bottle of champagne. "Just in time to help me christen the *Hillbilly Titanic*." He popped the cork on the bottle, tentatively stepped closer to the side, and offered up the bottle to Skade.

Skade held up her hand and turned her head, still smiling. "Nope. Can't. Still got a few weeks to go before I get my thirty days. Gotta get my token. Can't blow it now. Plus, I just came from a meeting with the court officers. I'm good so long as I keep passing drops."

"Hell yes!" said Jerome, hoisting the bottle and taking a swig. "Here's to you and your straight and narrow path. That can be a tough one, I know."

"Not too bad yet."

"Yeah, well, don't let it sneak up on you," said Jerome, with a knowing squint in his eyes. "So how'd you like my boat?"

"It looks—"

"It's fantastic! A feet of extreme redneck engineering if ever there was one!"

"So, you decided on *Titanic* for the name finally?"

"No, no…I just call her the *Hillbilly Titanic* as a sort of nickname. It's bad luck to use the real name before the christening. So, with that…" Jerome stood up as straight as he could, placed one hand on his heart, capped the mouth of the champagne bottle with the thumb of the other hand, and closed his eyes. "I hereby give you," intoned Jerome solemnly, "*The Clear and Present Freedom*!" and he shook the champagne and sprayed it all over the deck of his craft.

Skade clapped. "Jerome, that is a seriously great name for this boat."

"Yeah, it came to me in the end. It describes everything right now."

"It certainly does," said Skade, looking off down the creek. "So, what's the plan?"

"Cast off and down the river I go!"

"But this isn't a river. Where are you going?"

"Last year I got into a discussion with the professor over here," said Jerome, pointing to John Doe, still sadly holding his rope. "I suggested that you could set out in a raft on Stevens Creek and make it all the way to New Orleans. All the water here eventually drains into the Mississippi, and for a boat like this with next to no draft, it ought to be doable. There's a couple of spots where it might get tricky, but I got it covered. I will let go of my need to control and let the current take me exactly where I am supposed to be exactly when I'm supposed to be there. And I'll enjoy the ride!"

"Then what? What happens if you make it to New Orleans?"

"*When* I make it, you mean? I dunno. Something will come to me on the way, I suspect. What about you? How you doing? What's your plan?"

"I'm feeling rather new, you know? As much as I hate the idea of sitting in church basements drinking shitty coffee and listening to advice that rhymes, that idea of *one day at a time* is pretty accurate right now. I'm leaving for New York today. Kit leaves tomorrow. I'm meeting with my agent about my book, and Kit's got her interview all set up next week. I'll be there to hold her hand, not that she needs it."

"Then what?"

"Don't know. Something will probably come to me on the way." She smiled. "Depends a lot on Kit, I guess. I've got a friend who lives on Munjoy Hill in Portland. Might go that way. But first, New York. When I ran away twelve years ago, the farther I drove, the smaller I got. I think this time I'll reverse that and try to get larger. Or at least get to know myself better."

"Honorable," said Jerome. "And now, it's time to launch! Professor, cast off!"

John Doe tossed his end of the rope into the boat and watched with the same sad expression on his face.

"Professor, I leave you with this: There are no fools or wise men. Only the absence or presence of inner space," said Jerome as he grabbed a long garden hoe and used it to push off from the bank. "Stay spacious, Professor! Stay spacious, Skade!"

"I have no doubt you'll be the most spacious person in New Orleans," Skade called out.

Skade and John Doe watched Jerome capering about joyfully on his slow-floating raft as it caught the current and began spinning away downstream. As he made the first bend in the creek and waved one last time before they lost sight of him, Skade waved back and turned to John Doe. "Clear and present freedom," she said. John Doe looked sadly at her and didn't say anything. Skade turned and walked back up the slope to her Jeep, now packed and ready. She'd packed her bags from the beginning again, this time with the smells of ink and puppet breath and wet grass and heat, always a citizen of her own suitcase.

She climbed in and turned the key. The engine fired up right away. Corphael sat neatly buckled into the passenger seat beside her as she pulled out onto a road heading east toward a clear and present freedom.

ACKNOWLEDGMENTS

If it's true that it takes a village to raise a child, then it seems as though it takes a small city to write a novel. There are dozens and dozens of people who should be thanked for their help, support, and companionship throughout the process of crafting this book. Every writer I've ever shared work with so we could give each other feedback, so many I cannot thank you all by name, but know you are in my heart and my work.

I would like to thank a few people directly: Jaynie Royal and everyone at Regal House for taking a chance and making this happen. Anna Zimmerman for the feedback and for knowing what it's like. Elizabeth SanMiguel and Jennifer Malin for their inspiring writing talent, insight, and friendship. Carole de Monclin for giving me that one idea when I was stuck. Everyone at the Indiana Writer's Center. Everyone associated with the Solstice Low Residency MFA program, especially Anne Marie Ooman, for the invaluable expertise, support, encouragement, and education. And most importantly my community, the Equinox writer's group: Dean Raat, Cindy Abdalla, Ellen Parent, Charlotte MacDonald, Megan Leduke, and Rhonda McDonnell, all of them insanely talented writers with whom I'm proud to be associated, you all make me better. And as always, Amy.

Book Club Questions

- Excerpts of Skade's written text are interspersed throughout *American Still Life*. In those excerpts, Skade's mental state and personal thinking begin to rise to the surface. How do these diary or journal-like moments in her text mirror how she behaves? How does she suppress them?

- Several times Skade expresses a feeling that "something is missing" from her work and that she is unable to fully convey what she finds at the descansos. What is missing? Is this missing element actually in her work, or is it more deeply in herself?

- Does Lane have genuine feelings of fondness, love, and compassion for Skade initially? Or is he motivated by revenge and/or lust immediately?

- Is there any parallel between what is "missing" in Lane and what is "missing" in Skade?

- When Kit makes the Wonder Woman puppet in the image of Skade it sets off a host of complex reactions in both of them. Why does Skade become so enraged? Is she even aware of the answer? Why did Kit create the puppet in the first place? Is she even aware of that answer? How does the interaction in this scene change the dynamic between Skade and Kit for the rest of the story?

- Camille and Jerome both offer reflections back to Skade. What are these two supporting characters trying to convey? How are their messages similar and how are they different?